Reviewers Love Melissa Brayden

"Melissa Brayden has become one of the most popular novelists of the genre, writing hit after hit of funny, relatable, and very sexy stories for women who love women."—*Afterellen.com*

The Forever Factor

"Melissa Brayden never fails to impress. I read this in one day and had a smile on my face throughout. An easy read filled with the snappy banter and heartfelt longing that Melissa writes so effortlessly."—*Sapphic Book Review*

The Last Lavender Sister

"It's also a slow burn, with some gorgeous writing. I've had to take some breaks while reading to delight in a turn of phrase here and there, and that's the best feeling."—*Jude in the Stars*

Exclusive

"Melissa Brayden's books have always been a source of comfort, like seeing a friend you've lost touch with but can pick right up where you left off. They have always made my heart happy, and this one does the same."—*Sapphic Book Review*

Marry Me

"A bride-to-be falls for her wedding planner in this smoking hot, emotionally mature romance from Brayden…Brayden is remarkably generous to her characters, allowing them space for self-exploration and growth."—*Publishers Weekly*

To the Moon and Back

"*To the Moon and Back* is all about Brayden's love of theatre, onstage and backstage, and she does a delightful job of sharing that love… Brayden set the scene so well I knew what was coming, not because it's unimaginative but because she made it obvious it was the only way things could go. She leads the reader exactly where she wants to take them, with brilliant writing as usual. Also, not everyone can make office supplies sound sexy."—*Jude in the Stars*

Back to September

"You can't go wrong with a Melissa Brayden romance. Seriously, you can't. Buy all of her books. Brayden sure has a way of creating an emotional type of compatibility between her leads, making you root for them against all odds. Great settings, cute interactions, and realistic dialogue."—*Bookvark*

What a Tangled Web

"[T]he happiest ending to the most amazing trilogy. Melissa Brayden pulled all of the elements together, wrapped them up in a bow, and presented the reader with Happily Ever After to the max!"—*Kitty Kat's Book Review Blog*

Beautiful Dreamer

"I love this book. I want to kiss it on its face…I'm going to stick *Beautiful Dreamer* on my to-reread-when-everything-sucks pile, because it's sure to make me happy again and again."—*Smart Bitches Trashy Books*

Two to Tangle

"Melissa Brayden does it again with a sweet and sexy romance that leaves you feeling content and full of happiness. As always, the book is full of smiles, fabulous dialogue, and characters you wish were your best friends."—*The Romantic Reader*

Entangled

"Ms. Brayden has a definite winner with this first book of the new series, and I can't wait to read the next one. If you love a great enemies-to-lovers, feel-good romance, then this is the book for you."—*Rainbow Reflections*

"*Entangled* is a simmering slow burn romance, but I also fully believe it would be appealing for lovers of women's fiction. The friendships between Joey, Maddie, and Gabriella are well developed and engaging as well as incredibly entertaining…All that topped off with a deeply fulfilling happily ever after that gives all the happy sighs long after you flip the final page."—*Lily Michaels: Sassy Characters, Sizzling Romance, Sweet Endings*

Love Like This

"Brayden upped her game. The characters are remarkably distinct from one another. The secondary characters are rich and wonderfully integrated into the story. The dialogue is crisp and witty."—*Frivolous Reviews*

Sparks Like Ours

"Brayden sets up a flirtatious tit-for-tat that's honest, relatable, and passionate. The women's fears are real, but the loving support from the supporting cast helps them find their way to a happy future. This enjoyable romance is sure to interest readers in the other stories from Seven Shores."—*Publishers Weekly*

Hearts Like Hers

"Once again Melissa Brayden stands at the top. She unequivocally is the queen of romance."—*Front Porch Romance*

Eyes Like Those

"Brayden's story of blossoming love behind the Hollywood scenes provides the right amount of warmth, camaraderie, and drama."—*RT Book Reviews*

Strawberry Summer

"This small-town second-chance romance is full of tenderness and heart. The 10 Best Romance Books of 2017."—*Vulture*

"*Strawberry Summer* is a tribute to first love and soulmates and growing into the person you're meant to be. I feel like I say this each time I read a new Melissa Brayden offering, but I loved this book so much that I cannot wait to see what she delivers next."—*Smart Bitches, Trashy Books*

First Position

"Brayden aptly develops the growing relationship between Ana and Natalie, making the emotional payoff that much sweeter. This ably plotted, moving offering will earn its place deep in readers' hearts."—*Publishers Weekly*

By the Author

You Had Me at Merlot

by

Melissa Brayden

2024

YOU HAD ME AT MERLOT

ISBN 13: 978-1-63679-543-0

THIS TRADE PAPERBACK ORIGINAL IS PUBLISHED BY
BOLD STROKES BOOKS, INC.
P.O. BOX 249
VALLEY FALLS, NY 12185

FIRST EDITION: FEBRUARY 2024

CREDITS
EDITOR: RUTH STERNGLANTZ
PRODUCTION DESIGN: STACIA SEAMAN
COVER DESIGN BY INKSPIRAL DESIGN

Acknowledgments

Forgiveness is a complicated mechanism. It's certainly not one size fits all. Exploring the theme and how it affects this particular pair of characters was a rewarding experience on a personal and professional level. I hope the story of Jamie and Leighton and who they become to each other resonates.

After twenty-four books, my relationship with my publisher, Bold Strokes Books, and Radclyffe, who started it all, is a special one to me. I am already coming up with future stories that I hope we can tell together. It's been a fabulous partnership.

Sandy Lowe gets credit for the whimsical title. I'm so glad for your input and guidance with every book.

Working with Ruth Sternglantz as my editor has taught me a great deal, not only about storytelling, but also about kindness and friendship. I treasure our chats, Ruth, and very much appreciate your ideas and support along the way.

Inkspiral Designs has put together a cover that captures the world of the book so wonderfully. Thank you for the whimsy and creativity.

To the crew of behind-the-scenes professionals at Bold Strokes (Cindy, Toni, Stacia, Gina, and the proofreading team), your work has not gone unnoticed. Thank you for the attention to detail and for making me look better than I probably should. I adore each of you.

A special paragraph for Nicole Little, who is not only a best friend, but who is my eagle-eye proofer who works with me on every book. Get better soon, Nikki. I'm here waiting for you, ready for more amazing board game battles and tackling in the snow. I'm so glad you're still here.

To Alan and the short blond people in my home, I love you immensely. Thank you for the endless daydreaming time you afford me. The cartoons and cuddles on the couch aren't bad either.

Georgia and Rey, what a time we've had these past few months. Thank you for the support group and the words of encouragement. But most of all, thank you for your friendship.

To you, dear reader, thank you for taking another journey with me on the page. I'm so appreciative of all you've brought to my life: the messages, the hugs, the kind words, and the exchanges. I look forward to so many more.

For Nicole. My Friend.

PROLOGUE

Jamie Tolliver had no idea how important today would be," the voice-over inside her head said in that deep throaty voice of his. She liked the sound of that, hoping the day would be memorable. So far, everything had been status quo. The quick train ride to work. The three-block walk past businesses not yet open. The sun giving them a tiny glimpse on the horizon. As Jamie pushed open the double glass doors to the bar just before six a.m., she took a deep inhale. Heaven on Earth. The aroma of freshly brewed coffee served as her greeting each morning, and she never got tired of it. She gave her shoulders a happy shake. The streets of New York were still sleepy and empty for the most part, which meant it was time to get her coffee bar ready to bring caffeinated goodness to her customers, whom she adored. They'd be arriving soon. She dropped her bag behind the counter and stretched like a cat. "Morning, Leo."

Her longtime employee and friend was already behind the counter, hard at work on a blueberry latte for her and his traditional Americano. Dependable.

"Morning, James. Incoming."

She opened her hand and blindly accepted the warm drink like impeccably executed choreography, perfected over years of working together.

The voice-over didn't miss a beat. "The world better prepare. Jamie Tolliver was the kind of person who saved the day." She took a satisfying drink of the warm liquid and grinned. The espresso was rich and deep, a perfect balance of bitter paired with the sweetness of the blueberry. Harmonious in all the right ways. That's right, voice-over. She was a day-saver.

As she powered up the point-of-sale station for opening, the deep voice continued. "In fact, she stunned the world regularly with her fast-acting, problem-solving, crime-fighting prowess. Small business owner by day. Sexy superhero by night." She nodded along happily as if bopping to a great song. "In fact, Jamie rarely slept and liked it that way. Citizens of New York City cheered when she arrived on the scene, knowing justice was on the way." She flexed her muscles. "Women threw themselves at her feet." Record scratch. He'd gone too far with that.

And unfortunately, very little of the rest was true either.

Except the small business part. Jamie did have one of those and was incredibly proud of it. But alone in the privacy of her thoughts, the voice-over inside her head took over, and she pretended to be a badass ninja, capable of executing a lethal roundhouse kick, dark hair flying until she landed with catlike stealth. She'd then sign autographs for adoring children and advise them that they could be just like her one day. "Stay in school," she'd say, with a ruffling of their hair.

It was a fun little fantasy she kept going, knowing full well that she was not necessarily a brave person, nor did she live an extraordinary life. She was just Jamie. Not a lot of people stopped and took notice, but that was okay. She counted her blessings. As a New Yorker, she was one of nine million souls moving around an awesome island, anonymous and driven. It was a fun club to be part of and, in many ways, made her a different brand of badass.

"Ready?" Leo asked, moving to the door, poised to open with his keys in hand. His dark hair was coiffed to perfection and his black T-shirt hugged the impressive biceps he fought for nightly in the gym. There were already three or four people lined up, ready to snag a coffee or a doughnut on their way to work, school, or just life. But they'd be a part of their morning, and Jamie liked that.

"Let the people come," she said, positioning herself behind the register. Their customers were great, and so was the neighborhood. Talk about a lucky score. They'd carved out a space in Chelsea, chock-full of history and culture. These days, the area was super trendy and more than a little gay. It had quickly embraced Bordeauxnuts, her funky coffee bar that turned into a cozy wine spot at four p.m. A change in music, a dimming of the lights, glasses swapped for mugs, and voilà. The vino flowed while the coffee slid into the back seat until morning. Two vibes in one.

Inside, the café was fun and eclectic. A chalkboard menu, redecorated weekly, blasted their seasonal offerings as well as the drink of the day. The tables and chairs in the main dining area came with cushions for comfort and extra space for laptops and friend chats. Just to keep things interesting and give their customers options, a second room jutted off the first, designed for comfort. Couches arranged in multiple sitting areas offered soft spaces to lounge for those wanting a more laid-back experience. There was also a seven-foot bookcase on its far wall, overflowing with books and games for the grabbing. Jamie adored the ever-changing decor. The walls featured the work of local artists in a monthly rotation, all available for purchase. Lots of fantastic pieces had been sold off the walls of Bordeauxnuts, some for impressive prices.

As a result of good food and drink, warm service, and an immersive atmosphere, people loved spending time in what Jamie affectionately referred to as *the bar*, tick-tacking away on their laptops, watching the world go by out her picture windows, or staring into each other's eyes on a quiet date night out. Outside, the city bustled, deals were struck, and lofty dreams were coming true. Jamie often scrunched her shoulders to her ears just thinking about it. There was an energy on the streets of New York that couldn't be upended. It sent vibrations through the soles of her feet and had Jamie convinced that she lived in the most exciting city in the entire world.

But even that didn't make her a superhero.

"But didn't it?" the voice-over asked.

She shook her head. The only brave thing she'd done was come out to her parents a decade earlier. They'd made her tomato soup, argued about what brand of crackers Jamie would like best, and told her that they supported her one hundred percent. So maybe she'd given herself too much credit declaring the proclamation a brave act. Still. She'd been proud of herself that day.

"Morning, Marvin. Are we feeling the skim today?" Marvin was often her first customer of the day, a dedicated regular. Jamie popped a cup into her hand from the tall stack to her left and grabbed her trusty Sharpie with her right. Leo geared up at the drink making station, primed to pounce on the impending rush. He was the fastest barista she'd ever seen and would soon be going hard with cups lined up and the steam wand screaming. A master behind the espresso machine and the best in the biz, there would often be a trickle of men just wanting the chance to watch him work. This was Chelsea, after all.

"No skim. I'm cheating today." Marvin sighed dramatically. His curly hair was about three inches taller than normal. "I'll walk home instead of taking the train. My penance. Give me the two percent so I can wallow in calories."

Jamie nodded. "You got it, and don't you dare feel bad about that." She scribbled his name, the letter *U* for usual, and checked his big milk splurge box on the side of the cup before sliding it into Leo's queue. "Big day?"

He grimaced, making the lines on his forehead turn wavy like Charlie Brown's. It tracked. He'd always reminded her of a nervous cartoon. "It's looking ominous if I'm being frank. I don't like the trends." He had a copy of *The New York Times* firmly tucked beneath his arm and red glasses perched on his nose. Marvin was a day trader slash finance blogger and would stow away in the corner of the shop for the next three to four hours, ready to move and groove once the markets opened. He'd order a second hazelnut latte in about two hours and sometimes an order of mini-doughnuts, which were responsible for the amazing aromas that grabbed folks from the sidewalk and dragged them inside. Jamie's secret weapon. She didn't try to understand Marvin's life or work. She did, however, appreciate his continued patronage.

In fact, Jamie *treasured* her group of regular customers, who in many ways had become an extended family. They knew each other's habits, quirks, and coffee orders. They were a unique breakfast club, as unlikely as they were dedicated. No one in the group could predict what might turn up in the news or flip the world on its head next, but they knew they'd see each other each weekday morning. It was their glue. What more did a group of humans need?

Marvin sniffed the air. "Doughnuts come out in the last five minutes?" She glanced behind her at Mikey, their industrial mini-doughnut machine. Mikey wasn't fancy or even gourmet, but he turned out the most heavenly miniature fried doughnuts that Jamie and co then dusted with cinnamon sugar or powdered, customer's choice. When served hot and fresh, as they should be, nothing made for a tastier breakfast. Five doughnuts in a waxed paper bag for four dollars flat. Because of the bar's unique concept—the trinity of coffee, wine, and doughnuts, implemented way before the format became trendy—Bordeauxnuts had been featured on the local news multiple times as well as on a variety of food blogs and podcasts over the years. That kind of coverage kept new customers coming in, but it was their product that kept them coming back.

Jamie glanced behind her. "Less than five. You in?"

"I'll take a bag," Marvin said, using his hand to waft the smell his way. Mikey's powers always came through. People couldn't say no. "Cinnamon sugar. A dash extra. Three napkins. No fork needed."

"You're cooking now, Marvin."

Jamie rang him up and moved to the next customer. "Flat white," the businessman said. She asked him about his morning, and he let her know that his assistant was out and he'd have a lot on his hands.

"You take it one task at a time. I know without a doubt that you're gonna have an awesome day." A conservative smile blossomed, and he moved on.

The next woman was gorgeous and ordered an iced cap with almond milk. No doughnuts. Her loss. A man in a ball cap opted for the house roast, black, with a blueberry muffin on the side.

"You've gotta try these doughnuts, too. Fresh batch." She handed him a bag on the house, knowing full well he'd be back for more another day. Jamie was no fool. She didn't set out to be a tiny doughnut dealer, but that's who she'd become. Once folks got a hot bag, the suckers sold themselves.

"Thank God you're on register," Clarissa Rivera said at ten minutes to eight, scurrying up to the front spot. Her dark hair was pulled back on one side and she wore a brown dress with bursts of colorful flowers, likely from her family's clothing store a few blocks down. She knew how to make a fashion statement in a way that consistently impressed Jamie, who was not nearly as adventurous.

"What would happen if I wasn't?" She arched a brow.

"I'd have to hunt you down." Her bestie and semi member of the regulars club looked like she had something exciting to impart. An impossibility in New York, but still.

"Riss, what?" Jamie squeezed her hand across the counter. "You're dragging this out to torture me."

"Midtorture, I'll take a triple shot latte with two pumps of coconut."

Jamie took care of the drink order on automatic mode, her eyes never moving from Clarissa. True, Clarissa leaned toward hyperbolic reactions, like the time she said there was a small alligator in her bedroom when there was, in fact, a cricket, but Jamie did her best to always hear Clarissa out. She slid the cup to Leo. "Done. Now spill. You have my heart thudding because it's looped in with yours." She had a line of customers, but she could do both. Years of practice served her well.

Clarissa stepped to the side while Jamie helped a teenage girl who wanted what amounted to a milkshake with a tiny hint of espresso. She was a purist herself but refused to judge. "You got it. Can I add some whip to that for you?" she asked, as she wrote on the plastic cup.

"Extra whip. Double."

"I like it, I love it. You're gonna have a great morning."

"Awesome," the girl said. "Please be right."

Jamie's eyes flitted to Clarissa, who took a breath and placed both palms on the counter in preparation. "Here goes."

"I'm ready."

"So, I was doing our charts like I always do, and your month ahead is a game changer. You have a lot coming your way and need to be ready."

"My horoscope?" Jamie asked. She grinned and relaxed. "You're panicking over my horoscope. Got it."

"This is no regular reading, James. Listen carefully. Venus is going to have a field day with your spirit. You're going to be *thrown*."

"Well, that's unnerving." She rang up a couple of college students and handed over two bags of doughnuts. "What should I do about it?"

Clarissa leaned in, meeting her gaze with intense brown eyes. "Be on the lookout. Proceed with caution." She straightened. "But also don't hold back from stepping out of your comfort zone. You should feel free to handle whatever life throws at you in a new and different fashion. Abandon old practices."

She pointed her Sharpie at Clarissa. "You realize this is contradictory. You're telling me to be brave but to proceed with caution."

Clarissa nodded. "Yes. It's both. Big month for you. It may

change your entire life." She held up her hands and wiggled her fingers. "You heard it here first. One day we'll look back on this important conversation."

Humoring her best friend, Jamie nodded. "That would truly be something. I will surely take your advice whenever it's possible."

"It's going to be big," Clarissa said, backing away. "Take this seriously. Maybe write a note on your fridge. And your bathroom mirror. I can text you reminders."

"I feel confident you will."

Clarissa balked. "You're not taking this seriously."

"I am. I will. You have my word." And she wasn't lying. She wasn't at Clarissa's level of unwavering trust in the zodiac, but she did believe that the stars influenced a lot of what life brought their way. "Venus better go easy on me," she murmured before greeting the next customer with a bright smile.

Twenty-five minutes later, the line had dwindled, and Jamie hit her midmorning lull, which meant she had time to either stitch together a few to-do items in the back or relax with her regulars until the beast roared back to life.

"Back in ten, Leo."

"I got you, James," he said, tossing the new batch of doughnuts a few times to help them dry. He'd perfected the technique. Tons of flair in his movements, popping the doughnut basket high and in a circular motion the way only the very polished Leo could. She'd even put a video of him on their Insta page in slo-mo. She was no fool when it came to marketing their strengths.

"Jamie was every bit as suave as Leo," the voice-over said. She nearly laughed out loud. Was Venus already messing with her? She could never compete.

"You're the brains. I'm the talent," Leo once told her, with an arched brow that would rival the handsomest of villains. His signature. "The part-timers are the supporting players." They had a handful of those, all likable and young.

But Leo wasn't only the talent, he was also the show. His all-male fan club would show up midafternoon just to watch him work, stealing glances and conversing in whispered tones. As long as they bought a drink or a snack, Jamie was fine with feeding their Leo addiction.

Jamie surveyed the place and stretched her calves, always the first to burn. The bar wasn't big, but it could accommodate about eight tables and a few bar seats along the front window, plus another dozen and a half in the lounge area. The regulars were nestled comfortably in their traditional spots. Marvin was at a table in the corner, laptop open, worry lines activated. Genevieve sat in the center, surely working on another hot romance novel, generally with a contemporary slant and smutty scenes galore. The faraway look in her eye meant she was in another land full of sexual tension and—perhaps—passion, sex, and nudity right there in public. *Go, her.* To Genevieve's right sat Lisa and Chun with their heads together over a large construction plan that covered their table. They were a married lesbian house-flipping team who used their mornings to scour listings and wrangle their contractors in don't-mess-with-me voices that Jamie had learned to admire. Marjorie, always near the window, was a retired schoolteacher who'd harnessed Bordeauxnuts as a way to fight against loneliness and surround herself with other humans. She read the paper each morning before transitioning to her knitting project du jour. Kindhearted, she also never missed any one of their birthdays. This year she'd given Jamie a personalized card she'd hired out and had drawn up just for her along with a small Kermit the Frog she'd knitted right there in the coffee bar.

Yep. Jamie's core group of regulars had assembled today, as always. They were her rock, her comfort zone.

Lisa, who said *dude* a lot, broke into a grin when Jamie approached. "Break time at last. Dude, that line never quit. Busy this morning." Next to Lisa, Chun chatted away on her phone about fixtures and *not fucking it up, Jimmy.* "I feel like you haven't had a second."

"I won't complain." Jamie passed Lisa a tired smile and rubbed the back of her neck. She refused to see hard work as anything but a blessing. "Hey, did you two close on that Brooklyn property? Is it off your hands?"

Lisa's dark eyes flashed victory. "For fifteen percent over ask. Boom."

"Nice one. One day I'm gonna snatch up one of your flips when I'm rich and comfortable." She laughed. "Just any day now." Jamie took a seat at an empty table and let herself melt into the ambiance. It felt like the most wonderful exhale to just *be* among her people. Not just customers, either, her friends.

"Hey, G." She glanced at Genevieve. "You haven't said a word about your date last night. The swipe right."

She sat back and considered the question, hesitation apparent. "Swipe Right had nice hair and was a good conversationalist."

Jamie squinted, sensing Genevieve wasn't sold. "But...?"

"He worked his mom into the conversation a bit too much and then kissed with the overeager slobber lips."

"I hate the slobber lips," Jamie said, frowning. Not that she'd done much kissing herself lately, but she'd been on enough awful dates to sympathize.

Marjorie dropped her knitting and leaned in. "I'm telling you, Jamie, you need to meet my niece. She's a schoolteacher in the Bronx who dances like a wild woman. You would love her. No slobber."

"Could be your soulmate, James," Genevieve said from around her laptop. "Everyone has a happily ever after out there. Their gardener. An old flame. Their accountant with a penchant for public sex."

"That's so specific." Jamie blinked.

Genevieve continued, "The stranger in the grocery line. Mortal enemies are always promising prospects. Do you have any of those?"

"Not yet."

"Work on that. Most definitely try for a mortal enemy."

"I could try to start a few feuds and see what materializes."

"Do." Genevieve's gaze deepened to a smolder. "Great sex in the meantime doesn't hurt either. How long's it been for you?" Jamie balked. Leave it to Gen to pop in with a lust-laced question in front of the whole world. It was, after all, her life's work.

"I'm not divulging the details of my s-e-x life," she said with conviction, all the while hoping that the heat from her cheeks didn't make her look like a circus clown.

A new grouping of customers had wandered in, extending the line. That meant it was time for Jamie to get back to work and relieve Leo from double duty. She returned to her spot at the counter and grinned. "Hi! Welcome. What can I get for you?" she asked a woman who would forever be Fuchsia Lips.

"We don't get to hear the answer to the question?" Fuchsia Lips asked, pointing at Gen.

"Just offering coffee and doughnuts today, I'm afraid." She wished she was as sex-positive as Genevieve or even Clarissa, frosting the world with details from her spicy bedroom like decorations on a cake-o'-lust. She'd work on sexy frosting, too.

Chun studied her. "I'm estimating it's been a year."

"I don't tell you everything," Jamie said pointedly. She wrote out Fuchsia Lips's double shot Americano order and slid it to Leo.

"Collectively, we have a lot of information," Lisa said with confidence.

Marjorie, reaching for her knitting, nodded. "It was that Amy woman. The last time."

"Don't help them, Marjorie, or I'm taking back my Netflix password."

Marjorie scoffed. "You can't. I gave you Paramount Plus."

"Damn. I'm not willing to give that up." There was no winning.

Mikey dinged, signaling a new batch of doughnuts, yanking Jamie back to the flow to tend to the newly arrived gifts from the doughnut gods. "Do not talk about my personal life while I'm wrangling baked goods."

"Amy was the one with the eight cats?" Marvin asked Chun.

"I'm serious," Jamie tossed over her shoulder.

Her back was to the café door when she heard it open, inspiring her to spin around with a smile that evaporated from her face. There, standing at her register, was the most beautiful woman in a forest-green trench coat, sash tied. Tall. Dark blond hair. Stunning.

Jamie swallowed, remembering herself. "Morning. Hi there. What can I get for you?" *Smile. That's it.* Tons of pretty people came and went from the bar every day. This was like any one of those moments.

"Oh"—the woman scanned the blackboard menu overhead, decorated with little snowflakes for winter—"I think I'll give your peppermint latte a try."

"Yum," Jamie said with simply too much enthusiasm to be natural. She'd face-planted that response in glorious form. Why couldn't she function like any other person? "Any milk preference on that? We have lots of milks." Dammit. Her heart danced around in her chest like a professional tap dancer had moved in. What was happening? The woman had the softest smile. Big brown eyes which were a nice contrast against the soft color of her blond hair. A model, maybe? She had the height. Jamie was guessing five foot nine.

"Two percent would be fine," the woman with the perfect lips said. She pursed them briefly and relaxed. "Our default milk. Of the milks. The many. Perfect." She grabbed for the cup on top of the stack, prepared to pop it into her hand—a move she'd made thousands of times. Yet this go-round, she bobbled the catch, corrected, and knocked the whole stack over. "Whoops. And down she goes." Jamie laughed, but it was too much. "Let me just…" She dove to the floor, collected the cups, reformed the stack, and shot up to her feet again. "Tricky. Cups are."

"I see that." The woman was sweet enough to toss her a conservative laugh. She even showed joy like people in the movies. Restrained and perfect. Probably an actress. "Well done."

"Anything else? A pastry? Doughnuts? People line up for those suckers."

"Don't tempt me. Just the coffee." The woman tapped her credit card on the machine with the grace of an angel. Who tapped like that? Was elegant tapping a learned skill? She was certainly a believer now.

"Your order will be right up. Um, over there."

She turned to see Leo staring at her with focused interest, a small smile playing upon his lips. She glared at him and busied herself straightening the prep counter. When the woman picked up her drink and left the bar, Jamie exhaled. She turned to the dining room to find her regulars staring at her in wide-eyed amazement.

"What in the world just happened?" Marjorie asked. Her jaw fell open in glee. "Did you see yourself with her just now?"

"Well, that's physically impossible, so no," Jamie said, wiping her hands on her apron for no real reason. "Of course not."

"Girl, you had the 3D heart eyes going." Genevieve applauded as if she'd just watched a really satisfying film. "I'm about to write down everything I just saw for my next book. All of it. Sweet girl-next-door type loses her ability to speak properly when a quiet blond vixen arrives at her register."

"That didn't happen," Jamie said as nonchalantly as possible. "She was pretty, though. Anyone can see that."

"Don't minimize," Lisa said, standing and tossing her empty cup. Almost time for property visits. "It takes a lot to visibly rattle you. You're the most grounded human being any of us has ever met."

Chun studied her, thoughtful. "Either that or you usually cover it well."

"It just wasn't like you," Marvin said. "But I'm awful at dating and love and life, so don't ask me for tips. Fun to watch it play out, though. Interesting character study."

"Don't study me. I'm clumsy and uninteresting."

He went soft. "No, you're not, Jamie." Marvin was a gentle soul beneath his neuroses.

Lisa laughed. "I just want to watch you drop the cups again, dude. And then pop back up like a pogo stick."

Oh, they were all enjoying this way too much. "Fine. I can admit to being unnerved by our last visitor."

"Well, now we know your type," Chun said.

"I don't have a type."

Lisa leveled her with a stare. "Well, here's the takeaway. If you didn't before, you do now." She fanned herself. "Off to sell real estate to the people of New York."

Jamie exhaled. "All praise to the brownstone."

"Overrated." Lisa delivered a fist bump. "You behave yourself around the pretty ladies."

Jamie absorbed the semi-embarrassing advice. She really must have turned into a cartoon character earlier. "Very funny."

"Kiss your mom and tell your dad that the puzzle in the *Times* is harder than usual."

Jamie knew her dad would have devoted at least ninety minutes to the puzzle, and if it was extra difficult, he might have just tossed it right into the trash with a *to hell with ya* added in. She smiled at Lisa. "He will appreciate the empathy." Everyone loved her parents. They were warm to everyone they encountered and best friends to each other.

The rest of Jamie's day was certainly mundane compared to the four minutes of excitement she'd experienced when the pretty blonde had breezed through. Maybe this was a sign that she needed to get out there more. A string of bad dates over the past few years had turned her off the idea that she was a candidate for real romance. She gravitated instead to comfy clothes and a thoughtful movie on the old couch each night after work. Indies were her favorite, the lesser-known gems that the masses hadn't yet discovered. She briefly imagined the impeccable blonde sitting next to her in her apartment and nearly laughed out loud. The two simply didn't fit.

"At least I know I'm still alive," she told her cozy little apartment later that night. She popped a bowl of buttery popcorn on the stove and grabbed a blanket, remote in hand. "And it's kinda nice."

She looked skyward, remembering her conversation with Clarissa that morning.

"Don't mess this up for me, Venus."

Chapter One

Leighton Morrow arrived at her desk on the fourteenth floor of Carrington's corporate office in Midtown just before eight a.m. She had a cup of coffee in hand, but it wasn't nearly as good as the latte she'd enjoyed from Bordeauxnuts in Chelsea, which definitely stood out from the coffee pack. She'd be back there soon enough. For now, she'd have to just remember it fondly and deal with the less than perfect latte she had instead.

"Little something for you on your desk," her assistant, Mindy, told her in an overly sweet voice when she arrived. Leighton set Mindy's toffee nut mocha on her desk and frowned. "And I'm sorry."

"Oh no."

"Oh yes."

Sitting smack in the middle of her desk was an oversized bouquet of red roses in a box the shape of a giant L. The thing took up most of her desk. "Please tell me the *L* is for Leighton."

Mindy stood behind her in the doorway. "Oh, sweetie. I don't think so."

With trepidation, she read the card. She really hated rejecting anyone, but she and Harris Gilman from accounting were not meant to be. He just wasn't getting the message, no matter how politely she dodged his texts, visits, and detailed emails about his day. Their lone date was over a month ago. *Love is in the air this week, and I wanted to beat everyone to the punch. Want to go on a date with me? How 'bout we go to a Valentine's lunch? Love, Harris.* She turned slowly to Mindy and stared. Hard.

"It rhymes," Mindy said conservatively. "We can say that for him. Bless the second grade and Harris Gilman. He doesn't give up, does he?"

"What am I going to do?"

"We've been through this. You have to be straightforward. He usually swings by midmorning to see if you're in. You tell him that there can't be anything romantic between you and that you'll see him in the break room on the fourth floor."

Leighton was confident in every aspect of her life, except when it came to hurting people's feelings. That part, she simply couldn't face.

After she'd agreed to go out with him, Harris had pursued her with a vigor she wasn't quite sure what to do with. The fact of the matter was, there was no chemistry. Harris was enthusiastic about, well, everything, which made telling him this was never going to work out feel like stepping on a happy little butterfly.

"Incoming," Mindy said, glancing behind her.

Leighton straightened, preparing for the honesty battle she was determined to win against herself.

"Well, hello, hello," Harris said, stepping past Mindy and into her office, beaming. He wore a lot of brown, which was standard for him. Today, it was in the form of a dark beige suit jacket, white and brown tie, and pointy brown shoes. Even the tufts of hair on his head were brown. "What do we have here?" he asked in an overexaggerated tone reminiscent of a surprised kindergarten teacher. There was no way she could make out with a person who spoke that way half the time, even if he was incredibly nice.

"Well, someone sent me flowers," Leighton said, holding up the card. "It was sweet of you, but you shouldn't have gone to the trouble."

"I thought a pre-Valentine's surprise would be even more of a shocker."

She tapped the card against her hand. "And it was." A pause. "I'm going to decline lunch, though, because as much as I like you, I don't want to give you the wrong impression."

"Well, we both have to eat," he said, clearly dodging the implication.

"Harris. You're great. So is your poetry. But I don't think we have a romantic connection." There. She'd done it. Honest and up-front.

He seemed to take this in. "Are you sure?"

She nodded. "I like you very much, but our connection is friendship based."

He slid his hands into his pockets and rocked forward. "You don't think about us when you fall asleep? I imagine our vacations. We seem like beach people."

"I've always kind of been a city girl. But no. I don't."

He looked like a kicked puppy. Why was honesty, when it came to matters of the heart, so difficult? "I suppose you can keep the flowers."

"Are you sure?"

"Hmm." He touched his chin, thoughtful. "Well, I suppose Valentine's Day isn't until tomorrow."

She saw where he was going. "They're yours if you want them."

His eyes lit up. "Laurie who manages the cafeteria is really pretty."

"And starts with an *L*. There you go," Leighton said, bypassing the thought of Laurie receiving recycled flowers, and trying to act as Harris's cheerleader. Maybe they would make Laurie's entire day.

"Do you think we could maybe not…"

"My lips are sealed," Leighton told him, turning the lock in front of them. She made eye contact with Mindy just outside the door who did the same.

"I hope you have a great Valentine's, Leighton, and find the love of your life."

"I appreciate the vote of confidence, but I'll be flying solo tomorrow. Best wishes with Laurie."

"I hope she's not allergic to roses. I am."

"Okay, maybe not so close then," she said, pulling the large box away from his chest.

Once Harris floated away to the cafeteria, Leighton turned to Mindy. "I'm not good at that."

"You battle toe-to-toe with executives on a daily basis, yet Harris tugs at your sentimental side."

"They're entirely different. Updates?"

"Yes." Mindy picked up her tablet and scrolled. "Bryce upped your project meeting to three. Apparently, they want to move faster on permits in Chelsea, so they want your reports expedited."

"I'll try. I visited the coffee-wine bar briefly. Bordeauxnuts. Cute name. But, as you know, I want to spend more time inside to get a true feel for the space and its potential."

"I let him know."

"I will say this. The interior looked to have a reusable design, especially if we're holding to the café on the back wall of the store as originally planned."

"Bryce will love it. So will your cousin."

"Courtney's good at the grand scheme. That's for sure." Her first cousin, Courtney Carrington, was the CEO and face of Carrington's Department Stores. A good egg. As the cousin with a *different* last name, Leighton preferred to fly under the radar, keep her head down, and do her job. Only half the people who worked alongside her had put together her family connection, and that was just fine with her. She didn't feel the need to advertise.

"So if you're not going out with dear Harris, what are your Valentine's plans?"

"A glass of good wine alone at a bar before I head home and bury myself in work. Sounds ideal, no?"

"Sounds very Leighton. I was just hoping for a new sexy leaf. Time to get you out from behind your desk and into the heart and sheets of someone special."

"Well, I am dating."

"Not enough. We need more. My boring married self is not getting enough vicarious action. Please work harder."

"Well, there's no one special enough for a Valentine's outing. Those kinds of dates are special."

"I'm gonna give you a pass. I love that you're secretly a romantic."

"What about you? Billy taking you out?"

"We're going to his favorite restaurant that he continuously thinks is mine. Close your eyes and imagine that beautiful restaurant in the distance...Behold, the Olive Garden."

"Oh no, Billy."

"Oh yes. At least there are unlimited breadsticks."

"The key to any woman's heart." She turned. "Can you turn off my morning calendar? I'm gonna do a bit of research on the current leases on the Chelsea properties in question."

"I'll hang up a Do Not Disturb sign."

Mindy was a rock star at her job and always had Leighton's back.

As she settled and made a few key calls to the owner of several buildings along Sixteenth Street in Chelsea, she flashed back to the cute little coffee bar. It really was a shame to displace it. She got the feeling it was at home in the heart of the neighborhood and a cozy hangout to its regulars. "Nothing lasts forever," she murmured and she crunched the numbers she'd been provided on her call. Still, this time it ate away at her a little more than others. That was strange. Business was business. Since when did she let her emotions factor in?

❖

"Oh, Valentine's Day. Damn you," Jamie murmured to her alarm clock at four forty-five a.m. It had the nerve to say nothing back. No good morning kiss. No sweet nothings whispered in her ear. Not even a card or box of candy or saucy limerick. A deep sigh as she stared at her empty bedroom. That was okay. Single women everywhere had learned to turn a blind eye to the over-the-top displays of affection that showed up around every corner on February 14. It didn't mean Bordeauxnuts could do the same. She was no marketing fool and would capitalize on every damn holiday she could, even if this one did make her feel much smaller for being unattached. The bar had had cardboard hearts hanging from the ceiling, a chalkboard decorated with Cupid and his arrows, and love jams going on subscription radio all month.

Jamie spent the morning selling caffeinated beverages and piping hot mini-doughnuts to her customers who arrived carrying flowers, stuffed bears, and giant cardboard hearts. It was quite the parade. But Jamie hadn't ignored the holiday altogether. She'd ordered a bundle of cookies and brownies and had them delivered to her parents' apartment, only to have her father call and ask the name of the chocolatier because he wanted to send a handwritten card complimenting them on their work.

"It's a little place a few blocks away, but I promise you do not need to write to them, Dad. This is just what they do, especially on V-Day."

"If everyone took that attitude, how would anyone know when they'd made a contribution to the world that someone else noted and appreciated? You must take the time, Jamie, to reach out to your fellow human."

"Got it," she said. He was right, as always. "I'm sure they would love to hear from you."

"You're a good girl to us, Jamie. Thank you for your thoughtful treats."

"It's just because I love you both and adore the way you love each other."

"I'll tell you a secret if I'm not keeping you from work."

She had a line forming and her part-timer, Shannon, was in the weeds, but it would have to wait. She always made time for her dad. "Dying to hear it. Tell me."

"Your mom has already eaten two brownies, but I'm about to pass her up and steal a third. Don't tell." He laughed, and she grinned, hand on her forehead. She was their only child, who they'd had a little bit later in life, putting them close to seventy now. The truth was, they got sweeter each year. There were no two people as earnest and adorable as her parents, who played intense gin on weeknights and took long walks no matter how cold or hot it was outside. She wanted a partnership like theirs one day.

"I promise I won't tell her. Enjoy your day of romance."

"Is that Jamie? Tell her you had more brownies!" Her mother's voice drifted in from the distance.

"I did not!" he called back before returning to the call. "I hope you enjoy yours, too. I love you. Bye, sweetheart."

It had been a boost to her morning, speaking with her father.

By early afternoon, they were approaching transition mode from quirky coffee bar to cozy little wine nook. In a couple of hours, she'd switch her board to highlight their featured flights and pours of the day. She tried to keep the specials fresh and interesting. Today, she had a Merlot and Behold flight she planned to roll out. She'd also chosen a really rich red blend to debut for the Valentine's couples. They'd offer seven-dollar glasses from four to six, when they'd get hit hard by the after-work crowd before transitioning to customers in search of an after-dinner drink or bottle. At ten o'clock, they'd close for good, an appropriate time that put them in the semisophisticated column rather than the late-night party zone. Jamie, who'd opened, would sneak out once their happy hour hit its stride. Her capable team would take it from there. The only time she stuck around was when she was having too good a time to leave. She'd clock out and maybe enjoy a big, bold glass of red with whoever happened to be around. Sometimes that was better than going home to her empty apartment.

"Happy Valentine's! What can I make you today?" Jamie raised her gaze to a familiar pair of brown eyes. Beautiful ones, like a doe in the woods serenely staring back at her. She blinked to clear her field of vision, but no, the woman remained. Not a mirage. Today her blond hair was pulled back to her neck and twisted in that fancy way Jamie could never quite master. Her own dark hair had a secret method of messily escaping anytime she pulled it back. "You're back," she blurted.

The woman's eyebrows rose. "That's right. You have a really good memory."

The striking customer had no idea that she was *extra* memorable to Jamie. Time to play it off. "Everyone always tells me that." She touched her temple and the Sharpie behind her ear fell to the counter. Embarrassing. "Um, drink? I mean, what can I make you?" she asked, finding her normal stride. "It's a holiday, so the sky's the limit." She grinned, hoping for friendly rather than strange.

The woman scanned the blackboard. "The Chocolate Kiss sounds promising. Love is in the air, after all."

"Right," Jamie said, proud of her mocha-coconut espresso drink and happy to hear the selection. Her stomach went tight, making her more aware of the flutter of butterfly wings, multiplying by the second. "That's a fantastic choice. 'Tis the kissing season, right?"

"Exactly my thinking." They shared a smile that didn't feel so weird, which was nice. The woman—who Jamie was now calling Bambi's Mother, because those *eyes*—changed it up on her. Instead of taking her drink to go, she found herself a table and took out a MacBook. What was happening? The blonde was staying? This wasn't what Jamie had planned on. She'd worked to survive their brief exchange, but now she'd have to be a normal person for so much longer. Her regulars seemed to notice as well, shooting her do-you-see-who-is-seated-among-us stares. Eyes went wide. Seats were adjusted. Marjorie dropped her knitting needles with a clang onto the table. Seated just behind the woman, Genevieve, always the boldest personality, tossed an excited fist in the air. Marvin scratched his neck nervously, and Lisa and Chun quietly high-fived. They'd been infiltrated! Jamie held up both hands, palms out, sending the silent gesture to force them to keep calm. *Nobody panic.* Potential embarrassment loomed, and she had to get in front of it. After a squirmy moment or two, they slowly drifted back to their respective mornings. Ninety minutes later, when Bambi's Mother took her leave, the dining area erupted in a flurry.

"She came back," Chun hissed. "She likes your bar, Jamie. Get her number. Then a house and kids."

"No. Not in the realm of possibility." Jamie came around the counter, leaving Shannon on register. Shannon was very capable and knew her coffee, even if she was a bit of a food snob. She'd been working with Shannon on smothering her overt judgment when she didn't jibe with a customer's order. Jamie kept her mainly on mornings since she didn't know much about wine. "You have to understand that there are leagues. We're in different ones. That woman"—she hooked a thumb at the door behind her—"is Fifth Avenue. I'm downtown all day."

"Go downtown on her then. She'll love it." Genevieve licked her finger and let it sizzle in the air.

"Genevieve. Seriously?" Jamie blinked. "You cannot."

"Can. Did. People pay me good money for dialogue like that."

Jamie pinched the bridge of her nose. "I always forget who I'm dealing with." She slid herself into a chair simply to recover from the sexy image that had been placed in her head, while her cheeks flamed and her heart thudded. What she needed was a cool-off thought...like the hairbrush when it needed cleaning out. A fly landing in her water. Anything the opposite of sexy. Jamie didn't even allow her own brain the leniency of those kind of thoughts about Bambi's Mother. "The point is that even if she does come in here again, I'm not equipped for...*her*. So we have to put an end to the overt cheerleading, okay? It's a dead end."

"We're here for you, Jamie," Lisa said. She turned to the group, which now included several customers who knew none of them but seemed invested. "Tone it down, dudes. We're embarrassing her. She's all red and twitchy."

"I'm not twitchy." She caught herself midtwitch and hugged her arms to her chest. "I'm just stretching. It's a midmorning stretch. I do it daily." She stood and committed, doing a pronounced reach for the heavens.

"You're like my favorite Peloton instructor over there," Marvin said dryly.

Jamie straightened. "You exercise, Marvin?"

"No," he said and slid back behind his screen.

The morning marched on with a giant heart around it. At least for everyone else. That part was cool. Love, companionship, and happily ever after on display everywhere. All those smiling faces, customers coming and going with an added spring in their steps. Jamie smiled and tried to imagine someone thinking she was the most special person on the planet.

"She wasn't so bad," the voice-over said.

"Gee, thanks," she responded.

"Talkin' to yourself again, James," Leo called to her, midfroth.

"I know. It's a thing," she called back over the piercing noise.

"You do you."

She turned back to her line only to find Clarissa staring back at her from the other side of the register with panicked saucer eyes.

"Uh-oh," Jamie said. "What now? Is it Mercury today? What's the word on this side of the galaxy?"

"Worse. I heard a rumor that's starting to feel real." She gestured with her head for Jamie to step down the counter, which she did. "Others have heard it, too."

Jamie frowned. "Okay. What's the awful rumor?"

"I heard that there's a Carrington's headed to South Chelsea," Clarissa said. "A Carrington's, James."

Jamie frowned and checked her line. She only had a minute. A drink was ready next to her at the bar, and she slid it to its owner. "You have a fantastic day and enjoy that mocha frappé." Back to Clarissa. "The department store?" With every year that went by, another commercialized business invaded their small neighborhood. Starbucks had opened a flagship store just a few years back, for heaven's sake, which set Jamie on her mission to be the anticorporate coffee bar.

Clarissa shook her head as Jamie tried to examine the domino effect. "And a store like Carrington's will be massive. It could completely take us out. Our business can't withstand another financial hit, and a new location would be exactly that. We're struggling as is." Clarissa managed her family's boutique clothing store, De Colores, a few doors down Sixteenth Street. Chelsea real estate was a hot commodity these days. Luckily, the smaller independent stores like Bordeauxnuts and De Colores were on long-term leases that protected their terms. Unfortunately, that wouldn't always be the case, and the clock was ticking. Jamie's plan had always been to stay popular and relevant, keeping her chin above water with really good coffee, wine, and atmosphere. So far, it had worked. She was profitable and steady. However, De Colores had fallen on harder times lately, struggling to stay open. Dwindling receipts month after month had her worried for them. The Riveras had been a second family to Jamie for many years, and she'd never seen them with their spirits quite so low.

This was bad news. She worked to tame the crocodiles she now saw circling. "Well, don't panic." Even though Jamie was. "Maybe the Carrington's thing is just what you called it, a rumor."

Leo slid Clarissa her standard on-the-house latte and jutted his chin. "My buddy heard the same thing. He's a bike messenger and says word is out there. Get ready for another corporate giant to stamp out this neighborhood's culture."

Jamie hid her wince, headed down the counter, and brightened to greet her next customer. "Good morning. Welcome in. What can I make up for you?"

"Americano," a serious looking man said, refusing to smile. His tie was tied within a quarter inch of his life. Excessive, but his prerogative. She'd name him Tight Tie.

Jamie smiled at him for a good two seconds before the lines around his mouth relaxed a hint. *There we go.* And that was what her job was all about, making a tiny difference in the course of a day. If her moment of connection, that smile, made him loosen up even a little, it had been well worth it. "You got it. Love the tie." As if on cue, he grabbed the knot and gave it a small tug, offering a tad bit of relief. *Even better.*

Off to the side, Clarissa sighed, walking backward toward the café portion of the bar. "What's next? Is Amazon going to take over The High Line for outdoor storage? Will our precious landmarked buildings be stripped of their status so the corporate bullies can put up the loud signage they prefer? We're gonna be Times Square by next year."

"No. We're not," Jamie said. It was her job to balance Clarissa. The sky was not falling.

"The world is crumbling!"

Jamie laughed. "Don't jump to the worst case. Wait and see before expending the negative energy."

Clarissa crossed her arms like a child whose lollipop had been stolen. "It's my Thursday vibe, and I'm running with it. It's raining daggers, and we don't have steel umbrellas."

Jamie squinted. "Weirdest imagery ever."

"Well, it applies!" Clarissa said dolefully.

Regardless, Jamie refused to believe any of the gloom and doom until it was on her doorstep. She prided herself on her positive disposition. Change was a part of life. She'd never been a huge fan of it personally, but she was working on finding the value in new things. The rumor did quietly have her on edge, however. She was thirty-four years old and happily attached to things just the way they were. They didn't need a giant department store in their midst. She loved their little corner of the city and its historical, personal touches. The new Vans location had already taken out one of her favorite bars on the planet. Hopefully, the Carrington's buzz was a nothingburger. She touched her stomach. It felt weird, like she was careening down the giant drop of a roller coaster. Was this the Venus interference? For the past few days, she'd had a gut feeling that something was on the way, a giant wind about to blow in and topple everything in sight. She just couldn't pinpoint *what* and prayed it wasn't a robbery. She'd had two in the eight years she'd been open, and that was plenty. "Whatever happens, we're going to be fine. Do you hear me?"

Clarissa didn't appear convinced. "I will defer to your level head."

"I'm serious. Do not let this ruin your day. You deserve a good one. Look how adorable you are. They don't make 'em like you anymore." She gave Clarissa's cheek an affectionate squeeze.

Clarissa exhaled and settled in to enjoy her latte before heading back to finish out her day at De Colores. On her way out, she slammed a hand on the counter, snagging Jamie's focus. "Call me if you hear anything about Carrington's or even if you don't. We can gossip relentlessly."

"You got it. Sending smooches."

"Catching them." Clarissa made a show of smacking her palm to her cheek. "You're such a good kisser."

"I know." She grinned.

"Here's what I say about the whole drama," Marjorie said, gesturing to the door Clarissa just vacated. "If Carrington's posts something official, that's when you worry."

"Exactly where I'm coming from, too," Jamie said, coming around the counter to the café.

Marjorie gestured around the winter hat she'd been knitting all week. "And I need to come by De Colores for those bright green shoes Clarissa was telling me about. I need more pop in my life. I can't be the boring schoolmarm." She raised a finger in the air in declaration. "I refuse!"

"You're gonna love 'em. My mom has them in pale yellow, and she's on her feet all day, still giving lectures at the college. Like little pillows from whatever God you embrace. That's what she says, anyway."

Marjorie's eyes lit up. "Sold. I won't be buying any from Carrington's."

Marvin scoffed, unable to resist the lure of the conversation. "If Carrington's was making the leap to open a downtown store, I'd know. They're happy with their midtown arm, even if it is a bit small. Nothing to worry about."

"If you say so."

"I feel like I'd sense it in the air," Genevieve told her. "We're all good here."

The troops had rallied to assuage her fears. It had honestly helped, too. She shoved the concern to the side and focused on the customer traffic, which was always more plentiful on a holiday.

By early evening, she was uncorking a bottle of her favorite merlot for a cute couple dressed for a date, rang them up, applied her Valentine's Day discount, and for good measure, handed over a bag of cinnamon sugar doughnuts on the house. Fresh and hot.

"These pair perfectly. Trust me." She had a mushy heart, after all, and smiled wistfully at the cute pair as they found a quiet table by the window. When she ended her shift an hour later, they were sipping and chatting quietly, passing each other the sweetest smiles. As it should be on a night like tonight.

She walked the twelve blocks home rather than taking the short train ride, smiling up at the stars that were peeking out, ready to make their big debut. The streets were more crowded than usual, and she did her best to dodge the people heading here or there, looking their sharpest. Palpable energy zigzagged across the crowded sidewalks. She smiled and wished them well, enjoying the contact high she got from their excitement.

When she arrived at the door to her third-story apartment, her next door neighbor, Marlene, was locking up her place. "Where are you off to, Marlene? Big date?" Her question had been lighthearted because Marlene was seventy-three and lived a fairly quiet life, aside from visits from her grown children. She'd never seen her with a partner or prospect.

"Yes. His name is Edward and he's taking me to a jazz show at Birdland. We're gonna drink the liquor and have a time."

Jamie went still. The universe had to be kidding. Even Marlene had Valentine's plans. "That's amazing. Order a fancy cocktail for me and enjoy the music." Her heart swelled for her neighbor.

"I'm so excited. I can't wait. And Jamie?"

"Yes?"

"He has *hair*."

"Get out."

"I couldn't believe my luck." Marlene laughed. "I met him at a funeral. Can you believe it? We had the same friend in common and never even knew it until she was gone. Guess she was our guardian angel." She passed Jamie's door. "You have a fantastic night, sweet girl. Don't stay out too late. Or, maybe, do!"

Jamie decided not to correct the assumption that she'd be anywhere except on her couch watching sitcom reruns. "Oh, I don't know. I'll see what I can do."

"Love is in the air," Marlene called from down the hall. "La la da dee, la da," she sang in a melodic voice.

That, it was. But Jamie's own personal Valentine's Day didn't feel special. She watched a little TV, read a few chapters of her Michele Obama biography, scrolled social media, liking all the photos of her friends and their significant others at fancy restaurants, and climbed in bed with a small smile on her lips. Her solitary evening didn't matter. The world was a good place, and days like today where positive energy rushed through every nook reminded her of it. And there was even that semi-awkward exchange with Bambi's Mother that she could laugh about now. That's what life was about. She shoved the melancholy aside and decided she'd instead wait and see what tomorrow delivered.

You never knew when something wonderful was about to be dropped right into the middle of your lap. She hugged a soft pillow to her chest and mumbled the word *lucky*. Because that's exactly what Jamie was, and she would not allow herself to forget it.

Chapter Two

A nd what about the coffee and, uh, wineshop place? Is it a grocery store, too? Damn," Bryce asked from the head of the conference table. He had two empty Red Bull cans next to him and was popping a third. "Who do we have on that? Leighton, right?"

Leighton snapped her focus to the conversation in the room. Usually a very attentive person, lately she'd been daydreaming a startling amount. She was savvy enough to play it off, snatching up the file in front of her. "Bordeauxnuts on Sixteenth. Yeah." She slid a strand of hair behind her ear. "I've swung by a couple of times. Low-key place. Charming. There are portions of the design that are salvageable, especially if we hold to keeping the coffee shop at the back of the store. The dining space is solid, just need to redesign the counterspace and build in a walkway. Very doable. The numbers are certainly not a problem. Investment is solid."

"Encouraging," Bryce practically barked. He overdid everything, and it was starting to wear thin. "Any red flags?"

She consulted her notes on her laptop. "The owner seems personable and friendly. I can't imagine her being a problem."

"Not when a big fat buyout check is waved in front of her face," Jeffrey said with a smirk. Her colleague and complete opposite in every way proceeded to balance a pen on his knuckles, entranced. They were on the same team, unfortunately, but saw the process very differently. She frowned at him. He took too much pleasure in these swoop-ins. For Leighton, displacement was a necessary but unfortunate part of corporate expansion. Her job on the development team of Carrington's was to assess each new property, its risks and rewards, and make her recommendation to the higher-ups. Little Bordeauxnuts was in the way of the incoming Chelsea store and would have to go. Facts were facts. The little coffee/wine bar would hopefully land on its feet and seek out a new storefront once Carrington's bought out the lease. Hopefully, the owner would be grateful for the handsome payout and call the whole thing a financial win.

That would all be handled by their real estate attorneys, however. She'd file her report, make her recommendations, a few projections, and move on to the next project.

She leveled Jeffrey a stare. "Not everyone is an ant beneath your shoe."

He laughed. "Leighton, you robot. Try to enjoy what we're doing here," Jeffrey said, hands in a grabbing gesture, which was a metaphor for how he went through his whole life. Taking what he wanted. He also chewed with his mouth open at parties. "We're the big guys swinging our dicks around. Enjoy it."

The room of eight people cringed in unison. Jeffrey was a shark, and that's why he was here, but it was certainly hard to like the guy.

She leaned in. "That's a visual I will spend years trying to erase from my brain."

"Can we move on?" Bryce asked.

"Please," Leighton said. "I need more time with the coffee/wine bar, but the pizza place on the corner is definitely an easy wrap-up. Bored teenagers running the counter, no one who cares in sight. Business is close to nonexistent."

"Perfect. Mary Ann, how are we on our upped timeline?" Bryce asked, moving their meeting forward with his no-nonsense approach. As her colleague shuffled through her file folder, Leighton's thoughts casually drifted back to Bordeauxnuts and their amazing lattes. In fact, she had a surprising urge to swing by after the meeting, maybe finish the rest of her afternoon from a spot facing the counter. Was that awful, given that she worked for the company she knew was about to swoop in and evict? She swallowed the kernel of guilt. Everyone would be taken care of, and a brand new department store would service the good people of Chelsea. Plus, her job was to scout, and visiting the space was part of that task. She wasn't *exactly* a double agent. Plus, she needed coffee, and they had some. Easy.

When she arrived at the coffee bar, the late morning showed considerable traffic. The woman behind the register, whom she ascertained to be Jamie Tolliver, the owner, was just as cheerful as always. Adorable, too. Today, her dark hair was pulled back in a ponytail through her cap, which she hadn't worn before. A very cute look. Her blue eyes sparkled brightly. God, Leighton was a sucker for blue eyes. Even more so today, apparently.

"I'm back again."

"You are." Jamie swallowed. "I guess we're doing something right." A pause. It got longer. "Oh, sorry. What can I do for you? I forgot to ask." She touched the top of her cap. "What can I have made for you? It's been a morning."

Leighton laughed. "Universally. I'll take a pistachio latte if you think that's a good choice."

"I applaud it. Not enough people appreciate pistachio. The underappreciated flavor on our board. What can I get you to eat? Some of our warm doughnuts?"

Leighton inhaled the heavenly scent. She also spied the source, a machine dropping tiny fresh doughnuts into a tray behind Jamie. Her appetite and soul coveted and reached. "Well, now that I've laid eyes on them, how can I resist?"

"All part of our master plan," Jamie said, stone serious.

Leighton tapped her card and caught several framed news articles on the wall, all about the bar and its unique approach to coffee and wine. "Wow. You were featured in the *Times*?"

"Several different features over the years." Jamie pointed across the room to the other wall where Leighton spotted more framed media. "And *Time Out New York* and a whole host of others. We're incredibly famous." She was joking but wasn't entirely wrong given this coverage.

"You must be really proud."

Jamie relaxed into the most radiant smile. She had subtle dimples. Leighton went still as the happiness pulled her in. She was a sucker for people who carried passion for what they did. Maybe it was one part envy. Her job was important to her, but passion was unique.

"More than proud. This little bar is my family." She winced. "Sorry for the gushing. I probably sound like a human needlepoint, but it's my truth, and I can't smother it."

Leighton rushed to reassure her. "It doesn't. It sounds like someone who knows a good thing when she has it. Very cool." She nodded and moved down to the drink station to wait on her latte.

"Thank you for saying that," Jamie said. A moment later and Jamie's gaze was still on Leighton. She could tell without fully turning to find out. There was a warmth against her cheek. Was it possible she was being checked out? Well, well. Jamie might just walk on the queer side. She passed an appreciative smile that she hoped didn't say *You might be checking me out, and I don't mind.*

"What was your name?" Leighton called over the whirling and whistling of the espresso machine. Of course, she already knew but couldn't exactly stay so.

"I'm Jamie."

She softened at the way Jamie said it. "I love that name."

"You do?" She watched as Jamie's cheeks dusted the cutest shade of pink. She wondered what else she could say to elicit that same result, because *yeah.*

"Very much." She touched her chest. "I'm Leighton. Nice to meet you."

"Same," Jamie answered. She blinked a few times with those big blue eyes, almost as if ordering herself to get her head in the coffee game. Finally, Jamie nodded and brightened to a farewell smile and moved on to help the next customer. Leighton was sad their exchange had ended but had enjoyed the sparks of energy that moved between them. She'd noticed Jamie on their first couple of meetings, but now she *really* noticed her.

Leighton spent the next two hours catching up on paperwork and putting the finishing touches on her report for a property, currently doing business as a clothing store, a few doors down. During her short mental breaks, she rewarded herself by watching Jamie interact with customers from behind the counter and sometimes even in front of it. She was the perfect host, vivacious, warm, and actually really cute, especially in that cap. Energy like hers was contagious and captivating. Leighton had a feeling that the store's success was not just due to its unique, ahead-of-its-time concept, but because Jamie herself came as part of the package. Observing her in her element was an interesting character study. In fact, she lost more time than she cared to admit to stolen glances. Her phone, unfortunately, vibrated and pulled her away from her covert Jamie gazing.

She glanced down at the readout and slid on to the call. "Courtney."

"My weekly check-in. How are things in New York?" her cousin asked.

"Are you asking about *me* or the progress on the new project?" Leighton dropped her tone to maintain her anonymity in the bar.

"I'm always going to be more interested in you. You're one of my favorite humans ever."

Leighton smiled. She and Courtney were just two years apart. She had no siblings of her own and, growing up, always cherished Courtney for that reason. She looked up to her, and always trailed after her during those visits to their grandmother's house in California. When Leighton had formally requested to join the family business after completing her master's program, it was Courtney who'd made sure there was a prime spot for her, harnessing her skill set and placing her on the development team. Leighton had paid her dues diligently, working from the bottom up. No special favors. Courtney Carrington took the business very seriously and didn't believe in handing out unearned promotions, which had Leighton pulling some pretty hefty hours.

"Well, I wish I had more to report. I had a date two nights ago." She knew that would perk Courtney up, a die-hard romantic these days. She loved Leighton's dating stories.

"Any potential there? We're supposed to raise our kids together, but we're both falling short."

"At least you have your person already." Courtney really did have the perfect, most enviable relationship. She and Maggie had been married for several years now and had a life bursting with love. They made eyes at each other across any table, strolled the length of the strawberry farm Maggie's family owned on their off weekends, and took on the big cities whenever Carrington's demanded Courtney's attention. The perfect hybrid existence.

"I take it two nights ago did not deliver yours," Courtney said. She could hear the disappointment in her voice.

Sensing the need for privacy, Leighton began to pack up her table. "A setup from Mindy, who means well. He took a bite of my mushroom ravioli without asking and then used all the butter for his own bread. All."

"Bastard."

"There was no good-night kiss, needless to say. I made sure of that. Not with a butter absconder."

"Always a fan of your vocabulary, Lay. No one should abscond."

"How's Maggie?" Leighton slid her attaché onto her shoulder, and with a quick wave to Jamie. who smiled warmly back, Leighton emerged from the cozy coffee bar to the busy sidewalk. A blast of frigid air hit her face, and she fell in line with the pedestrian class of Chelsea. She was seven stops on the train from her place but had business at the office in midtown first. She signaled for a cab, deciding to dodge the chaos of the station.

"Maggie is getting a much-needed massage. She's earned it after going so hard this week. She sold three properties and listed a handful more. I set her up with a surprise intervention."

"See? Butter guy would never do that."

"He wouldn't. Cut the cord and move on. Life is too short. He or she is out there for you. Just gotta keep looking." Courtney paused. "And the Chelsea store? Bryce says the progress is steady."

"As it can be. I was sitting in what would likely be your new café when you called. Currently a coffee and wine spot loved by the locals."

"Well, they'll love us, too, once they give us a chance."

Leighton was prone to agree. Still, she had a dose of sadness about the loss of Bordeauxnuts as it currently existed. It was an uncomfortable pill she was trying to swallow and so unlike her. Why was this one business standing out in her mind over all the other businesses they'd have to displace to make this store a reality? "I think this one might be a tough sell. The owner seems to love her job and the bar."

"Then let's make sure we take care of her generously on the lease buyout. I trust your gut. Add it to your report. I'll make sure Bryce signs off on it. We're not heartless. I don't ever want to be that."

"On it." She sighed and tried to shake herself out of the melancholy. "Hey, get to the city sometime soon so we can have fake birthday cake." A throwback to when they were preteens and would save up their allowance to buy an entire birthday cake from the grocery store, lie on the floor, and eat it with two plastic forks while watching a movie marathon full of teen heartthrobs. Dammit. Those were the days she cherished. Life was simple, and everything felt possible. Now, she couldn't even count on her date to spare a sliver of butter.

"I'm in! It's on my schedule for next month. And God, I miss having fake birthday cake with you." Courtney laughed.

"And don't forget chocolate milkshakes for breakfast when the adults slept in."

"We're lucky we still have teeth," Courtney said.

"I stand by the gamble. Grandma let us buy those cakes, knowing full well we'd attack them."

Her cousin laughed again. "That's why she was the greatest ever. Oh, damn. I'd love to chat longer, but I have a reporter calling in five."

"A reporter? What's that about, Ms. Sophistication?"

"It's kinda cool, actually. *The New York Times* is doing a piece on corporate succession within families and using me as the centerpiece example."

Courtney had ascended the ranks of the Carrington corporate ladder over the years once her father had passed. She'd made impressive changes to the stores as well as the structure of the company. She'd spent time learning from the company's top executives and eventually took the reins fully. Leighton continued to be in awe of Courtney's instinct and prowess. "I can't wait to read it. But yes, get outta here. We can catch up later."

"Okay. Just understand that I'm smooching all over your face, and Maggie can't wait to show you the new pool this summer. She's in heaven imagining us in the warmer weather in chaise lounges. Love you tons. Please don't work too hard."

"A challenging request, but I'm holding her to that pool time. I love you back."

Leighton ended the call, finished her day of work, and emerged from her office just after the afternoon fully faded into the evening rush hour. As congested as the city became, and despite how long it would take to get anywhere, it was her favorite time of day. Final deals were being made, last minute theatre tickets were being scored, and people from all walks of life made the mad dash to their evening destinations.

For Leighton, she'd head home to her apartment on the Upper East Side with the killer view and the really impressive ceilings. She'd paid a pretty penny for those. In addition to her salary at Carrington's, she'd also inherited some family money on her mother's side plus her mother's Carrington shares. Money would likely never be an issue, but loneliness was, on occasion. She had friends, but no family nearby. Colleagues, but no significant other. Not even a dog to cuddle with because her work schedule would make it unfair. So for now, it was just Leighton, her apartment, and the career goals she'd set for herself. Life was a little less colorful than she'd imagined for herself at thirty-six, but she hoped there was still time to shade in the lines.

Was her person out there somewhere in this great big city? She hugged herself and looked to the stars, partially visible through the wisps of dark clouds.

She laughed off the thought and savored the view from her too-big apartment that seemed lost on just her, no one to share it with. She had standards, though, which was why her relationships never ended in a forever romance. Simple things mattered. For example, she valued true connection and thoughtful behavior. She grinned and sipped her freshly poured glass of merlot. Priorities mattered. So did butter sharing.

Chapter Three

"G orgeous," Jamie murmured to herself, clutch held nervously at her side. Her high heels were already chafing the backs of her feet, but she could ignore all that for the beauty of the space in front of her. The private room on the rooftop level of the Driskill Hotel was clearly designed to impress and did. With its floor-to-ceiling windows and opulent crystal chandelier, Jamie felt like she'd been dropped into a fairy tale as she arrived at the cocktail party in celebration of her friend Elise's engagement. Sometime in the next year, Elise would become Mrs. Jeremy Turner and join all the other married people in the happily ever after club. She had seen much less of Elise since Jeremy had appeared on the scene, but that was okay. Her friend was happy, and that was the main goal. Tonight, they'd raise a glass in honor of the newly engaged couple in a setting that had turned out to be much fancier than she'd expected. Jamie's eyes went wide as jumbo shrimp, lobster crostini, and brisket poppers were whisked around the room by astute servers along with trays of wine, every shade one could imagine. Oh, and what were those little cocktail glasses with sprigs of rosemary propped against the side of the glass? She'd have to investigate further. The foodie in her celebrated.

After taking in the scene, Jamie scanned the room for Clarissa, realizing quickly that she'd arrived first. That was okay. She chatted happily with the mutual friends she recognized, enjoying herself until the inevitable record scratch.

Jamie didn't actively cringe when she crossed paths with too many people, but her ex-girlfriend Laurel Kippling made the top of the list. Unfortunately, they still ran into each other every so often, despite the size of the city. Symptom of sharing friends prior to the big, bad breakup. In their case, the relationship had ended over three years ago. Yet it was becoming clear that Laurel was likely going to be a permanent fixture in Jamie's life simply due to social proximity.

As a plan of action, Jamie forced herself to forget about the ugly breakup, after which Laurel had immediately taken up with their good friend Lara and bought a damn Goldendoodle, the same breed Laurel knew Jamie had always adored. She'd gone on to flaunt the new relationship in Jamie's face until it had thankfully ended, too. Laurel, with her overly highlighted blond hair and big green eyes, was an attention seeker who was often rewarded with throngs of it. She was likely on her fifth or sixth girlfriend since Jamie. But who could keep count? If anything, that circumstance should make Jamie feel better about the bullet she'd dodged. Nothing personal, right? Just another ex-girlfriend to Laurel, a number. Except Jamie walked away from every Laurel interaction feeling like a very small and undesirable insect. Laurel's gift.

"Look! Jamie is here!" Laurel said, scurrying over and leaning in for an air-kiss. "Sweetheart, this is Jamie, um"—a pause—"Tolliver. Yes. Where is my mind these days?" She added a flippant laugh.

"Hi." Jamie smiled at Laurel and her sweetheart du jour, refusing to wince at the name stumble that was in all likelihood an intentional mistake made to belittle. They'd lived together for a year and a half, and now Laurel couldn't come up with her last name? Par for the Laurel course. "Nice to see you both."

When she'd received the invitation to the engagement party, she'd known there was a likely chance of a Laurel sighting. She'd strategically selected her royal-blue fit-and-flare cocktail dress that showed off her shoulders, which Jamie was convinced were her one truly stellar feature outside of her smile, which she was proud of as well. "This is cute," Laurel said, thumbing the fabric near her thigh.

"Thank you. Just something I picked up."

"Jamie's great with a sales rack," Laurel told the sweetheart. Only the dress hadn't come from one. Jamie had saved up for it. Another jab landed by Laurel.

Luckily, she had Clarissa arriving shortly for backup. *Please hurry.*

She scanned the busy room for any sign of her best friend, who had a similar distaste for Laurel Kippling. Clarissa would quickly rescue her or go to battle in her honor. No sign of her yet.

"How do you know Laurel?" the stunning brunette sweetheart asked. She was about five inches taller and Jamie felt every damn one of them.

"Oh, we lived together a very long time ago."

"Roommates?" the woman said, her eyes lighting up. She sidled up to Jamie. "You'll have to tell me all of Laurel's little faults around the house. Does she remember to turn the dishwasher on at the end of the evening?"

Jamie was pretty sure that Laurel was unaware how a dishwasher even worked, nor how to wash a dish by hand, but this was not the moment to be petty. "I'll never tell," Jamie said, to a laugh from Laurel.

Laurel leaned in toward her date. "I think we can arrange for you to find out all those details personally." She squeezed her date around the waist, making her laugh in a high-pitched tone. "Now leave little Jamie alone."

Little Jamie. Jamie nodded, absorbing the passive-aggressive slight. "We were together, though," she said.

The sweetheart, who'd still not been introduced by name, raised an eyebrow.

"Not just roommates. Laurel's my ex. We were together for two years." Jamie had no idea why she needed to make that information known but did. Something about claiming her identity, her truth. She needed to be recognized as someone who had once mattered to Laurel, in the midst of the insults.

"Oh?" the woman said. "That's very cool. So glad you're friends now. Très mature of you both."

"Isn't it great?" Laurel said, placing a hand on her hip and narrowing her gaze. "We were just too different to make it work. Jamie's a barista in Chelsea."

She was also a successful small-business owner who'd won awards and garnered major television and print attention for her bar. However, Jamie didn't correct the statement because barista was also a great gig. She was every bit as proud of interacting with her customers and making drinks as her other accomplishments. The part that bothered her was Laurel didn't seem to think so. "That's true. If you're ever near Sixteenth Street, swing in for a drink and bag of hot doughnuts. I'll make them myself."

"Oh. So kind. We don't go downtown much." Laurel added a wince. "It's just become so…well, *you know*."

"Got it. No downtown." And that would be all she planned on listening to. "If you'll excuse me, I see someone I need to…" She gestured absently across the room to a woman taking in the view from the gorgeous windows. She made a beeline for her, and at the last minute eased her progress, imagining Laurel and her date had shifted their focus. The skyline in its clarity snagged her attention, however.

"Sparkling rosé?" a server asked, offering a selection from her tray. Both Jamie and the woman at the window turned.

"I don't think I can say no," Jamie said, selecting a long-stemmed glass from the group. After that interaction, she deserved a pink treat.

The woman also reached. "Don't mind if I do, too. Cheers."

She raised her glass to the woman's, remembered her manners, and met her gaze on the clink. *Hold up.* Her brain stuttered and started again. Her stomach went tight and fluttery. "It's you. Oh my God. You're Bambi's Mother."

The woman blinked. "I'm not. But I do know you. Trying to place where." She wore a beautiful red dress that fell to midthigh, making her look like a celebrity. Her hair was gently curled and pinned. She was breathtaking. Jamie's heart thudded in happy discovery.

Her actual name hit. "Leighton. You're Leighton. And I'm Jamie."

The most beautiful smile blossomed on Leighton's face. "Yes! You're Jamie from Bordeauxnuts. Hi." She blinked several times as if trying to orient herself to Jamie in the wild. "Wow. You look… stunning."

"Thank you."

"That dress."

She looked down, warmed. "It's new." A pause as they stared at each other happily. "Probably like running into your teacher at the movie theater."

"No. I'm just used to you in—"

"A T-shirt and apron rather than a cocktail dress and heels?"

Leighton opened her mouth and closed it. "When I said stunning, I meant it."

"Oh." A pause. Jamie twirled her hair in an exaggerated fashion. "Sweet of you."

Leighton laughed, which was a fantastic sound. Quiet and melodic. "Not that you're not equally stunning in cotton."

"Bless you." She looked around. "What are you doing here?"

"Why did you think I was Bambi's mother? I don't have children."

They'd asked their questions at the same time and smiled to acknowledge the overlap. "I'll go first," Leighton said. "Jeremy is one of the first friends I made when I moved to the city years ago. We were neighbors who grabbed dinner a few times."

"It seems our friends are getting engaged."

"What a small world. Elise?"

"Yep." Jamie nodded. "We grew up together and maintained our friendship into adulthood. We run in the same social circles now, but back then, her mom and my mom would watch movies while we pretended to fight off pirates in my bedroom."

"I hate it when pirates invade bedrooms." Leighton's brown eyes went wide. "I trust you won."

"Always. Our umbrellas were sharp."

Leighton sipped her pink bubbly with measured elegance, and Jamie tried to mask her captivation. "You're a city kid? No accent."

"Watch out. It slips in every once in a while. Just hang out with me some more." She'd said it with too much bravado, like she was a woman with moves. She wasn't. They would likely never hang out, but she could dream.

"Now I'm going to have to pay attention." Interestingly, that sentence hinted at continued interaction, and Jamie wouldn't mind that at all. "But back to Bambi's mother. Did you mean the cartoon deer, or is there a literal child you had me attached to?"

Jamie pinched the bridge of her nose, searching for a plausible explanation that wouldn't fully embarrass her in the middle of a really nice exchange. "Here's the thing. My regulars and I sometimes have nicknames for customers based on initial impressions or the nature of their order. Sometimes we learn their real names and the fake ones fade away, sometimes they override their real names for all time. Just depends."

Leighton's eyes went wide and her perfect lips pulled in amusement. "Aha. You named me Bambi's Mother?"

"Yeah. You're with me now. And because I know your actual name, we can lose that one."

"Unless it supersedes."

"It won't. Trust me."

"But Bambi's Mother? Why in the world?"

There was no way around this. Jamie decided to dive in headfirst. "You have these really pretty, luminous eyes. And long lashes to go with them." Jamie gestured to her own. "Wasn't a long leap."

Leighton nodded, turned, and faced the window as she tilted her flute into a sip. "Were you checking me out the other day?"

"What? Ha! Why would you say that? Ha again!" Jamie realized her voice was much too loud. "Funny, but...I mean..." Her words trailed off because, damn it all, the Wicked Witch of the East was headed their way with a curious look on her face. "I'm warning you now. The woman who will be here in four seconds is my awful ex-girlfriend, and she's probably going to make passive-aggressive comments in order to disparage me and elevate herself. It's a dance we do."

"Oh, she sounds lovely." Leighton straightened and turned.

Jamie leaned in and kept her voice low. "She's not. I promise. Here we go. Incoming."

"Jamie, is this your date?" Laurel said with an overabundance of enthusiasm.

"Laurel's intentions were not good," the voice-over said.

Oh, you don't have to tell me.

Jamie opened her mouth only to have Leighton beat her to the punch. "Yes. Her date. That's me. Leighton Morrow. Pleased to make your acquaintance."

Laurel's plastered-on smile lost wattage. Leighton had just greeted her with the serenity of someone dripping with both confidence and grace they didn't need. She spoke like royalty. Maybe a kind heiress. "Laurel Kippling. Jamie and I go way back."

"How interesting. You're lucky." Laurel blinked, and Leighton smiled, completely unfazed by any of this. Wow. She then threaded her fingers through Jamie's possessively, and the world went still. Jamie's body came instantly alive, electricity pinging off the scale. "We were just taking in the view. Very romantic up here." She turned to Jamie, kissed her hand. Heat scorched its way up her arm. "We need to come stay for the weekend. I'm told they have a gorgeous penthouse with a park view and a strawberry shortcake not to be missed and"—she lifted her shoulder—"I love robes and room service."

"They're wonderful," Laurel said. She prided herself on being the prettiest girl in any room. Always had. She didn't love competition, and Leighton's presence had surely thrown her off her game. "My girlfriend is around here somewhere. I'll have to introduce you. She's a model working on a tire commercial this week."

"Tires. Wow," Leighton said in an overly enthusiastic voice. "Well. I suppose we all need them."

Laurel looked from Jamie to Leighton, her eyes like darts. "Maybe we can all get together sometime."

"We'd love it. Right, baby?" Leighton asked Jamie, who wasn't at all sure what planet she was on right now but hoped she could live here forever. Leighton was her pretend date, calling her baby and kissing her hand, and Laurel was here to hate every minute of it? Should she buy a lottery ticket next? What had she done for the universe to bless her with this gift of a moment? She planned to relish every second of this exchange, like juice from a ripe nectarine.

"That would be fantastic, but I know your schedule at the office is jam-packed this month," Jamie said and realized she had no idea what Leighton did for a living. She did know, based on Leighton's standard wardrobe and hours spent on a laptop, that it seemed corporate in nature. Maybe an attorney. Or an accountant. Both just upped her sex appeal by a thousand.

"It is crunch time." She turned to Laurel. "Jamie's always so sweet to me after a long day." Laurel blinked several times, swimming in misery and indignation. Jamie was surprised she hadn't started hopping with anger by now.

"Oh, we're the same. Just like that. Too," Laurel added just as Clarissa raced in, scanned the room, and headed straight to Jamie.

"Hey, train delay, but I'm here." She looked to her right. "And so is Laurel." She looked to Jamie's left, saw her holding hands with Leighton and paused. "Oh. Hello." Her gaze flew to Jamie, who calmly explained.

"Yes, *Leighton* is here, too."

"Hi," Leighton said. "Good to see you."

Clarissa simply stared and nodded, surely trying to piece this silly little story together and failing. She'd never met Leighton and was likely struggling with why Jamie was holding hands with a stranger when she knew everything about her life. Luckily, Clarissa was good at taking a cue and did. "I'm thrilled to see you as well." She turned to Laurel and her smile faded. "Laurel," she said flatly.

"Fab to see you, Clarissa. Was it windy out there?" she said, surveying Clarissa's hair.

"Probably from a spell you cast. We all have our gifts."

"Well. I'll leave you all to your evening. It's so exciting to see Jamie with a date." She scrunched her shoulders with false joy and glided away.

Once they were safely alone, Jamie exhaled and laughed. "What in the name of the Bonus Jonas just happened?"

A proud smile played on Leighton's lips, but she held her composure. She was good at that. "I think we just made your ex-girlfriend a tad jealous, which was more fun than I ever would have guessed. She's something." She released Jamie's hand, causing Jamie to grieve.

She turned to Clarissa. "Leighton is friends with Elise's fiancé. Total coincidence, running into her here. She's come into the bar a few times."

"Is she Bambi's Mother?" she practically squeaked, finally putting it together.

"Apparently, yes," Leighton answered for her. "I'm the one who told Laurel we were dating. That was my doing. Sorry for the confusion. Leighton Morrow. Nice to meet you."

"Clarissa. The best friend." Clarissa took her hand. "And in that case, you're my hero. Laurel's the worst and perpetually awful to Jamie, who, by the way, is the sweetest ever."

"Oh, stop," Jamie said, making the keep-it-coming gesture. She was on a high.

"That part's apparent." Leighton beamed. She gestured a few feet away. "I'm going to give Jeremy a kiss and sneak out if that's okay with the two of you. I have a work call across the country. It's much earlier in San Diego." She turned to Jamie. "It was good to see you, and you look incredibly beautiful." A soft smile. "I mean it." She held eye contact for a few delicious seconds, and Jamie felt her knees liquify.

"Yeah. You, too. Hey, Leighton?" She turned back. "Thank you."

Leighton nodded. "Anytime. I mean that. Enjoy your evening. I wish I could stay."

Once alone, Jamie and Clarissa turned to each other with identical shocked expressions.

"She is so into you," Clarissa said, eyes wide. "The last few moments were like something out of a movie." She looked behind her, the same direction Leighton had traveled. "That woman was sexy and gorgeous and poised and quietly flirting with you every second she was here."

"No. Really?"

"Yes."

"We don't know that she's gay."

"She's definitely bisexual at least. I can guarantee it. The interest was on display."

Clarissa was kinda right. She'd felt it, too. Jamie surrendered. "She was a little bit flirtatious, though, right?"

"Jamie. The chemistry was screaming. You two are fire. This is it. This is Venus upending your life. It's tossing you out of your comfort zone, but in the most wonderful way."

"I think I like Venus." She closed her eyes, trying to memorize this moment and the cloud she'd found herself floating on luxuriously above the city. How had such an awful beginning to the cocktail party led to this really gratifying moment?

"Girl, I think you've earned another glass. We have to celebrate." Clarissa looked around for a server.

Jamie laughed, still levitating. "Yes, please."

❖

Leighton woke the next morning with a euphoria she rather enjoyed. She stretched, drank her coffee in her favorite pair of black short-shorts and a tank as she watched the sun rise over the rooftops of a sleepy New York City. She took her time getting ready with the daily news playing on her TV in the background while she ruminated on her time at the Driskill the night before. She knew unequivocally that it was the source of her positivity. How unexpected it had been to run into Jamie of all of the people at the private gathering. Leighton had about fallen out of her heels when she realized that the gorgeous brunette in the blue dress was actually the gorgeous brunette from the coffee bar. She hadn't been cheating on one with the other! Not that it took her that long to make the connection. Jamie was Jamie. Unique in the way she carried herself, spoke, and smiled. In fact, Leighton had trouble taking her eyes off her the whole damn time. Those blue eyes that matched her dress. Her dark hair swept back. Dimples. Leighton tapped her lips as she toyed with the idea of swinging by Bordeauxnuts this morning for a quick coffee stop. Out of her way? Sure. But her whole morning seemed lighter at just the thought. She got a hit of excitement imagining her exchange with Jamie, who—she had to admit—had captured her attention more than anyone had in years.

Of course, at some point, they'd have to discuss Leighton's job and the reason she'd been pulled into the shop in the first place. She dreaded that part, secretly hoping Jamie had always wanted to move and that this was just a very lucrative vehicle to help her take the leap. It was a long shot, but it gave her something to hang on to.

She hopped the train downtown, soaked up the sunshine on her walk, ignored three calls from Bryce, and found herself happily on Bordeauxnuts' doorstep. Maybe she should just get it out of the way. Slip in the Carrington's name and go from there. She nodded once with confidence and pushed open the glass door to the warm atmosphere that enveloped her like a hug. The heavenly smell of espresso and doughnuts coupled with the chatter of people happy to be there put a smile on her face instantly. She'd not been in the place this early in the days before and was surprised that the line stretched all the way to the entrance.

She scanned the café section as she waited, recognizing many of the same faces from her other visits. Curly haired guy in the corner. Knitting lady. The couple always on their phones. Probably more that she missed. Leighton was starting to understand that this was a favorite spot for lots of people. She ignored the pang of regret that nestled in her chest. She'd be filing her report with Bryce that week about her assessment. The architects were already hard at work and this mammoth of a project was about to make itself known when Global Newswire sent out a press release which would confirm any and all rumors that were likely circulating.

"Leighton. Thank God you're here," Jamie said with a wink once she reached the front of the line. Now that they were friends, Jamie

YOU HAD ME AT MERLOT

seemed more confident. Playful, even. Leighton liked it a lot. What she also liked? Flirting with Jamie, watching her cheeks color pink before she perhaps even flirted back.

Leighton laughed. "I had no idea I was in demand. I'd have come sooner. I wish I had now."

"This is the perfect way to brighten my morning." They held eye contact for an extra beat that made Leighton want to scrunch her shoulders against the shiver and slash of heat it brought on. This woman did things to her, and she wanted to do even more.

"How's the blueberry latte?"

Jamie didn't hesitate. "My favorite drink on the menu."

"Then I can't resist."

"Perfect." Jamie reached behind her for a bag of mini-doughnuts and handed them to Leighton. "Latte on the way. And doughnuts just because. On me."

Their hands touched briefly and probably for a beat too long on the handoff. "No one's ever gifted me warm doughnuts before."

"That's the saddest thing I've ever heard. It's lucky you met me." The way Jamie said that last part made Leighton's thighs tingle and other parts of her ache ever so slightly.

"More than lucky. I completely agree," Leighton said, moving down the counter to beverage pickup. The chiseled barista, who wore a name tag that said Leo, offered her a playful wink as he tossed cardboard cups around like a highly skilled magician. Behind him, a cheerful young woman dusted sugar and cinnamon onto two different bags of doughnuts. They were a well-oiled machine, beautiful to look at, and choreographed like a ballet. She wished she could stick around and enjoy the company, by she had a ten a.m. Another project meeting, and Bryce would need updates.

"What do you have going on today in your world?" Jamie called over.

"I have a meeting back at the office," she called back.

"Are you nearby?" Jamie turned to the next customer. "What can we make for you today?" The guy looking back at Jamie wore what had to be a three thousand dollar suit.

"Closer to midtown," Leighton told her, stepping back over, "but I try to get down here as much as I can." That seemed to pique Jamie's interest. She gestured to the young woman to take over on register and came around the counter to speak with Leighton, who honestly began to panic. That was new. Not much was able to flap her, but explaining who she was to Jamie did.

Jamie opened her mouth with another question and before she could get it out, Leighton rushed to beat her there, elbowing her way to prime focus. "Are you free tonight? Would you want to grab a drink with me later?" Yes, she'd panic-asked Jamie out, but it was also something she very much wanted. It would be the perfect opportunity for them to get to know each other better and would give Leighton a more personal platform to explain everything before they went farther. Because she did want to take things to the next step, if Jamie did.

The question had shut Jamie up. Her eyes went wide, which only made her cuter. "As in a *drink*-drink?"

She stepped closer to be sure the conversation was just between them. "I'm thinking two women on a date. What would you think of that?" She waited. Nervous. Excited. This felt like an important moment.

A small smile appeared on Jamie's lips, a seeming expression of quiet happiness. It made Leighton's morning. Warmth wound its way around her midsection and twisted. "I'd love to get a drink with you. I just wasn't a hundred percent positive that you—"

"Have a crush on you?" She said it purposefully without looking away. Direct eye contact was best. When Leighton focused on something important, she didn't let shyness intrude. Jamie was someone she wanted to get to know, and she had no time for guessing games.

"I was going to say *dated women.*"

"I'm attracted to interesting people. Women included." Leo silently slid her latte across the counter with his head down.

"In that case, yes. I'd love to." Leo popped his head up with wide eyes, then dropped it right back down again.

Leighton checked the time. "Better run. Can we meet at Puzzles? It's a very quiet and cute wine bar in the Village. Have you heard of it?"

Jamie nodded. "I love Puzzles. Um, how about six?"

"See you there." Leighton wiggled four fingers over her shoulder as she walked through the door. As she hit the sidewalk, she thought she heard applause erupt from inside the bar. Couldn't be. Likely just in her head.

With a happy spring in one step, and a slightly worried feeling coating the next, Leighton went about her day, counting the moments until she could spend time with the woman she couldn't seem to stop thinking about. Jamie was warm, smart, down-to-earth, and beautiful. Not only that, but there were the alternating feelings of calm and excitement that came over Leighton every time they were in proximity of each other. But before she got ahead of herself, she'd have to find a way to deal with the potential catastrophe of it all, right? Because their career objectives were in opposition. But before dropping the bomb, she wanted Jamie to get to know her first, to *like* her. Maybe that would give them an honest chance without her job instantly painting her as a villain. A true opportunity for Jamie to see Leighton for who she was and vice versa. The real world and all of its dicey confrontational waters could hold the hell on for just one night. That's all it would be.

Chapter Four

As a wine bar owner herself, Jamie appreciated a nice spot for a good glass. Plus checking out the friendly competition was always fun. Puzzles was a secret oasis tucked on a side street in the Village and frequented by locals who knew better than to broadcast its glory. She hadn't had time to go home to change, but as a rule, she kept a stash of clothes in the storage room in case something came up. She had one option that fit a date-I can't-believe-I'm-going-on occasion, and that was her army-green slim cut pants and semisleek black top. It would have to do. Maybe she could dress it up with jewelry. She located a simple necklace in her bag and stole ten minutes in the employee restroom to apply makeup and tame her hair. The results weren't bad, and she made her way to Puzzles with unfamiliar confidence and excitement. Not only was Leighton everything she was attracted to on the outside, but she was nice, funny, smart, and even a little bit mysterious. Maybe they could eliminate that last part tonight. She hoped to learn a lot more about her.

She stood in front of the bar, took a deep breath, smoothed down her pants, and moved inside only to spot Leighton sitting along the window looking like a fantasy. Beautiful. Pensive. Sexy as fucking hell. Was this whole thing real? It did not appear that Leighton had yet ordered. It also meant she'd likely watched Jamie prep, which she refused to let bother her.

She hooked a thumb behind her as she approached. "That was me fluffing my hair on the sidewalk." She added a laugh. "Hi. I hope you haven't been here long."

Leighton legitimately brightened, which made Jamie feel about ten feet tall. "You should stop and pull that hair number in front of every building you enter. Ten out of ten."

"Dinner and a show. Tada."

"I won't complain."

"You're flattering me before I even sit down."

"Can't help it." Leighton gestured to the chair across from her. Jamie happily took a seat and slid out of her navy leather jacket that her mother had given her for Christmas the year prior. "Nice jacket."

"Thank you. Don't be fooled. It's probably the most stylish thing I own, and I didn't even pick it out."

"Hopefully, I'll find out." Jamie went still and then basked in the way her stomach dropped out from under like a free fall. Meanwhile, Leighton perused the small leather-bound menu. "Shall we order a bottle?"

"I'd love that. You choose."

Leighton handed the wine list to Jamie. "Absolutely not. You're the wine expert here. I'm a dabbler who would hate to make an embarrassing choice."

"I very much doubt you would."

"But here's the thing. I want to drink wine *you* picked out."

Heat hit her cheeks. "You're making me tingle," she confessed.

"I want to make you a lot of things just so we're clear, but I'm going slow."

She blinked, holding on for the ride. "Fair enough." Jamie studied the menu, attempting to focus. "I don't know that I'm an expert, but I would love to flaunt what little I do know and impress you."

"Please do. I think you're full of good ideas tonight."

"Really? Well, this is already the best date." They exchanged a purposeful stare, the kind that felt like electricity had been unleashed and now ran the length of the room, crackling the whole way. She scanned the list. She didn't plan to pick out the most expensive bottle, but her choice needed to be something worthy of the occasion. How often did a gorgeous woman walk into Jamie's life and ask her out? "What do you think about a bourbon barrel reserve merlot?"

"What do I think? You had me at merlot. That's what. Yes." Leighton added a heaven-sent sexy smile that was worth every ounce of the intimidation that came attached to her.

Jamie squinted. "See, you don't seem like the kind of woman to embrace a good old-fashioned pun."

"Except I am. Stick around awhile. I'm incredibly proud of myself for that one." She sat back and exhaled. "I also might be a little nervous."

"You? Don't try to pull that. No one would ever believe it." Jamie certainly didn't. Leighton had a calm energy about her at all times. She was this cool, beautiful cucumber who glided places and offered treasured smiles as gifts. Nerves wouldn't dare encroach upon her in-control mellow.

"Well, then I'm excellent at faking it. What about you?"

"I'm nervous, too," she said quietly. Jamie grinned, harnessing her bravado, the same energy she put on for her customers. "But I have a proposition."

Leighton leaned in. Was it possible Jamie detected the delicate scent of watermelon? Intoxicating. Jamie could do a lot with a scent like that urging her on. And wanted to. "I'm listening."

"We throw those nerves out the window and revel in good wine and good company because life is too damn short for anything less."

Leighton didn't move. She seemed to be measuring the words. "I'm on board and so impressed with that proposition. Not only is my answer yes, but I'm buying tonight. Decided."

Jamie grinned. "Are you sure? We could split that sucker right down the middle. It's fair."

"No. My treat." A pause. "You look really pretty tonight." Her voice had gone soft, which caused Jamie to melt into the sound of it. She wanted quiet words like that in her ear. "But I'm not going to be nervous about that, per our arrangement."

She liked very much that she had an arrangement with Leighton. They were *arranged*. "Thank you. You radiate, but then you always do."

"Have we made decisions?" the server with the sweet smile asked. She had a Rapunzel amount of hair twisted in a bun on top of her head. Jamie remembered her from her last visit a couple of months back, which felt so mundane compared to the energy pinging tonight.

She pointed to the menu. "We'll take a bottle of Tangle Valley merlot."

The woman pressed a few buttons on her tablet. "You're in luck. Last bottle."

"Meant to be," Jamie said and handed back the wine list.

"It truly is. I have a friend in Tangle Valley. I'll tell you about her someday."

"I'd love to hear."

In just a few short moments, they were each poured a gorgeous glass of full-bodied red wine. Jamie held it up to examine the color, giving it a soft swirl. "Good legs."

"Mine?" Leighton arched a brow and winked.

"Without saying. Yes." Leighton was quick and more fun that Jamie had imagined. The playful and flirty vibe they'd established helped her relax, a ping-pong game she never grew tired of.

Leighton took a sip, closed her eyes, and savored. "Perfection. You did great. This is exactly what I needed after my day."

Jamie rested her chin on both fists as if ready for story time. "What is it that you do anyway? I realize I don't actually know."

Leighton took another sip while looking thoughtfully at the ceiling. Apparently, her job was complex enough to require a short planning session to explain. "I work in real estate development. More specifically projects beneath that umbrella."

"Interesting." Also, vague. She pressed for more. "You buy and sell buildings?"

"I make recommendations to interested parties on what areas would work best for their projects, and of course, how to go about making that happen."

"And how do you do that?" Jamie quirked her head. This was intriguing. It meant Leighton was an important person that others listened to. The whole thing sounded impressive. She liked the idea of Leighton having that kind of expertise.

"Well, I write a very detailed report."

"You're very businessy."

"So are you. Bordeauxnuts is really great. I loved the place from my very first visit forward."

Jamie sipped and grinned. "You did come back. That must mean it spoke to you in some way."

"There's just something about it." She tapped her wineglass with her nails. "So much personality. Very warm, but it also feels like you've stumbled into the hottest new hangout. I don't know how it's both, but it is. You should be incredibly proud."

She nodded, ruminating on the compliment. "I am. If there's one thing I can look at in my life and latch on to with pride, it's the growth and success of my little business that could. And now, did." She shook her head thinking back. "My parents thought the name was a horrible idea. That no one would get it. They begged me to go with something tame like Coffee Commotion or Sips in the Night."

Leighton laughed and covered Jamie's hand with hers. "Thank God you didn't." Jamie went still, hyperfocused on the contact. Their first of the night. Her skin heated and her center ached ever so slightly, reminding her that it had been a while. "Bordeauxnuts is creative. Snagged my attention right away because it's unique."

She turned her hand over in Leighton's and let their fingers intertwine and play. "You weren't confused by the concept? Doughnuts and bordeaux?"

"Not at all. And if I was, the wine bottles along the wall and aroma of fresh doughnuts would have served as helpful context clues."

"See? People are savvy. They get it. I once hired that very PR firm, Savvy, and it was the best decision of my life."

"I know those women. They're go-getters."

"Yes! They got me on the third hour of *Today*, and it helped put the shop on the map."

"That's amazing. I'll YouTube that interview."

"Oh, don't. I talk too fast, and my hair was a travesty that day, but I own it. One of the best days!"

Leighton topped their glasses off. "Let's see. In addition to Savvy, I worked with Peters Brothers and The Lennox Group on small projects back when I was doing a little in marketing. I think two of them are married, right? One of the Savvy execs and Jessica Lennox. Jessica's become a friend."

Jamie nodded. "Yes! They've come into the shop a handful of times, always holding hands and grinning at each other. I can report that the honeymoon phase has been extended indefinitely with those two. I love watching them flirt in line."

Leighton seemed to enjoy this report and got a faraway look in her eye. "That sounds like the dream."

"Are you a romantic?" Jamie asked around her glass.

"Most people would guess no." She paused. "But they would be wrong. I am." In that moment, she wasn't just beautiful, she was cute. "A closeted romantic. What's your favorite romantic film?"

"Too many to name. But I have watched *Pretty Woman* with my mother more times than I care to admit."

Jamie widened her eyes, pleased with the choice. "The grand gesture at the end? Is that the pull?"

Leighton's cheeks dusted with rose. Maybe she *was* a romantic. "Vivian deserved that and more"—she held up a finger—"but I also love *The Fast and the Furious*."

Jamie blinked. "I'm trying to find the common thread."

"The long game, maybe?" Leighton tapped her chin. "I think when it's meant to be, it's *always* meant to be. Friendship, romance, cars. Doesn't matter what the thing is if it was ordained for you."

"So that means you believe in fate."

"It does. Don't you? We all have a destiny just waiting for us to discover it."

"And what's yours?"

Leighton let her gaze linger, caressing Jamie from across the table. "I'm not sure, but I might be sitting across from her this very minute. Time will tell."

Jamie forgot to breathe. "How does it look so far?"

"Promising. Very promising."

Jamie touched her glass to Leighton's. "To fate."

"To fate."

As she sipped, Jamie pondered the concept, examining it slowly. Intrigued. "I'm not opposed to the idea of an ideal path. I just think there's maybe more than one path for each of us. We choose our own."

Leighton shook her head. "No. I'm looking for the one. The only path I'm supposed to be on."

Oh, Jamie could definitely lose herself in those soulful brown eyes when they searched hers with such intensity. Leighton clearly had a lot of feelings about destiny, and it was turning Jamie on. "Oh, you *are* a romantic. Your friends are wrong."

Leighton's lips offered a hint of a smile. "Which is why I had to ask you out. I said there was something about your bar, but there's something about you, too."

Jamie took a steady breath. "What do you think it is?" She lifted her glass, hoping the casual movement masked her utter captivation.

"Beyond the obvious"—she gestured to Jamie's face—"I think that's what I'm here to find out. There's this instant likability and quiet charisma that radiates off you. It made me, I don't know, want to be around you more."

"Are you saying what I think you're saying?" The wine was starting to make Jamie bold and flirty, a fun combination slightly outside her wheelhouse. She planned to enjoy every minute of it.

Leighton tilted her head. "I might have a little crush. And I'm not someone who fears failure. I fear *regret*. And I don't want to have any, Jamie." Could this woman please say her name again?

For an extended moment, they stared at each other, testing out their connection that took off like a spark in a dry forest. She swallowed. Leighton was truly someone to take in. Her skin was near flawless, a freckle next to her left eye. Her semilong blond hair fell in perfect layers, and the subtle lines around her eyes when she smiled made her even more beautiful. She still had her fingers mixed with Jamie's and must have noticed. She pulled her hand back slowly, confidently, in absolutely no rush. It took Jamie a moment to shift her gaze and focus on the fancy charcuterie board that arrived, looking like something off a Food Network commercial.

"Please eat every bite. You'll thank me," their server said with a wink and floated away to give them time to enjoy. Jamie gazed at the array of hard and soft cheeses and their accompaniments. Prosciutto, salami folded in the shape of a rose, olives, honey, jam, mustard, almonds, spiced cashews—and were those pickled vegetables? It made her want to step up her own cheese selection, but she remembered doughnuts were her customers' favorite wine pairing and she couldn't betray the culture. Puzzles had an entirely different vibe and target customer. Mainstream and posh. As it should be. There was room for both.

"It's too good to ruin," Leighton said. "We can't do it."

"All the more reason. We must. Food was meant to be consumed, devoured, savored." To demonstrate, she stole a bite of the nutty Gouda and closed her eyes, letting the flavors take their time.

When she opened them again, Leighton seemed transfixed. "Look at you. Showing off your foodie skills."

Jamie went very serious. "Can't help it. I eat more than I should and make no apologies."

"Nor should you if it looks like that when you do it."

The next two hours flew by. They killed the bottle, did their best on the amazing tray, and swapped stories about their exes.

"So, Laurel was actually a promising partner at one point or...?"

Jamie sighed, trying to figure out how to explain Laurel and the number that relationship did on her. There was a reason it had been over three years since Jamie had entered into a relationship with anyone. "She made me feel that because I was with her, I was important." She exhaled slowly, trying to organize the words that would explain the very unique feeling of being dependent on another human for self-worth. "I felt small and, in a way, lucky to be with Laurel, whose personality was larger than life."

"That's one way to put it."

Jamie pressed on. "She was someone who always pulled in a lot of attention, and my identity became this extension of her, which she reinforced every chance she got."

Leighton sat back, dejected. "That's not my favorite story. I think we need chocolate lava cake and another top-off."

"You don't have to say much more than *chocolate cake* to get me to sit here for another hour."

"How did you finally break away?"

"Well, I started to see my existence, my identity, slipping away. I was standing in quicksand, and a little bit more of me disappeared every moment I was with Laurel. It was only a matter of time before I lost myself entirely. So, one night, I quietly packed." Jamie shrugged. "She made sure I understood that I was nothing, and that without her, my life would have zero interest or meaning. I still walked out of there, tears streaming down my cheeks."

"Oh no. And yet you still have to run in the same circles."

Jamie closed her eyes. "New York turned out to be smaller than I thought, especially when we still have a handful of the same friends. She'll never get over the fact that I left her and uses every interaction we have to try to point out how boring I am."

Leighton shook her head. "I don't find you boring at all."

"Thank you. I don't either." They clinked glasses again. "In fact, I kinda like me."

"Perhaps the sexiest sentence ever." She rested her chin in her hand. "We've covered a lot except where's home?"

"I have an apartment down here. It's small, but it's actually a really nice place to land. If I look to the right and crane my neck, I can see the Flatiron Building. Where do you live?"

"Upper East Side."

"Ooh la la." Jamie raised her eyebrows. "I'm dining with the upper class." She looked around the table for show. "Did I use the right silverware? Your job is a bigger deal than I thought."

"I do okay, but if we're talking about my apartment, well, I inherited some family money."

"A trust fund baby in the flesh?"

She sipped her wine. "Hi."

The way she said that, almost shyly, sent a very welcome shiver down Jamie's spine and back again. She laughed, which made Leighton smile along. They had a nice give-and-take, and Leighton had no problem taking Jamie's teasing. She never would have predicted on that first day Leighton had arrived in the coffee bar that she'd ever be this comfortable with her. Life was a pretty amazing thing. It had a way of sneaking up on you, and in this moment, Jamie felt blessed it had tapped her on the shoulder. Even if tonight was all they ever had, a one and done, she'd still feel lucky. She'd needed this date, this connection, to believe that romance was alive and well for her. Beyond that, she really liked Leighton. She was so much more than an attractive woman in her line.

"Are you thinking about how awesome a time you're having?" Leighton asked. She glanced at the clock near the beautiful bar across the room. "Or that I kept you out past your bedtime?"

"To the first question, yes. Stop reading my mind. It's creepy." She tossed in a grin. "Second of all, yes, again. I open pretty early. But the truth of it is that I don't mind losing sleep. It's a nice night, and you are…"

"Also nice?" Leighton asked, using Jamie's word.

"No. Much more than nice," she said quietly. But she'd dropped the playful tone because Jamie wanted Leighton to know she meant it.

"Oh." Leighton matched her sincerity. She leaned in, making it feel very much like it was just them in the entirety of the restaurant. "I'd really like another one of these."

"Bottles of wine?" Jamie asked in order to not be too presumptive. Leighton didn't hesitate. "Another night like this. With you."

"My turn to say *oh*." A pause struck because Jamie was a little drunk, and it had nothing to do with the wine.

"You haven't actually responded."

She was living happily in this moment of direct eye contact that felt decidedly like foreplay. "I'm supposed to do that?"

Leighton nodded. "Customary."

"Good point." She pulled her gaze away for a moment to avoid combustion before refocusing with confidence. "I'm all in. I want another date with you, too. But I'm buying next time."

"Whatever you want, Ms. Tolliver."

Leighton handed the small leather portfolio and her credit card to their friendly server.

When she returned to them, she paused. "Why do I get the impression we're celebrating something. An anniversary?"

"No," Leighton said in amusement.

"This is actually our first date," Jamie told her.

"Wow. First? Because there's a very natural chemistry here. I'm just saying that you heard it here first." She placed a quick palm on the table. "Enjoy your night. Invite me to the wedding."

She scurried away, leaving them to laugh at the comment, which only confirmed to Jamie that the date had likely gone as well as she thought it had. When they arrived on the sidewalk out front, she felt like she was floating. Night had fallen, and the busy streets had thinned to only an occasional passerby.

Leighton looked up from her phone. "The app says my ride is one minute away."

"New York certainly excels at rideshare. Dammit." It wasn't the best thing she'd said all evening. But a new bundle of nerves swarmed her as they approached their good night. Would there be a kiss, and how would she possibly handle that without her everything short-circuiting?

"Oh, and I think that's me coming down the block. Your car is close?" Leighton asked.

"Two minutes out," Jamie said as a white sedan pulled up alongside them. Her least favorite car ever. Did tonight have to end?

"I had the best time with you," Leighton said, giving her hand a squeeze.

"I did, too. I still am," Jamie said, not wanting to let go of her hand.

"Good night, Jamie." Leighton slid into the back seat of the car and looked up at her.

"Night, Bambi's Mom," she said with a cheeky smile and closed the door. She stepped back onto the curb and paused to watch the car drive away. As it approached the corner, the brake lights flared, and it came to a stop. Leighton opened the door, exited the car, and walked to Jamie with purpose.

Jamie quirked her head. "Did you forget some—"

"I did forget something. Yes." Jamie's lips were then claimed, occupied by a kiss from the most entrancing woman she'd ever met. All that was left to do was surrender, and oh, she did. Their lips moved slowly together as the lights of the city twinkled around them. The surprising part was how well they kissed together, as if they'd had years of practice. That had to be a sign. Who kissed so perfectly the first time? Jamie could have kissed Leighton for hours.

"Sorry." Leighton pulled back, searching her eyes with a smile. "Just couldn't go home without doing that first," Leighton said quietly, her gaze alternating between Jamie's eyes and her mouth. "There was no way."

"I'm glad you came back."

Leighton stole another soft kiss before taking a couple of steps back. Jamie had to have hearts dancing in a circle over her head. The Earth had just shifted. She was sure of it. "Maybe I'll see you for coffee soon."

"We also have merlot, you know," Jamie said. "I hear you're a fan."

"All the more reason to mix up my visits. Sweet dreams, Jamie Tolliver. I have a feeling you might show up in mine."

Her heart soared. Jamie raised a hand in farewell and watched the sedan disappear down the street, leaving her alone, yet hovering somewhere above heaven. Her lips still hummed wonderfully, but the rest of her ached for more. She pushed her hands into the pockets of her favorite jacket and walked to the curb to wait for her ride. After a few minutes, the corners of her mouth hurt from grinning. Was this night meant for someone else? She laughed because they were never getting it back from her now. Jamie Tolliver was somebody as of tonight. She did a clichéd little twirl and held on to whatever these wonderful feelings were, so foreign and welcome. This was a night she'd never forget, a happy reminder that incredible things did happen. Life, apparently, had so much more it was waiting to offer her, and if she played her cards right, she'd have a second date with Leighton Morrow. A third. And then…who knew? She couldn't think of anything more wonderful. For the first time in years, Jamie felt like the universe saw her. *Little her.* She gave her head a disbelieving shake, checking her shoes because if this wasn't a Cinderella moment, what was? In the storybook of her life, she simply couldn't wait to see what came next.

CHAPTER FIVE

Leighton stood in her darkened apartment in front of the large picture window facing the river and replayed every moment of her evening spent with Jamie. She admitted to herself that the date had far exceeded her already hopeful expectations. Jamie, who made her toes curl and her stomach flutter, was smart, witty, down-to-earth, and thoughtful. When was the last time she'd run into that combination? Jamie had also been the perfect conversationalist and dinner companion. The kiss she'd run back for had proven incredibly satisfying, inspiring daydreams about what would have happened if they hadn't said good night and Jamie had come home with her. Would she have pulled Jamie into her lap and slid her hands up her thighs, inching higher and higher until she took what she wanted?

After such a fantastic night, why was Leighton now clutching a glass of ice water with a needle threaded with dread moving through her midsection? She knew why. She hadn't been forthcoming with Jamie at all about who she was, her job, or what brought her into Bordeauxnuts to begin with. It had been fantasyland tonight on their date, which allowed her to pretend none of those factors existed. She got a taste of what she and Jamie might be like together, and now she couldn't erase that knowledge. But this scenario had her waiting for the other shoe to drop. What was going to happen to them when it did? Would Jamie blame her for Carrington's decision to open a store in Chelsea? It was entirely possible. Would she be furious Leighton had sidestepped important details about her job when directly asked? She sighed and pinched the bridge of her nose because who wouldn't be?

She'd gone about this all wrong. Everything was out of order. Dammit. Now what was she supposed to do? Upend it all before it even had a chance to get going?

As she thought through the situation, it almost felt wrong to allow herself to enjoy the memory of Jamie's smile, the sparks that flew when their gazes connected, or the kiss that had rocked her fully—because it hadn't been earned. None of it was rightfully hers, and that hurt. She'd been dishonest, and now it colored everything like black paint tossed on a beautiful painting.

Leighton now knew she should have never asked Jamie out without supplying her with all the pertinent details. That was on her. She slid her fingers into her hair and gripped, angry at herself and grieving.

The fact of the matter was that she had to come clean and soon. She got ready for bed, selecting her satin shorts set because the soft fabric against her skin felt like the pampering her soul needed. If only it had helped. She slipped beneath the cool sheets and stared at the shadow shifting on her ceiling for what felt like hours. Sleep was not to be. All was not right in the world, and Leighton had to fix it. The stakes were too high. Her heart was already hoping, reaching.

When she arrived at her office in midtown at quarter to eight the next morning, her plan was to lose herself in numbers and notes until she could summon the courage to swing by the bar and see Jamie before the evening traffic picked up. Maybe they could steal a glass of wine together and have an honest and important conversation. Leighton would come clean and apologize, and hope Jamie would understand.

When five o'clock rolled around, Leighton gave her shoulders a roll and stopped at Mindy's desk on her way to do what she should have from day one.

"I'm gonna take off for the day."

"You're early. This is nice. You're trying for a life and are to be commended."

Leighton offered a curtsey. "Trying. There's a woman I can't stop thinking about, and I have to go see what I can do about making sure she doesn't hate me."

Mindy's fingers went still on her keyboard. "What a weird sentence. Do you want to rewind? Why might she hate you?"

Leighton, needing to hear the story out loud for clarity, recalled all that had happened with Jamie up until this point. "So I'm headed over there now."

"Wow." Mindy offered up a Snickers from her desk. "You might need this for later. Put it in your bag."

"Recovery chocolate?" She deflated. "You don't think this ends well for me, do you?"

"Lay, I'm gonna hope it does, but she needs to know the truth and fast. Strong, awesome women like straight shooters. You're going to have some ground to make up. And rightfully so," Mindy said with a small glare. "Now go make it right, and next time consult me about this kind of thing."

"I hear you. I will." Leighton sighed. Mindy's outrage was telling and warranted. She'd screwed this up and knew it.

Along the way to the bar, she stopped at a sidewalk flower sale and picked out a single long-stemmed rose for Jamie. Nervous energy bounced from her head to her toes, and when she rounded the corner to Bordeauxnuts, she found Jamie clicking off a call in front of the storefront. Leighton paused, holding the rose and waiting for Jamie to look up from her phone. When she did, Leighton watched her whole body relax and a smile blossom. She was everything. It was dusk, and the light was fading fast, but Leighton took a moment to memorize Jamie, haloed by the oranges and pinks of the setting sun. Leighton opened her mouth to speak just as Jamie burst into tears.

"Oh no," Leighton said, letting the rose fall to the side as she moved to Jamie. "I hope I didn't do that."

With a hand to her forehead, Jamie seemed to surrender to the emotion and allowed her face to crumple and tears to fall. Leighton guided her to a bench a few yards away, her own heart tugging. She couldn't stand to see the anguish on Jamie's face.

"Not you," Jamie whispered through the emotion.

Leighton instantly took her hand and held on. "Well, I don't know what I walked up on, but I'm here. We can just sit together." Jamie nodded, the emotion seemingly stealing her voice. A siren wailed in the distance. Pedestrians passed by on the sidewalk as rush hour ramped up to a roar. Through it all, Leighton refused to let go. Occasionally, she'd rub Jamie's arm or toss out an encouraging few words. "You're gonna be okay. I got you."

Eventually, Jamie took an extra-deep breath and turned to Leighton. "This was embarrassing."

With her thumb, Leighton dried Jamie's tears. "You have nothing to be embarrassed about," she said quietly. "Just me here."

A soft smile touched Jamie's lips. "That's true. Hi."

"Hi. Want to talk about it or no?"

"I'm very close with my parents. My dad's been moving a little slower these days, but we all just thought age."

"Is there more?"

Jamie nodded. "He's been struggling with catching his breath more than normal and went in a few weeks ago. They found a spot on his lung that the doctor didn't like the look of, and now the biopsy is back." She lifted her shoulders and let them drop. "It's bad news."

Leighton nodded. "I'm so sorry. Does that mean lung cancer?"

"Yes. God, I hate that word."

"Me, too."

"They're gonna start treatment right away. His new doctor said they caught it at a good time, but I just can't imagine my little dad going through this. I just want to protect him, you know?"

"I do. I've been there with my mom." Her gaze dropped to their hands and back. "We lost her to ovarian cancer six years ago. But I have a different feeling about this. Your dad is going to be just fine."

"I hope so." Jamie's blue eyes were still glistening with tears when she met Leighton's gaze. "I'm sorry about your mom."

"Thank you. She was a great mom. We laughed all the time growing up. I was lucky."

"She sounds wonderful." Jamie disentangled their hands and stood, walked a few feet, and turned back. "I just can't believe this is happening. It feels like there's an elephant sitting on my chest."

"Be gentle with yourself. Do you have to work anymore today?"

Jamie shook her head. "I can hand over the reins to my evening staff and head home. I'll change and then visit my parents." Her gaze fell to the rose next to Leighton on the bench. "You brought a rose?"

"I brought *you* a rose." She stood and extended it to Jamie. "It's not much, but I wanted you to know I was thinking about you. Can I walk you home?"

"I'd really like that."

Jamie scooted inside, and Leighton, alone on the pavement,

closed her eyes. There was no way she could tell Jamie that there was a department store about to take over her storefront and Leighton was part of the team. Not on a day like this. She pinched the bridge of her nose, deciding she had no choice but to stand down.

They walked the few blocks, quietly discussing all their favorite parts of living in the city.

"When I wake up after it's snowed the night before. The streets are beautifully blanketed and mostly untouched because no one's up yet."

"A perk of your job," Leighton said. "You get to see it first. I like Central Park in the spring. Sometimes I'll stop and watch a random softball game, just because."

"This city does have some great park action."

It was at that point in the walk that Jamie quietly took Leighton's hand and threaded their fingers in a move that was natural, wonderful. They walked the remaining six blocks, holding hands and stealing quiet glances. Finally, they arrived at a building with four steps leading up to the entrance, and Jamie gestured to them. "This is me."

"Delivered safe and sound. Can I have your phone?"

Jamie handed it over with a questioning stare. "I wish there was something scandalous for you to run into, but alas, no."

"A shame." Leighton laughed. "But I'm putting my number in here in case you need anything, okay?"

Jamie grinned. "So now I have your digits."

"If you send me a text sometime, I'll have yours."

"You're on."

Jamie headed up the stairs and turned back. "While it was embarrassing to cry in front of you, I'm really glad you were there today."

"Me, too. I hope things get easier. Take care of yourself, Jamie. I'll see you soon."

"I hope for that as well." She lifted her hand in farewell and disappeared inside the building.

Leighton blew out a breath. It wasn't what she'd planned on, but she was glad she had been there for Jamie in a difficult moment. As for her big confession, well, it would have to wait for a more appropriate moment.

Hours later, just as she went to turn off the lights in her apartment and head to sleep for the night, her phone notified her of a message.

Thank you for today. Always, Jamie.

She placed the phone against her chest and let the words wash over her.

"Always," she said back.

❖

The last week had been a whirlwind. Leighton Morrow had waltzed into Jamie's life and taken her breath away. She'd taken her out, brought her a rose, been there for her when she needed support, and now they were on-and-off texters. Did she check her phone eight times more throughout the day than she ever had before? Possibly. Did she mind? Not in the slightest. On the flip side, she'd had a sobering punch in the face in regard to her father's health that had her more worried than she'd ever been before. The combination of the two factors had her distracted and screwing up at work exponentially.

"James, did you leave this milk out overnight?" Leo called to her in the early morning hours from the walk-in.

She smacked her forehead. "Did I?" A wince. "I think I must have. How many gallons?"

"Eight."

She shook her head. "Totally my fault. I'll have more delivered this afternoon. Are we good for the morning?"

Another pause. "Should be." He came around the corner with a patient hand outstretched. "Being in love is cool and all, but the milk, man. Don't forget our milk." He touched his chest as if the milk were his precious child left in the snow.

"I'm not in love."

"But you're grinning when you say it, which means you know it's just a matter of time."

"Too early to say, Leonardo."

"See, you never call me that. That's weird in love Jamie talking." A pause. A grin. "But it looks good on you, boss."

"I will screw my wayward head on tighter and focus on things like milk storage. Just a lot going on in here this week." Just then her phone vibrated, and she glanced down to a good morning text with a heart from Leighton. *A heart.* She'd been underwater at her real estate business and hadn't been able to get away for a few days. They had tentative plans to meet up that night, and Jamie, for one, couldn't wait to lay eyes on those beautiful brown ones. She had plans to kiss those lips and not stop. Their week of texting had brought them even closer, and she couldn't wait to explore their new, more intimate dynamic.

How do you feel about lingerie? Leighton had asked mid-text conversation the night before. *No wrong answer.*

I love it when there's someone to appreciate it, Jamie had typed back. *Do you appreciate lingerie, Leighton?*

Can't answer. Too busy imagining you wearing it.

Jamie had sent her a trio of flames. *What about reading?*

I love to read. Especially on a lazy Saturday. Maybe we could read together one morning.

You're giving me something to look forward to.

Us both.

She'd sighed happily and checked the clock. *Four a.m. comes early. Night, Leighton.*

Good night Jamie. Sweet dreams.

She could feel Leo staring at her as she typed her own good morning message back.

"So, are you hitting it already?" he asked.

The bar hadn't opened, and it was just them in the room, but the question still caught her off guard. They'd talked about his love life before, his inability to settle down and preference to live alone, but never her own personal life. Maybe it was because she hadn't had much of one.

"Wow. You're really going for it this morning." She considered the question and decided a guy like Leo, suave and unaffected, would likely have good advice for someone like Jamie who'd been out of the game awhile and didn't want to seem needy to a catch like Leighton.

Leo shrugged. "Just checking in on you."

Jamie smiled, because he'd always been one to look out for her, hadn't he? "Not yet. But I think we're inching our way there. We've kissed. We flirt." She placed her palms flat on the counter. "I'm more than a little into her, Leo, and I don't want to blow this. The problem is I get so nervous just thinking about us…together."

He nodded. "So, it's easy. You make the first move in that department."

"The sex department?" she squeaked. "Why would I do that?"

"Because when it comes from you, you're the alpha."

"I'm not alpha."

"That's why you fake it. Force yourself to assume the in-control position and magically give yourself a little bit of confidence." He shrugged. "Trust me. Go after what you want, make the move, and watch the nerves fade away."

She nodded, absorbing. "You're telling me to harness my main character energy."

"Is that a book thing? I prefer flicks."

"Such a dude, Leo."

"Yeah, well, this dude is telling you to make the first move. Let me know how it goes." He bounced his eyebrows and fired up Mikey, prepared to start the first batch of doughnuts.

Jamie breathed deeply and mulled over his advice as the morning rush took over. Maybe playing the role of confident, sex-positive individual wasn't a bad idea. It was essentially getting out of her own way, and allowing her to act on her own feelings.

Are we still getting together tonight? she texted Leighton midday.

The reply was quick. *Yes, please. I miss you. And I want to talk to you about work.*

Jamie grinned. *Perfect. How about you come to my place?*

CHAPTER SIX

The day had been a rainy one in New York. Bursts of showers on and off made it hard to go anywhere without an umbrella, just in case. Leighton had already paid the price once when she'd dashed down to the deli to grab herself and Mindy a chef's salad for lunch.

In spite of the weather, she was excited and nervous to see Jamie tonight. She'd missed her in the few days they'd been apart but had lived for their text exchanges and getting to know the fun, lighthearted side of Jamie as well as the thoughtful, deep version. The more they talked, the stronger her feelings for Jamie grew, which was why it was so important tonight went well. She'd let them settle in with a glass of wine, sit Jamie down on the couch, and lay it all out there the way she and Mindy had gone over earlier that afternoon. She'd tell Jamie that she was becoming more important to Leighton than any job, and let her know that if Leighton had known how things would happen between them, she would have announced her identity from moment one. She'd say she was sorry and offer to do whatever Jamie wanted to make it up to her. And then she'd wait, because Jamie was allowed to have any reaction she wanted, even if it was to kick Leighton out of her apartment. Her heart dropped just imagining that scenario.

As she made her way to Jamie, she'd opted for a Uber to alleviate the risk of getting caught in the rain. Didn't matter. As she exited the car in front of Jamie's building, a torrential downpour coupled with aggressive wind flipped her umbrella inside out and near soaked her on what was only a short walk to the door.

"Dammit," she said, shaking herself off on the lobby's doormat. Her shirt clung to her body like a second skin. She couldn't even guess what her hair must look like. She found Jamie's door on the third floor and knocked, ready to apologize for the puddle she'd likely create. Was that music? Yes. Something mellow and nice, which helped her relax a bit.

The door opened, and there she was, looking drop-dead gorgeous in navy tapered jeans, heeled boots that gave her at least three inches, and a dark pink sweater with a generous neckline Leighton wanted to thank the universe for. "Wow, you're beautiful, and I'm sadly dripping."

Jamie's initial smile faded as her gaze moved from Leighton's face down to her probably now see-through shirt. She hadn't thought about that component, but Jamie seemed struck.

"No one is complaining in the slightest," Jamie said quietly as she stepped back to allow Leighton inside. "Please come in. I was prepared to offer you wine, but maybe I should pivot to a change of clothes."

"I wouldn't turn down a comfy shirt, if we could dry this one before we go anywhere."

"We can toss it in the dryer and make you comfy in the meantime." Jamie poured Leighton a glass of red and handed it off. "Back in a moment."

Leighton sipped, trying to stay positive, until Jamie reappeared with a cozy, worn-in sweatshirt that Leighton already loved because it was Jamie's. "Thank you."

Without giving it much thought, Leighton unbuttoned her own shirt just as Jamie said, "You can change in there if you—Oh. Okay."

"I apologize," Leighton said. "I can go—"

"No. Stay."

She did, and the temperature in the room shifted with each remaining button. When she slid the shirt off her shoulders, she felt Jamie's stare all over. Her skin went hypersensitive with her slightly wet bra now on display. Pale pink. Jamie took a step forward and, with a determined look in her eye, slid the shirt off the rest of the way until it fell to the floor. Leighton barely breathed as Jamie brushed her hair off one shoulder, leaving it bare. Her gaze dropped to it, and she leaned down and kissed it. A shot of arousal moved through Leighton, downward. Her eyes fluttered closed, as Jamie's lips moved from her shoulder to her neck, the soft sounds of her breath sending a shiver skipping across Leighton's skin.

She went still, sent into some kind of half panic, half wonder. This was an unexpected twist, but how was she supposed to press pause? "Jamie," she murmured, just as Jamie's mouth pressed to hers and the world flew off its axis. Her ability to reason skipped off with it. She stepped into Jamie and cupped her face and angled her own for better access. The kiss instantly took over everything, sending Leighton down the rabbit hole to lust and lust only.

The more they kissed, the more they needed to. Urgency took over. Their pace reflected the desperation at play as hands joined the mix, roaming, touching lightly and then with more purpose. The wine, the rain, Leighton's trajectory all forgotten. Thunder rumbled outside, and the candle Jamie had set on the end table flickered shadows onto the far wall.

With her tongue, Leighton urged Jamie's lips apart and slipped inside, exploring her mouth, a source of her captivation for weeks. "I love the way you taste," she whispered and deepened the kiss. There was no one sexier than Jamie Tolliver, she decided, and confident, in-charge Jamie was new and intoxicating. She was very much in control tonight, and Leighton loved it.

"Follow me," Jamie murmured against Leighton's mouth and gave her hand a tug. They didn't make it to the bedroom before finding each other again and stumbling their way there through the haze of lips and tongues and heat.

Leighton sat down on Jamie's bed and noticed a candle flickering next to it, as well. A whole scene. Distantly she wondered if she was being seduced, but in this moment, she had no problem with it. Jamie knelt in front of her and, as they kissed, worked the button on Leighton's pants, which honestly couldn't come off fast enough. Her body was on fire, but the tingling ache between her legs took center stage. She needed to assuage it and soon. She'd dreamed of making love to Jamie slowly more times than she could count, but it would have to wait for another night.

Cool air hit her legs as her pants hit the floor. Her bra followed seconds later. Jamie's mouth was on her breasts, kissing, licking, *God.* Leighton was eased onto her back and topped by the blue-eyed temptress she hadn't seen coming. When Jamie's weight settled over her, she decided there was nothing more satisfying than their bodies pressed together. For a brief moment, everything slowed down. Jamie met her gaze and nodded, to which Leighton nodded back. They were on the same damn page.

"I want to touch you," Jamie said in her ear. The sound alone had her arching her back. A request. A need. There was one thing that had to happen first, though.

"Can I see you?" Leighton asked, cupping Jamie's cheek, sliding her other hand up the back of Jamie's sweater. Her skin was smooth and warm. She wanted to kiss every inch. A crack of thunder hit and shook the walls. Jamie kissed her good and long before sitting up to oblige.

"I love kissing you," Jamie said. "There's nothing like it."

Leighton propped herself up on her forearms to watch. "Well, there's more where that came from."

She then had the pleasure of looking on eagerly as Jamie took off each piece of clothing. Her breath caught, and she tried to memorize every moment of skin being revealed to her, each curve, every aspect of Jamie now in front of her. She held steady against her body's cries. This moment was too special. When Jamie at long last removed her bra and her round breasts were bare, Leighton's arousal doubled. The increased wetness between her legs only proved the point.

Naked and gorgeous, Jamie slid onto the bed next to Leighton, whose hand went immediately to Jamie's breast. She needed to touch Jamie intimately, to know every inch of her body and own it. At least for tonight. With one finger, Leighton circled the nipple as Jamie hissed in a breath. "You're beautiful," she said in reverence. "Just look at you." She palmed Jamie's breast, closing her eyes at the wash of heat that toppled her. Jamie murmured her appreciation in a tone much lower than her voice, and it sent a potent shot of need to her center. With determination, Jamie supported herself on one forearm and slid her other hand straight into Leighton's underwear, easing her legs apart with a knee.

"You feel amazing," Jamie said, dropping her head, reveling. Her touch was everything. At first, she simply explored. Light touches, soft movements. Leighton heard herself moan. Her hips rocked, searching for a rhythm they'd yet to establish. Cruel and wonderful. Jamie removed her panties entirely, tossing them to the floor. The look on her face changed to one of determination. As Jamie increased the pressure of her touch, Leighton had to grasp the bedspread beneath her to keep from levitating off the bed. She pushed herself in earnest against Jamie's hand, feeling the torturous pressure climb. She didn't ever want it to end, and yet she needed it to. "I might come," Leighton said after several thorough strokes. She slid across Jamie's hand. "I'm going to."

"Good," Jamie said, entering her with purpose. It was too powerful. Leighton tossed her head to the side as Jamie took her higher and higher with each firm, smooth thrust. "You're so wet."

"How could I not be?" she managed, loving the feeling of being taken by Jamie. *Taken.* When was the last time that had happened?

She opened her eyes, took in the visual of Jamie's naked body, her hand moving between Leighton's legs. It was the hottest image ever, like molten lava. She broke. She was knocked right over the edge, spiraling into wonderful oblivion.

"I was literally just caught in a thunderstorm," she said through the satisfied haze. Leighton shook her head. "And now I'm in your bed."

"Surprised?" Jamie said and placed a soft, open-mouthed kiss on Leighton's neck.

"Among other things." She gave her head a shake. "I'm still feeling it."

"Yeah?" Jamie asked in the sweetest voice. Her hand returned to between Leighton's legs and softly played.

"No, no," she said with a laugh. "I can't." But it was only a couple of seconds before her hips began to rock. What was happening right now? She was wet all over again and felt the distant tug of need inch closer. Already? This wasn't like her at all.

"You can do it," Jamie whispered. "Leighton."

"Yes." Her eyes slammed shut.

"I want you to open your legs and come for me."

Those words coming from sweet Jamie's lips let her know it was possible. She pressed back against Jamie's hand and the delicate touches, no more than a fondle really, easing her along until, out of nowhere, she shot like a star, tumbling all over again as pleasure rained down with an intensity she couldn't quite comprehend. "How did you do that?" she gasped, vulnerable, still lost in the most unexpected payout.

She heard a soft laugh as she came down. "That was the best."

Leighton turned her body to Jamie's so they were face-to-face. "Oh, you think so?"

"I will never ever forget the perfect details of tonight."

"I know a way to make it even better," Leighton said, crawling on top.

"Oh, I like this," Jamie said.

Leighton settled her hips between Jamie's legs. "And this."

Jamie closed her eyes and took a moment. "Even better," she managed, but her tone had dropped. Leighton smiled and began to rock against her. "Yes," Jamie said in a near whisper. She wrapped her arms around Leighton and held on. "I'm close," Jamie whispered, moments later. That was Leighton's cue. She kissed her way slowly down Jamie's body, savoring every moment, before arriving at her destination. She parted Jamie's legs and licked her softly, lingering. "Fuck," Jamie said.

Leighton couldn't have even told you her own name at that point. She was lost and happy and on a mission. She kissed Jamie's center once, twice, three times to the sound of her whimpering quietly above. Jamie found a rhythm and Leighton matched her, tracing circles around Jamie's most sensitive spot. Fast then slow. Leighton could have done this for hours.

"I need you," Jamie said. Leighton knew exactly where, yet she withheld. She looked up.

"What is it you need?" Leighton asked innocently.

"You," Jamie said.

"You might have to be more specific."

"Your tongue. Make me come."

Leighton nodded and captured Jamie in her mouth, swirling her tongue for only a moment before Jamie went still and called out. Leighton smiled and memorized the wonderful sound. She rested her head on Jamie's stomach and brought her back from the orgasm with soft touches.

"Come up here," Jamie said finally, opening her arms. Leighton slid beneath one and they shared a kiss. "I didn't expect you, ya know."

"I didn't expect you either," Leighton said honestly.

There was a lot to say. Much to discuss. But for now, Leighton opted to live in a land where she and Jamie were the only people who existed. They lay in each other's arms and talked and laughed for the next hour or two before Leighton dressed, this time in Jamie's soft sweatshirt, for home.

"Are you sure you don't want to stay?"

"Trust me when I say how badly I do. All I'm going to think about tonight is you. This. In fact…" She pressed Jamie to the wall and stole a searing kiss.

Jamie laughed when they came up for air. "You really know how to say good-bye."

"Just holding on a bit longer," Leighton said. "I wish we both didn't have an early morning."

"Me, too. The only reason I'm agreeing to this is because I'm hoping we have many more nights ahead of us."

Leighton nodded. "That's what I want so badly, too."

Another kiss that gave way to another. When they paused, Jamie quirked her head as if remembering something key. "We didn't talk about your work thing. You said you wanted to."

"I do. But it can wait." A heaviness came over her, a reminder that all of this wasn't fully real. At least, not yet.

"Okay. If you say so." She opened the door and leaned against the side. Leighton moved to the hallway, and when she turned back, Jamie was squinting. "Clarissa was asking me the name of the company you work for, and I didn't know what to tell her."

"Oh, it's named after my family," she said automatically. It was the best she could come up with.

"So, Morrow…?"

"And Associates. Yeah." She blinked and took a deep breath. She'd shocked herself because that was an outright lie and it wasn't like her. She'd panicked. "Um. I guess I better go before another storm hits. Probably any minute now." She took Jamie's hand and kissed the back of it. "It was a great night. I'll call you tomorrow."

"I look forward to it. Good night, Leighton."

"Night, Jamie." Leighton stole a last glimpse of Jamie and her warm smile before turning and heading for home. Guilt-stricken and falling hard for the girl she'd left in that apartment, Leighton felt like a tornado attempting to find the path of least destruction. She wasn't doing a very good job.

"What now?" she asked the dark clouds gathering in the sky. "What the hell now?"

CHAPTER SEVEN

Jamie was five minutes late to work that next morning, but she didn't care in the slightest. She'd practically floated her way from the train to Bordeauxnuts and now hummed to herself as she prepped the point-of-sale station for opening. She was on a high from her night with Leighton and enjoying every second of it. Nothing could smother her mood, not even if Rude Latte Face showed up and demanded they make his drink three times until he approved.

"You're humming," Leo stated, stroking his chin in thought.

"I am doing that. You're right. Strange." She sent him a sweet grin.

He continued to study her. "You're also moving with big gestures and smiling a lot."

She lifted a shoulder. "So I am. Interesting." She was being playful and reveling in it.

"I'm gonna guess somebody here got laid, and it wasn't me."

"Ding, ding, ding!" Jamie said and placed a finger on her nose. She scrunched her shoulders. "And I owe it all to you and your advice. I took control. I made the first move, and the end result was"—she stretched her arms and fingers, searching for the perfect descriptor—"like skydiving with a tub of amazing buttered popcorn."

He laughed. "And since we know you love both of those things, it was a fucking good night."

"Fucking good," she said loudly, mirroring his Leo voice. "I'm gonna ask your advice about everything from now on. What do I want for lunch, Leo? Should I get a dog, Leo? You better gear up."

He cracked his knuckles and grinned. "Gotta say. She looks good on you, James. This woman."

"Thank you. I think so, too."

The morning catapulted them to a busy start that kept Jamie on her toes. She was in her groove, though, and bonding with each and every human placed in front of her. These were the kinds of mornings she lived for in the bar. When Clarissa showed up during her midmorning break, she pulled her aside and gave her all the details.

"This is so unreal and perfect. No one deserves a huge dose of happiness more than you, Jamie."

"Thank you. I mean, this feels so shockingly right. No other person I've been with has fit quite so well with my personality, my life, what it is that I'm looking for."

"Sounds like she might be the one," Genevieve said, eavesdropping as always.

Jamie laughed. "I'm not going to go all the way there yet, but the thought has crossed my mind."

"Have you daydreamed about your future life together?" Chun asked, pencil to her chin.

"Yes," Jamie said matter-of-factly.

"That's serious, then."

"I concur," Marvin said. "You're very different. Jolly, even. I like this."

Jamie slid into a chair and offered what felt like a dopey grin. "Yes, it *feels* serious, Chun. And thank you, Marvin." She addressed the small group. "We talked last night about vacation spots and maybe taking one together this summer. I suggested an all-inclusive in Jamaica, and Leighton knows a great travel agent she's going to check in with if we ever do decide to jet away."

"Oh, can you imagine the photos?" Marjorie said, hand to heart.

Clarissa nodded. "You two would be gorgeous against those crystal clear waters."

Jamie stood. "Stop. You're making me want to head there with her now." She added a laugh. "I'm probably ahead of myself, but it feels really, really good."

"And you deserve it," Chun called after her as she headed to the counter, ready to take on the rest of the morning. Everything seemed so much more exciting now. Each interaction, each decision, each plan she made had more meaning. For the first time in a while, she also didn't feel alone. There was somebody out there thinking about her in the same way she was thinking about them, and that made her feel not just happy, but *important*.

"What can I make for you?" Jamie asked her next customer. "It's a great day, today."

❖

When Leighton arrived on the fourteenth floor of Carrington's Corporate, she placed a breakfast burrito on Mindy's desk just as she swiveled to Leighton's side of her L-shaped desk.

"Egg and bacon one for you. I already ate mine. Also, I found those fizzing bath bombs you told me about online. Planning to order." She purposefully didn't mention her amazing night with Jamie or the fact that she still hadn't confessed. Mindy would have a hard time understanding, and she wasn't sure how to explain it herself.

"Thank you for breakfast. We have an exciting development."

Leighton paused midstroll to her office and returned. "What's that?"

"Well, you're famous today. See the *Times*?"

"No. I know they were doing an article on Courtney and succession. Is this the profile piece?"

"It is, and guess who makes a decent sized cameo?"

"Me?" She paused "That's weird. They didn't call for a quote. Nothing." Then an awful feeling hit and spread like a flu. "Do you have a copy?" She didn't have the fortitude or clarity of mind to run an internet search. Not when she was in a full-blown panic. What if the article outed her as a Carrington's employee and fell into Jamie's hands? She'd landed upon the strongest connection she'd ever had with another person in her whole life. She couldn't miss the chance to explain things to Jamie personally and save the relationship. This could really be bad.

"Are you kidding?" Mindy reached down below her desk and grabbed the paper. "Bryce has it delivered to each of us every morning." She pointed. "Business section. Just below the fold."

It had been ages since Leighton'd held an actual newspaper, but she took it in her shaky hands and flipped to the article, locating it moments later. "Succession: Not Just a TV Show" the headline read. She skimmed the first few paragraphs, a profile on Courtney and how she started with her feet on the ground floor, working in a department store in small town California before ascending the ranks. Leighton was mentioned three-quarters of the way into the article. "Courtney isn't the only the Carrington carrying the family banner. Her cousin Leighton Morrow works as a real estate analyst in the company's development division. 'My cousin has a bright future ahead of her. She's going about it the right way, too. We're lucky to have her.'"

The mention was brief. That was something. It was entirely possible that, like most people, Jamie didn't read the daily paper. She was busy in the morning with the coffee prep, doughnuts, rush hour, who even knew what else? Even if she was a news girl, the mention was late in the article. Today's culture was all about quick news bites. Who was going to read that far into a below-the-fold business piece? She calmed herself in the knowledge that she was likely in the clear to still explain herself to Jamie personally and hope for grace. She refolded the paper and handed it off to Mindy. "They even spelled my name right," she said, attempting to remain nonchalant. Her pulse began to even out, and she relaxed her arms.

"Told you. Famous. Anything you need this morning?"

"What was that?" She was on an entirely different thought track now and was having trouble staying tuned in. "Oh, um, nope. Just going to get started on email."

Mindy studied her. She knew her too well to buy it. "Mm-hmm. You okay? Did things go okay with Jamie?"

"They went well. We're going to talk more later." She glanced behind her. "Gonna go try and hunker down, get some work done."

She was being weird, and Mindy knew it. "Happy hunkering."

"To you, too!" Nope. That didn't fit.

"If you decide you want to tell me what's going on, I'll be out here." Mindy eyed her with suspicion, and Leighton hightailed it out of there. She closed herself in her office for the better part of the day, only emerging for coffee, which made her think of Jamie, so she sent a *can't stop thinking about you* text. She tried for a light lunch but was in no state to eat. At quarter to five, she packed herself up and with determination and dread took the L train to the Fourteenth Street Station. It was nearly dark on her short walk to Bordeauxnuts, a signal that they were still clinging to winter. The air smelled wonderful as all the restaurants turned to dinner service. Her midsection rumbled, uncomfortably empty, not that she could stomach much until she threw herself at Jamie's feet once and for all. *God, please let her know my intentions were good.*

Leighton arrived at the bar and stood outside a moment, attempting to gather the perfect words that she knew didn't exist. Her overstressed brain wasn't much help, so she decided to simply speak from the heart.

She pushed through the glass door, relieved to see a line only two people deep. She joined it, shifting her weight until Jamie noticed her. The second she did, the room went ice cold. The smile Jamie offered the customer at the counter faded, and she shifted her focus to anything but Leighton.

Fuck. Fuck fuck.

She'd never once witnessed Jamie chilly to anyone, but if looks could kill, Leighton would be dead on the floor. The *Times.* It had to be. She waited the three minutes that felt like four days, and when she arrived at the counter, Jamie blinked.

"Leighton. Why are you here?" Her voice sounded tired, but her hands shook. No one off the street would have noticed, but Leighton took in every detail, searching for information.

"Can we talk? Please." Luckily, no one had joined the line behind Leighton, giving them privacy. She glanced at the dining room, which was mostly empty. The regular faces she'd grown used to seeing in the daytime hours had vacated their spots for the evening. A couple of women sat at a small table by the window, an open bottle of white next to them in a chilling bucket. It reminded her a bit of their own wine date, and sadness washed over her. The dynamic between her and Jamie felt entirely different tonight, and she hated that she'd put them here. All her fault.

Jamie glared. "Why? So you can spy on us small business owners a bit more? You're from Carrington's, Leighton. Hell, you *are* a Carrington, or did you conveniently forget again?" Her eyes were no longer ice. They were fire and burning right through Leighton.

"I get it. I want to explain." She ran her fingers through her hair, a nervous habit. "My intentions, as far as you and I are concerned, were one hundred percent sincere."

Jamie sighed. "You get how I would have a hard time buying that, right?"

Leighton nodded. "I do."

"But at least we can agree that they weren't so pure when it came to my business, my life's work."

Feeling uncomfortable at the counter, like there was a timer running, Leighton inclined her head to the dining room in invitation for a longer exchange. Jamie hesitated but finally led the way to a secluded table along the side wall. The young woman working alongside Jamie automatically stepped to the register, taking over just as another couple arrived. Behind them, a discussion about which wines were full-bodied played out while Jamie took a seat across from her and folded her arms, a fortress denying Leighton any kind of glimpse inside. She got it. In Jamie's shoes, she'd likely go into self-protection mode, too. But she had to try to undo some of this.

"I originally came into the bar because of my job at Carrington's."

"You are a Carrington. You don't just work there."

She took a moment with that. "Technically, that's true."

"Is that how you operate? In technicalities?"

"I think I just meant that I'm not my cousin. I care about my job, but the corporation isn't everything."

Jamie exhaled, the hurt in her eyes flaring. "Well, I think it's apparent that it's pretty damn important to you, or you would have told me what you were doing before we..." Her eyes welled.

"I should have."

"Does that mean that you want to take out this place and put in a giant department store?"

Leighton was caught. Because it was going to happen whether either of them wanted it to or not. "It's not what I want, but that's the plan. The lease buyout will be more than generous, and you will be compensated. You can pick out a fantastic new location, maybe even better than the one you have now." It was a stretch, and Leighton damn well knew it.

Jamie closed her eyes and stayed just like that, absorbing what had to be the worst kind of blow. It was clear this was all news to her. When she raised her face, her eyes carried nothing but sadness. "We all thought the store would likely go in three blocks from here. My best friend Clarissa, who you met at the party, has been terrified they'd lose their clothing store, when it was me all along." She pressed her fingers to her eyes. Leighton was paralyzed. There were no helpful words. She could point out the money again, but for Jamie this seemed to be so much bigger than finances.

"You can reopen. You have to."

"Yep. Thank you. When will I be hearing officially?"

"Maybe a couple of weeks. I'm really sorry. This isn't at all how I—"

"Let's not, okay?" Her smile was tight. Their familiarity, their connection, was nowhere in sight. Two strangers at a table in Chelsea.

Leighton's mind clipped along in chaos, trying to save a sinking ship and fast. This was all going sideways. "I get that you're upset. With me. With the circumstances. But I need to make one thing very clear. Every moment between us was real, and that's the part that I need to—"

"No. It wasn't, Leighton. How could it be? It was all bullshit, built on lies, and a secret I still don't even understand the depth of because this information is so new and actually horrific. Morrow and Associates?" She shook her head and stood. "How would I ever in a million years trust you again? You're a liar. Please don't call me. Please don't come by. I don't want to see you. If Carrington's needs to contact me, tell them to send someone else, for God's sake."

Defeat overwhelmed. Grief engulfed her almost instantly, and her stomach turned over, nauseous. "Jamie, I'm so sorry." It was all Leighton had to offer. She hoped the words meant something but understood the damage that had been done. All that was left to do was quietly leave the bar, which she did. The only sign of respect she could offer at this point was to honor Jamie's wishes.

When she landed outside on the sidewalk, she couldn't resist a last look. Her heart wouldn't allow her to walk away without one. And so, she watched through the glow in the window as Jamie busied herself behind the counter, pouring two glasses of wine and placing them on the counter, ready to be delivered to a waiting table. On her way, Jamie nodded and flashed a smile to a customer who'd asked a question. On either side of that smile, she looked devastated as she moved through the room. Leighton had done that, and she hated herself for it.

❖

The day had been a runaway train that had run right over Jamie when she hadn't been looking. Still shell-shocked, she hadn't gone home at her normal time. She didn't want to leave the bar. In a strange sense, she found comfort within its four walls, her most prized possession now under attack. She locked the door at ten p.m., having worked well over twelve hours, and followed with a flip of the light switch, bringing the bar to near darkness. The safety lights lit her way back to the counter as she poured herself a glass of California cab and then took a seat at a table by the window. The day had started off so wonderfully. She'd practically skipped her way through the early hours, laughing with customers, living in the excitement of her time with Leighton and all that was ahead for them. Hell, she'd been thinking about vacation destinations, and exchanging flirty texts in her head as she made a lavender latte for Jim, who worked as a chocolatier at the fudge shop across the street.

"Your day seems like it's going well," Jim said, as she handed him his drink just after lunch. He'd hit on her once upon a time, but after she explained that she didn't date men, he'd become a truly nice acquaintance.

"It's definitely one of my better ones. I hope yours is just as bright."

He grinned and lifted his drink. "It's always a little better once I swing by Bordeauxnuts. You all are just so cheerful in here."

"How we like it. Come back tomorrow." She raised a hand in farewell as he pushed open the door.

"It's a deal."

Clarissa, who swung by for an afternoon hug and gab session, not to be confused with her morning version, leaned her hip against the pickup counter. She'd arrived in enough time to hear a portion of the conversation. "James. I love this for you." She smacked the counter and laughed in celebration. "It's about damn time you got yours."

She stretched her fingers. "I feel like I'm gliding all over the place. Am I gliding?"

"Your feet haven't touched the ground all day."

"Well, Leighton's made me feel really special, and it's been a long time since that's happened. Plus, I'm a little obsessed with her."

"Rightfully so." Clarissa covered her heart with her hand and held it a moment. "I'm going to glide my way to work now, too, because I'm riding your high. Hey! Maybe we could double sometime." Her mouth fell open, seemingly in love with the new thought. "I'm on date four with Tara, and it would be so much fun to be couple friends with you."

"Couple friends! Yes! We could hit up that Italian place no one can get reservations to. Just let me get in a little more time with Leighton first. But that would be so much fun."

Leo slid Clarissa's standard afternoon blueberry latte between them and eased out of the conversation like a ninja. "I'm not listening in. I'm just dropping off."

"You are so," Jamie said, "and I don't even mind."

"We're listening, too," Lisa called over. She and Chun offered silent applause while the rest of her regulars smiled along. They'd become her cheering section, and she loved it.

Not long after Clarissa's departure, the day had taken a turn.

She'd learned about Leighton first. Marvin had been combing through the *Times* the way he did every day during his lunch break. Midway through, Jamie caught him throwing strange looks her way. A look to her. A furrowed brow. A glance at his paper and back to her again with worry. Something was clearly making him uncomfortable.

"Hey, Marvin? Is there a question from the back of the class?" she called from the counter during a lull. She grinned and waited for his response, which was sure to be something very Marvin-like. Maybe the espresso machine was making a stranger noise than usual. He was quirky about sensory changes.

He swallowed. "What's the name of the woman you're dating, again?"

"Bambi's Mother," Chun said easily, looking up from whatever notes she jotted in that very busy looking spiral notebook. She'd once confessed that she thrived on those chaotic scribblings and had a notebook for each house they'd flipped.

"No." Marvin cleared his throat. Something had his attention. "Her real name."

"Leighton," Jamie said and tossed a glance at the doughnut bin, just as Leo flipped the batch. "Leighton Morrow. She might be in, in a little while. You never know."

"She damn well better be," Genevieve said. "I need to see you two in action. You can be my own personal writing inspiration."

"Well, stick around then," Jamie said, "but don't be obvious."

Genevieve offered a salute. "Got it, boss."

"Jamie, could you come back here?" Marvin asked. His voice sounded weak and coated in hesitation. The anomaly snagged the attention of the other regulars, who stopped what they were doing and swiveled. "You might want to take a look at this. Um, right here." He pointed. "It's an article on Carrington's and the Carrington family."

Jamie frowned and accepted the paper, quickly reading the piece on the Carrington family and their business, when a name sang out to her like the high note in an opera. She paused. "I don't understand. Hmm." She read the section again and looked up. "It can't be the *same* Leighton Morrow, though. No."

Marvin just stared at her. Clearly, he had his doubts. She didn't, though. Right? "Morrow is likely a common name."

The others looked on with concern written all over their faces. Lisa, meanwhile, was typing something into her phone. "Oh my God." She turned her phone around, and Jamie moved to her table, eager to see what she did. There was a headshot of Leighton on one of those professional networking sites. *Development Analyst for Carrington's, Inc.* "Was she on some kind of undercover mission? Did she mention the new Carrington's going in?"

"No. Nothing." Jamie couldn't believe it. The hope she'd held on to with a vise grip the past few moments evaporated, and dread began to slowly overtake her. She tried one more time. "Hold on a second. Let's just think this through. Is it all just maybe a coincidence? That she works for Carrington's and they're putting in a store nearby?" The legitimacy of the question lasted only a few moments, even in her mind.

"I don't think so," Marvin said with regret. She returned to the article and scanned the rest. The last section made official mention of the future Chelsea location and the blocks that would be home to the new store. Hers. *Fuck.* It had been a one-two punch all along. The woman who'd swept in and stolen her heart was a fraud who wanted to put her out of business. How could it all have changed over the course of five minutes? She folded the paper and handed it back to Marvin, numb. Her brain lagged about three steps behind, shorted out on all the new information. In fact, now she felt a little dizzy, and her cheeks felt cold.

Marvin turned to the group and explained the final details in the story. Marjorie set down her knitting bag. She'd yet to even get started. "But what about Bordeauxnuts? It's home. To all of us."

"They're going to buy out the owner and evict us," Jamie said, flatly.

The room went silent, leaving only the sound of the milk frother, which now sounded garish with its high-pitched whistle, almost like a little scream.

"Hey," Genevieve said, whirling around. "I'm a believer in happily ever after, and this story is not yet over. Do not give up on this place, okay? It's ours. All of ours. Nothing's final."

"Yes. You're right. I hear you." Jamie tried for a smile, but her eyes were beginning to fill. She had to get out of there and fast. "If you'll excuse me for a sec. Leo, you got this?" He nodded once solemnly, which meant he'd heard the news. She walked quickly because the tears were threatening to fall any second, and embarrassment was queen. Jamie wasn't a regular crier, but this was beyond everyday scope.

As soon as she was behind the closed door of the storage room, she let go, reaching for the arm of the chair against the wall and blinking through the waterworks. Her throat strangled and her stomach swirled. She wasn't even sure what to focus on first. Her brain cycled between losing the store and feeling like a fool for falling for Leighton, sleeping with her, and foolishly believing she might just be the one.

The notices that were surely on their way were simply a formality. The freight train that was Carrington's was already en route to take them out, and it's not like a small business owner renting space in New York City could do anything to stop it. She had to figure out what her next step was, where she was going to go. Would her customers find her in a new spot? Would she be starting all over? There was too much to sort through, and her heart hurt. She loved this place, her neighbors, the local customers—even the little bench a few yards down was special to her. She sat on that very bench the afternoon she turned her first profit and smiled from ear to ear as the world shuffled past. She'd been on it when she heard the news about her father's diagnosis. How could this have happened?

Now, hours later, as she sat alone inside the darkened café, Jamie allowed herself to feel the feelings she'd had to shut off to get through her workday. She'd mustered up the fortitude to smile and engage with customers, all the while her heart was breaking.

But now, she let herself unwrap the day. Interestingly, of all of the moments, there was one image that played in her mind like a scene from a film on repeat. It stood out from everything else, and it was the look on Leighton's face when Jamie told her not to come back. She'd gone very still and placed her palm flat on the table as if the smooth, cool texture would ground her. Her brown eyes had been sad, but she'd left things there, quietly exiting the bar.

Jamie couldn't remember what varietal of wine she'd poured for herself just minutes earlier, but could recall every tiny detail of that exchange, etched into her brain like granite.

When she looked back on her time with Leighton, the woman who'd captivated her in every sense, all she felt was disoriented. Leighton claimed it had been real between them, but how could she ever believe anything that woman said now? She wasn't the person Jamie thought she was and was, in fact, the very reason Jamie was at her lowest. No. She had no plans to forgive Leighton Morrow now or ever.

Jamie Tolliver felt like a lost soul, sipping her wine in the dark, tending to her tears, and wondering desperately what was next.

Chapter Eight

Three years later

Jamie's girlfriend, Monique, was a lot of things, but quiet in movie theaters wasn't one of them. Everyone had their faults, and luckily Jamie could handle this one. Mo was just exceptionally curious when it came to dissecting even the simplest of plot lines. It was cute, in a way. It meant she was fully invested.

"Where is she going?" Mo whispered in Jamie's ear.

"I don't know," Jamie whispered back. "I haven't seen this film before. We gotta watch."

"Is she serious right now?" She clutched Jamie's arm. That was rhetorical, right? "Does she know her mom knows about him? I would so freak out. Does she know?"

"Um, I don't think so," she whispered back. The problem was that it was difficult for Jamie to lose herself in the story if her full-time job was question answerer.

She left the film she had very much wanted to see feeling like she'd just completed a school assignment. But Monique was beaming. That made the whole thing worth it, right? She threaded their fingers, and Mo squeezed her hand and hopped a little. She was a perpetual hopper. Lots of energy. That part was also cute.

"Hey, it's only nine thirty. Want to hit up The Bishop's House on Fourth? I know the door guy. He'll take us to the front. We can do shots off the shovel."

"The shovel?"

"You'll see."

Jamie blinked. Dating Monique had been a bit of a culture shock. First of all, she was seven years younger than Jamie, and it showed in how they approached their nightlife. Then again, Jamie had never been much of a partier at any age. Her mother once said she'd been forty years old since birth. "Sure. Let's go. Just remember I have to work in the morning, pretty early."

"I will have you home by midnight. Or maybe twelve thirty." She stole a quick kiss and started typing away on her phone. "I'm telling Kelly and Layla to meet us there." A pause. "She says they're bringing Tom-Tom and that one girl Lorna who sells fruit and always looks at me strange, but it's whatever. This place is fire, and we're gonna rage."

"Oh. Okay."

"Oh, and Layla's whole crew from the McDonald's on Eighth Ave is swinging over. You met them at that one party with the big straws."

"This is quite a group." She didn't mind. Much.

The Bishop's House had a steady beat emanating from inside when they joined the line. The group of friends all seemed to locate each other rather quickly and chattered in shorthand. Jamie smiled and nodded along, doing her best to fit in but feeling a tad like an outsider. They said the word *vibe* a lot. She started to count how many times for fun. Mo moved like a social butterfly between the women, hugging, catching up, fist-bumping, and shouting names back at Jamie as a reminder of who each woman was. "Remember Skinny Drew with the pizza box drama?"

"I do. Hi!"

"What's up, Jamie James!" Skinny Drew yelled, her hands cupped to her mouth. She had a lot of energy and apparently hated pizza boxes. There was a lot to keep up with in this friend group.

Jamie and Monique had been dating for five months now and had been an official couple for three. They'd met when Jamie joined Clarissa, Elise, and a few others for cocktails. Monique had approached her at the bar and offered to buy her a drink. Long dark hair, petite, and full of energy, Monique was a force Jamie was still learning to keep up with.

"Baby Jamie, I love your hair. Have I told you that?" Mo shouted the words because the music was so incredibly loud that Jamie could feel the beat pulsing through every inch of her body.

"Once or twice."

"What?"

"Once or twice!" she yelled louder in Mo's ear.

"Dark hair and light eyes? Good God, take me now." Somehow the volume killed the romance, as did the dancing-slash-hopping while she said it. Mo was also now three shots in and a little handsy. She ran her fingers into Jamie's hair, cupped her ass, and smiled.

Instinctively, her arms went around Mo's waist. "We could go now." She topped the comment with a smile that was only half playful because she really was missing her apartment and her bed about now. She wasn't cut from the late-night-club cloth and never realized it more than in this moment.

"No way. We have to dance, like, eight more times." Mo did a bouncy twirl to demonstrate.

"Do we?"

"Come on. Let's do another shot."

"You go ahead. I need to sneak into the restroom." She didn't actually, but she did need a slight breather from the wall-to-wall bodies and didn't want to drink anymore with literally just hours until she needed to open the bar. The journey to the restroom took three times longer than it should have due to the lack of space, but once inside, she found the distance from the crowd allowed her to think clearly. Alone in the stall, she took a deep breath and then another, forcing herself to relax.

A few moments later as she washed her hands, a woman about her age called over her shoulder with a laugh. "We have no business in a club like this anymore. We belong in quiet restaurants with piano players underscoring our mundane conversation. Maybe a library."

"I plan to visit so many more libraries after tonight," her friend inside the stall said back. "What were we thinking?"

"Can you take me with you?" Jamie said with a laugh.

"You're in," the woman next to her said. "Do you like conversation and libraries?"

"I love both. It's a match!"

The woman handed Jamie a paper towel from the dispenser next to her. "I can't believe I used to have the energy for these places."

"Well, you're cooler than me. I never did," Jamie said.

The stall opened, and the friend approached. She took the sink next to Jamie's and turned on the water. "I never did either, I was more—" The comment died. Jamie froze mid-hand drying. The paper towel had gone still in her hands. Her brain took a minute to understand that her eyes were locked in the mirror with Leighton Morrow's. A multitude of emotions charged her way and walloped her. Placed on momentary pause was her ability to speak. She'd imagined for years what she would say to Leighton if they ever ran into each other again. Here was her moment, and her words were gone.

"Leighton, everything okay?" Leighton's friend asked from a few feet away.

"Yeah. Um, yes. All good." A pause. Leighton clearly didn't know what to do or say either. She looked like a teacher caught smoking in her car.

"Hi," Jamie said evenly. She was nothing if not a cordial person and would remain that way, no matter the company.

"Hi," Leighton said. "It's been a really long time."

"Right?" Another conservative smile. Just two people who were friendly for five minutes in a restroom. No big deal. They'd get back to their lives in a moment. Was Leighton even more beautiful now? Her hair was slightly longer and her brown eyes still big and expressive. That was certainly annoying. Dishonest people shouldn't be rewarded. "Take care." She backed away.

"Jamie."

"Yeah?" She paused. So breezy.

"I don't know." She seemed to be stumbling just as much as Jamie. "I honestly don't know. Just…how are you?"

For whatever reason, that comment kicked her into gear, and she advanced again.

"Great, actually." She flashed a victorious smile. "The bar had a record year financially. I'm working fewer hours and enjoying every minute. I have an awesome girlfriend about twenty yards from here, too."

Leighton relaxed and nodded. "I'm really happy to hear that."

"Well, good. But it doesn't erase the fact that you tried to put my business out on the street." She offered a laugh as if remembering the good ole days. Okay, it was maybe unnecessary to go there. No need to be petty. A polite exit would suffice.

Leighton held total composure. Damn her. "It wasn't quite like that, but I'm glad the bar was able to keep its location."

The reality was that Leighton's efforts on behalf of Carrington's hadn't paid off in the end. The deal had fallen through, and the Chelsea store never did come to be. Carrington's found themselves caught in a great deal of red tape when it came to the preservation of landmark buildings and what could and could not be done to their exteriors. Apparently, vanity was a hidden agenda item in their mission statement. Jamie had celebrated when the news came through with a free glass of wine for anyone who'd stopped by that evening, putting out a *We're Staying* notice all over social media.

"Well," Jamie said, "everything worked out the way it was supposed to in the end. Enjoy your night."

"You, too." Leighton remained right where she stood, a faraway look in her eyes.

On her way out, Jamie nodded and sent a polite smile to Leighton's friend, whose gaze bounced between them in utter confusion. No reason the friend had to be caught up in this. "Maybe I'll see you at the library."

"Definitely," she said and then moved straight to Leighton on a mission, surely full of questions.

Jamie hightailed it out of there, scanned the club, spotted Monique, and pretty much crowd-surfed her way back to the group, which was jumping in unison and shouting the lyrics to a song she'd never heard in her life.

"Hey, you ready to get out of here?" she asked Mo, whose face fell in response.

"Dude. Why can't you just have fun with me? You really need to learn to play the good-time card more often, you know? Not really needing a babysitter."

Drink four—or was it five now?—seemed to have added an aggressive streak to Mo's personality. Jamie nodded. "So sorry. Just had a weird thing with someone I know."

Mo frowned. "What? I can't hear you. Tell me later." She pointed at Jamie as she danced her way back to the jumping circle. "You're fucking hot, though. Damn."

Jamie nodded, understanding she was sentenced to who knew how much longer of this overly hypnotic music, while she tried not to think about the woman she'd just run into so very unexpectedly. Feelings warred and circled. Sadness, anger, grief. It had taken her so very long to move on from her confusing emotions for Leighton, only to have the dust kicked up again. She pressed her nails into the palm of her hand and took a seat on a stool at the bar, bopping her head ever so slightly to the beat in an attempt to look like everyone else.

Only a few minutes passed before she saw them, Leighton and her friend, settling a tab across the bar and heading for the exit. Lucky library people.

She didn't want to watch. She shouldn't have, but Jamie couldn't drag her eyes away from Leighton as she moved—no, *glided*—through the crowded room. No one bumped into her. No one danced in her path. They simply moved out of her way as if ordained. Apparently, nothing had changed. Yep, Leighton had presence for days and owned whatever room she walked into. Several heads swiveled in Leighton's direction as she passed, only confirming Jamie's last thought.

"Yeah, I'd be careful there if I were you," she murmured to the rest of the people in the club.

She turned back to Mo, her *girlfriend* and the only one deserving of her attention. She was attempting to dance with a cocktail over her head and spilled a little on the guy next to her who turned around with an irate look on his face before moving away to safety. Jamie sighed because never had their differences been more on display. Was she noticing this even more because memories of the Leighton she once knew were swirling and swooping? What was the cosmos trying to tell her tonight? Was Venus lurking?

"You look so bored," Monique said, approaching and squeezing her knee. "You can jet. I'll catch a ride with Lorna."

"Isn't she the one who sells fruit?" she yelled in Mo's ear.

"Totally her. But she's chill tonight."

Jamie had no idea why she wouldn't be chill. "You sure?"

"Beyond. Get some sleep. I'll call you, babe."

She placed a quick kiss on Monique's lips and watched her bounce to the beat back to her friends. Jamie was heading home. She had a mild headache and a haunting case of nostalgia she needed to shake off, and fast.

All the wonderful moments with Leighton had been fictional. So why were they all up in her space now? Annoyed and out of sorts, Jamie headed for home, way past her bedtime.

Tomorrow, all of this would be in her rearview again. Thank God.

❖

"Lennox, you're late."

"I know. Take me to court. You'll win." Leighton's friend Jessica arrived at the bar, looking like an ad for women in kick-ass corporate America, in a black pinstripe suit with a white collared shirt underneath. Her dark hair was in a semitwist with tendrils escaping, an effortless look on Jessica.

"No litigation needed, but you might have to buy the first round to make it up to me."

"Done. Is there red? Beg the people here for it," Jessica said, searching for the bartender. "We need red."

"Down, girl. You're getting wine in mere moments. Have a day?"

Her dark blue eyes flashed in exasperation. "We've taken on a new client, this zany millionaire who opened a candy bar company with national distribution."

"I don't see the problem." She signaled to Stevie, the bartender she'd come to know well over the past three years. Stevie held up two fingers and Leighton nodded, knowing she'd just ordered two glasses of her favorite merlot. She and Stevie had fantastic nonverbal code, developed after many a night. Leighton loved Puzzles and spent her evenings here whenever she needed to unwind or feel better about something. Jessica, who had her own personal connection to the bar, joined her on occasion.

"Let me enlighten you." Jessica began to count off the issues. "This man insists on calling five times a day and refuses to speak to any members of my team. Only me. He also starts off every call with one of those two-line jokes and won't ever share the punchline, so I'm left to simply guess and guess."

"That's hysterical."

Jessica glared and carefully moved a strand of hair off her forehead. "Brooklyn thinks it is, too, because she almost went after his account." She shook her head. "I should have encouraged her."

Leighton laughed. Jessica and Brooklyn were married but worked for competing advertising agencies, which made for great stories. "Doesn't sound so horrible. Millionaires and candy."

"The money part isn't. He's throwing cash at us. But my time is valuable, too." Jessica sighed. "Lay, we can have a thirty-minute strategy session, and he will erase everything we decided one week later, and we're back to square one with me trying to figure out why the frog got on the elevator."

"Why did he?" Leighton asked.

Jessica dropped her head. "I don't know. That's the problem," she said weakly. Jamie laughed. This was too good. "He wanted a TV spot with dancing bananas eating the chocolate bars, and now we're talking about nuns and penguins. It's a lot, Lay. I need the wine." Jessica touched the space in front of her. "Is the red here? Where are you, little red?"

Leighton's laughter only grew because frazzled was not a version of Jessica Lennox that she was used to. Jessica was the calm, commanding type that sent competition quaking in their boots. Right on cue, Stevie appeared with a bottle of Tangle Valley merlot and a corkscrew. Jessica sat taller and regained her in-control status, leaving her lamentation in the rearview. Impressive how she turned it off so effectively.

"Leighton, that woman from last week asked about you," Stevie said. "She knew your name, too."

Jessica sipped the merlot and smiled in victory. "Perfection. I love this wine. I needed it." She exhaled in satisfaction. "Who's the admirer?" She turned to Stevie. "I've tried setting her up several times and have failed miserably. Not that I'm done."

"I'm not settling," Leighton said. "I want what you have, or I don't want it at all. Life's too short for mediocre relationships. And she's just a nice woman who bought me a drink. Cute enough. Nice enough. We flirted some, and she went on her way."

Reliable Stevie leaned in. "Until she came back looking for you."

Leighton took a sip and regarded them both. "I ran into Jamie." Stevie arched an interested brow and lingered close as they talked.

Jessica went still. "Did you now?"

"Don't give me the knowing eyes. It wasn't a big deal. A run-in at a club." Leighton paused. "She wasn't thrilled to see me." Leighton put up a brave front, but saying the words made her wilt inside. Jamie was a tough subject for her. She'd always wonder about what might have been if their circumstances had been different. Maybe that was one of the reasons she frequented Puzzles. She tried to learn from the mistakes she'd made, but also didn't allow herself to reminisce too often, having learned to keep her fingers off the bruise. It wasn't meant to be between them. That was that.

"She's the one who got away?" Stevie asked, as she placed napkins in front of two new arrivals down the bar.

"You could say that," Leighton said, reflective, her gaze brushing the bar and the swirl of its gray marble. The cool stone beneath her fingertips helped ground her.

Jessica held up a finger. "But I believe in fate. I've seen it at work. Hear me out."

"No."

"Maybe running into Jamie was fate's way of tapping you on the shoulder."

Leighton laughed. "I highly doubt it. I tried to fix things with Jamie once. It didn't work."

"Once." Jessica scoffed. "If I'd given up after a single defeat, my life would be very different today. Just ask Brooklyn."

"I wish I had your fortitude, your killer instinct. The truth is that I'm a softie, and if Jamie says to go away, I'm going to respect her wishes."

"We don't know what they are now, though."

Leighton scrunched one eye closed. "We kind of do after last night."

Jessica glanced over her shoulder. "Bordeauxnuts is just a few blocks from here. You could swing by for a cup of coffee."

Leighton sighed. "I dream about those little doughnuts."

"I had them last week."

Leighton swiveled. "What? You didn't tell me."

"I stop by now and then. Too good not to. I don't mention it because Jamie is an understandably delicate topic, and I don't like watching the sad little storm cloud appear over your head." She sipped her wine. "She's looking really great lately."

Leighton closed her eyes, flashing on the memory of Jamie at the club. Her hair was longer now. Still dark, thick, and beautiful. And the red top she'd been wearing? Yeah, well, an impression had been made. "Trust me. I know."

"And you're still not interested in testing the waters? Time has passed. It all worked out for Bordeauxnuts."

Leighton stared at the wine rack that stretched its way to the ceiling on the far wall. The servers had to climb the rolling ladder to retrieve the more expensive bottles. "Part of my job used to be risk assessment, and I think I'm pretty good at it. My chances with Jamie Tolliver make the endeavor nonadvisable."

"Before meeting Brooklyn, I think I would have understood that ideology." She shrugged. "But she changed me. The least I can do is pass on this advice because it's worth it. All the trouble, stress, grief, and heartache are worth it in the end. Brooklyn says it better with an ice cream/brain freeze analogy, but it's all the same."

Leighton allowed the words to settle over her. She valued Jessica's wisdom, and so she tucked the advice into her back pocket in case she ever needed it. But this wasn't the time to act. "I hear you, but there's a boundary in place between me and Jamie, and my plan is to respect it. Unless she asks me not to someday. That would be different."

Jessica turned to her with a gleam in her eye. "I like that last part. I'm hoping it happens."

Leighton lifted the glass to her lips and let it hover just shy. "Yeah, well. You'd probably have better odds of winning the New York Lottery."

Jessica smiled and watched Leighton, wheels turning. "I'm not so sure about that."

CHAPTER NINE

"What do you think I should do?" Jamie asked. The first hint of daylight shimmied its way in through Bordeauxnuts' street-facing picture window. Summer was cheerful—the sunshine joined them earlier these days. "I want your honest opinion. This is too important for unwavering support."

She stood across from Leo, her arms crossed, leaning back against the counter in the empty coffee bar fifteen minutes before opening. She had a decision looming and hadn't slept well, knowing the meeting with this Michael Stoneking guy was scheduled that afternoon. Her thoughts were all over the place about his offer, and she needed input and a clear direction and fast.

Leo, mirroring her position against the opposite counter, nodded. He'd been her right hand since the early days when she'd first opened. He knew Jamie. He knew the business, and what was more, she trusted him. "Well." He sighed, contemplating the question. "You've been wanting this second location for as long as I can remember. You talk about it all the time. Scout properties, neighborhoods. It's your vision for this place."

"That part is true." The reality was that she simply couldn't afford to open a second bar just yet. Every time she had a little money put away for that particular pipe dream, the price of milk would inch up, or her wine distributor would inform her of a nationwide shortage. Bordeauxnuts was profitable, just not enough to fund the new venture. At least, not yet.

"This is one way to make it happen," Leo said, meeting her gaze head-on. "You can't discard that just because it wouldn't be yours." He shrugged. "You'd pull in a nice fee, though."

"Yeah, but it feels a little like making a deal with the devil. Do I do devil deals? I'm not sure I can."

Michael Stoneking was a entrepreneur interested in opening a franchise location of Bordeauxnuts uptown, near Columbus Circle. He'd fallen in love with the café and its concept after stumbling upon an influencer's blog and visiting a few times. Apparently, he wanted to be a part of the Bordeauxnuts family and open his own branch.

"The upside is a franchise store brings in cash flow that could help fund an additional location of mine." She paused. "The downside is that he owns a piece of my brand. Do I want to hand over my baby to some man I barely know just because he has money? Bordeauxnuts is what it is because of us, the love we put into what we do every day." Jamie touched her chest, her feelings running away from her like water poured from a jug. "I believe in our store and our mission. Can he say the same?"

Leo touched his thumb to his chin. "Look, I think that's what this meeting might tell you."

"Okay, okay. Good point." She wrapped her arms around herself, a comfort mechanism that had become habit, and checked the clock. "Can you start the first batch of doughnuts while I take delivery of the pastries?" She eyed their supplier, pulling up to the curb in his white truck of goodies.

"Let's roll," he said with a game-time clap. The day got off to a whirlwind of a start with a line out the door, but she and her team were in their groove, bopping to Leo's hits playlist he'd designed especially for their morning grind, pun intended. Her regulars rolled in, followed by the semiregulars. Even Jessica Lennox made a dazzling appearance in maroon pants, a black shirt, and heels. The woman was a corporate rock star and always looked the part.

Jamie beamed as she approached the counter. "Ms. Lennox, looking like dynamite today." Her hair was down and formed the perfect S swish just past her shoulders.

Her eyes lit up. "You're always so good for my ego."

"I simply speak the truth. Americano for you this morning?"

"Yes, please. I have no idea how you keep everyone's order straight."

"My most impressive gift." She slid the cup down the counter to Leo.

But Jessica seemed to hesitate before she said, "Hey, Jamie. I'd love to talk to you when you're less busy about a charity event I'm spearheading. I'd love to have your insight on the committee. I feel like you have your finger on the pulse of this city."

It was a compliment. "Oh. Really? Me?" She'd never been asked to be a part of anything as important before, and she knew everything Jessica touched was.

"Yes. The commitment consists of a handful of meetings and the event itself, raising funds for Hope and Help. It's a leg up for formerly incarcerated women reentering the workforce. They do amazing work."

"Yes. I would love to help." Jamie perked up because this was an especially good cause.

"Do you have a card I could steal while I get out of this nice gentleman's way so he can order his coffee?"

"Here you go." She handed Jessica her business card from beneath the counter.

She held it up and picked up her Americano from Leo. "I'll be in touch."

"She looks important," Genevieve said from behind her laptop as Jessica breezed out of the café like a boss. "I might be about to put her in this book." She fanned herself. "Wowza. Inspiration in a pair of killer heels."

Jamie laughed. "Happy to help."

"Why do you think I come here?"

"Sex inspo and doughnuts."

"You know me well."

Three o'clock rolled around, and there was no Michael Richpants, which was the nickname she'd assigned to her potential franchisee. She sat at the table by the window in the sparsely occupied bar, sipping a hot blueberry latte, and waiting on a businessman to pitch her. What an odd feeling. She shifted, watching the sidewalk, wondering if she got the time wrong. Fifteen minutes after the hour, he breezed in with a charismatic smile, wearing jeans and flip-flops.

"Hi, Michael," she said, standing. Butterflies danced a salsa in her midsection. She still didn't know how she felt about this whole thing and didn't want to make the wrong decision. This was an important opportunity for her, but was it the right one? Why did this feel like such a huge crossroads?

"Jamie, there you are. Glad you agreed to this meeting." He held up a hand, not giving her a moment to respond, nor apologizing for being late. "You're going to love this offer. I'm telling you. We're gonna kill it together." He took a seat and began shuffling through his messenger bag for a manilla folder, clearly wanting to get right to it. She had the distinct feeling he was fitting her in.

"I'm interested to hear your offer, but I just have to be blunt and say that I'm concerned about—"

"I know. I hear you. That's what today is about, right? Making sure you're comfortable before we move forward."

She felt the urge to keep up with his fast pace and decided to get right to the heart of her concerns before he ran her over like a garbage truck late for its route. "My first question is who is going to run the bar? As in, be in charge."

He eyed her. "I'll hire a suitable manager, and a selection of employees." He said it easily, like it was something he did every day. He likely did.

"So not *you*?" That made her nervous. Who would be the keeper of the culture?

"I'll be around, but I do have other businesses to look after." He held up a hand. "Doesn't mean I don't have a very vested interest."

"Understood." She nodded and pressed on, tiptoeing the line between remaining his friend and protecting her legacy and reputation. "You seem to have a portfolio of many different businesses. Are any of them coffee shops?"

"No. That would be a conflict of interest. But I plan to just lift your system and apply it to the new store, which I imagine to be very similar to this one."

Part of her relaxed, hearing that last section. "Really?"

"With an added edge for the uptown clientele, of course." He added a knowing smile.

"Right." She hesitated. "What kind of edge?"

"Well, your blackboard menu for example. Very raw. Very hip. It works for Chelsea, but it doesn't have that uptown sophistication that Joe Trustfund on his way to the brokerage is looking for. Thereby, I'd want a more permanent menu."

"But that's part of the charm. There's nothing truly sophisticated about Bordeauxnuts."

"Yet." He waved her off. "But we're getting caught up in the details. All of that can be hashed out later." He tented his hands. "I want to be in the Bordeauxnuts business. That's what it comes down to at the end of the day. You have a reputation in New York, and we can blow that up and make a lot of money together." He slid the envelope her way. "I think my offer reflects that." He must have seen the hesitation come over her face. "Listen, we both win. And the world gets the best damn coffee, wine, and doughnuts ever made. Do you trust me?"

"Not really," Jamie said. "I don't know you that well."

"I'm an open book. Google me. Stalk me. Fuck, ask around until you're comfortable with the kind of businessman I am. I'm up for it." He tapped the envelope. "Look these over, show 'em to your lawyer, and get me an answer within thirty days. That's how long my offer is good for." He stood. "Can I get one of those blueberry lattes iced?"

"Um, sure. Leo, can we get an iced blueberry?"

"You got it," Leo called.

"I really like the cinnamon doughnuts, too. Can we toss in a bag for the ride uptown?"

"A bag of cinnamon, Leo. Anything else?" She passed him a smile, actually counting the moments until he was gone. She found Michael to be stressful and a tad annoying. Their energies didn't match. At the same time, he was her only option at the moment, and she couldn't discard that important little detail.

"Nah, that'll do it. Thanks, Lyle," he said, swinging by the bar. Leo didn't correct him, but it was another careless misstep to add to the unlikable column.

She wasn't sure what to do about that. She needed Michael almost as much as he needed her, and if it went well, who knew what one store could lead to? Expansion had always been her dream, which meant she had to examine this thing from every angle, even though the gnawing in her stomach told her this was all wrong, wrong, wrong.

"Interesting guy," Leo said, coming around the counter. "He was here for maybe eight minutes. What the hell?"

"I thought we'd have more of a chance to feel each other out."

"Guys like that don't do touchy-feely. Always late for someone more important." He touched his temple. "Keep that in mind. He's never gonna hold your hand."

"Which is exactly the vibe I don't want my business to come with. We're personal and fun and warm. We value people and good conversation over a glass of wine."

He held up his hands as if to say don't shoot the messenger, which of course, she shouldn't.

Jamie spent the next ten minutes stress scrubbing her countertops until a ping on her phone snagged her attention. Jessica Lennox had invited her to The Lennox Group's office for a committee meeting for the charity event that night. She checked her watch. If she did a quick wine inventory and got her order in for next week, she could sneak out early and might be able to swing it. Monique had hot yoga that night and would be unavailable. Why not? She needed a worthy project, and this one fit the bill.

❖

It was already early evening and Leighton hadn't come up for air since lunch. In fact, she hadn't even had one, working right through the break, lost in a report. She sat back in her soft black leather desk chair and exhaled slowly. She'd noticed herself spending more and more time at the office, most notably on the partnership portion of her job as the new Community Outreach Director. She valued her work but no longer wanted it to be her sole focus, and lately, it had been. She also valued her big-picture career and the journey she was taking with Carrington's, a company she'd truly come to care about under Courtney's leadership. However, she didn't want to wake up fifty years from now and look back on a lifetime of memories spent in front of a laptop or in a business meeting on her fourth cup of stale black coffee from the break room. She longed for a family, Christmas traditions, and lingering kisses before she left for work. Those were the things that mattered most in life, and though she casually dated, it was becoming more and more clear that she wasn't finding what she was looking for, and she had to ask herself *why*.

So, instead of calling up a friend, or using her dating apps to find a potential dinner companion, she was off to the Hope and Help committee meeting, which—double sigh—honestly felt like an extension of her job. Another meeting in a boardroom. Another agenda. Another set of tasks to complete. The cause was a good one, but she now had nagging regrets about agreeing to serve despite how wonderful an idea it seemed when Jessica had pitched her months ago. Time to pay the piper.

The Lennox Group was located in Midtown East, only two train stops from her own office in the heart of the city, which made getting to the office building easy enough. When she approached the bank of elevators in the lobby, she spotted a woman in jeans and cute slingbacks waiting there. She secretly checked out her ass because it was a thing to behold. Dark hair that fell in subtle layers, making the slight waves look shiny and full. What was it that she was just lecturing herself about an hour ago? Focus less on work and more on making those important connections. Well, here was someone smack in front of her that pulled her attention, and she didn't plan to let the moment slip away.

"These things sure take their time, don't they?" It wasn't her best opener, but a decent jumping off point. The woman turned, lips blossoming into a radiant grin. Just when she was about to speak, their eyes locked. *Jamie. Again.* Twice in one week? It now made sense why she'd been so taken. Dammit all. Leighton let her head fall to the side. "I swear I didn't know it was you. Nor am I stalking you."

Jamie nodded. She'd yet to speak, but the radiant grin had dimmed its wattage. To her credit, she'd been nice enough not to drop it entirely. "These things do take a while." She turned back around and resumed waiting. *Okay, then.* Leighton took the cue and waited silently as well. When the elevator arrived, they stepped inside, just the two of them. Jamie selected the twelfth floor and turned to Leighton, expectant.

"I'm going to twelve as well."

Jamie's gaze narrowed, and they seemed to get it at the same moment. "Did Jessica invite you to—"

"Yeah." Leighton nodded. "Yeah, she did."

"Coincidence or…?"

"Definitely *or*. She's an astute woman."

"So she used a *charity* to set us up to see each other?"

"If it makes it any better, it's a fantastic one. They've helped women across the country get a foot in the door when they really needed it."

Jamie swallowed, seemingly coming to terms with her fate. "I understand that part."

Leighton wanted to let her off the hook. "I can let Jessica know that you won't be able to serve on the committee. She'll understand." There it was. Jamie's get out of jail free card. All she had to do was snatch it.

"But I want to serve. I'm not going to put my own comfort level ahead of the greater good." She shrugged and faced forward as the elevator pulled to a halt.

"Great. Well. I'll be sure to give you space. You don't have to worry about—"

"Leighton. I'm grown up. You don't have to look after me, okay?" The doors opened and Jamie breezed out, leaving Leighton in the car, staring after her and trying really hard not to look at the jeans and slingbacks combo from behind.

"Got it," she said, a beat too late.

Jessica had a plate of enormous chocolate chip cookies sitting in the middle of the table like a fucking amazing hostess. Jamie sat right in front of them, making her Leighton's hero.

"Hi, you two. Just in time. We're about to get started," Jessica said, passing them each a navy folder with their name and the charity's logo embossed on the cover. When Jessica moved out of Jamie's sight line, Leighton passed Jessica a wide-eyed *what the hell* look to which she passed back a serene-eyed *you're welcome* reply, to which Leighton sent a *you shouldn't have done this* stare to which Jessica countered with a *well it's too late now* smile.

"Whatever shorthand that is, it's impressive," Jamie said, gesturing between them. The winsome smile helped. It also made Leighton's heart rate double. What was it about her and Jamie in one space that made the air feel heavy and kept Leighton at full attention?

Jessica brightened. "What? Hmm? Well, we should get started." She addressed the small committee. "We're a group of six women on a mission to make as much money in one evening as we possibly can for a very deserving organization. Open your folders and start the clock because we have six weeks until the Gala."

The group opened their folders in unison and were off. Surprisingly, Leighton enjoyed the contributions of everyone on the team. Jessica had assembled a group of smart and capable women—herself, Jamie, Leighton, Eileen, an established designer in the fashion world, Toni who was a tech executive, and Tess, a women's health physician. As they enjoyed the heavenly cookies from Jessica's favorite little bakery in the Village, they came up with a list of fundraising ideas.

"Obviously, a silent auction for cocktail hour," Eileen stated. "People love to jump right in over a glass of wine, which we should have hand passed. No waiting in line."

"Agreed," Leighton said. "The fancier the feel, the more they spend. We need to pamper these folks."

"Could the auction have an online component?" Jamie asked. "We have so many introverts come through the bar each day, and I can guarantee you'll snag their participation if they can bid from the quiet of their phones."

"I love that," Jessica said. "Exactly the kind of enhancement we need. Is there software?"

"There is," Toni said. "We can even start the bidding a couple of days before so we're up and running, ready to turn up the heat."

"But let's save big-ticket items for the live auction," Leighton suggested. "I'm pretty sure I can get Courtney to okay a Carrington's shopping spree in the midtown store."

"Perfect." Jessica nodded. "Hit up any big clients, friends, loved ones, and most especially corporations for donations."

Leighton watched Jamie jot down a few notes, taking in the way her lips pursed when she concentrated. It was everything, and so much more captivating than anything happening in the room. *Focus.* She couldn't. She was staring. It was rude, but she couldn't seem to stop.

"What do you think, Lay?" Jessica asked.

"I have no idea what you just asked me. I'll be honest."

Jessica's mouth pulled into a hint of a grin. Busted. "Just wondering if you thought we should leave a middle aisle between banquet tables. A runway to the stage."

Jamie looked up from her notebook. "To give the auctioneer room to stroll."

"Definitely," Leighton said. "Interaction is the key to getting people involved. Everyone wants to look good when called upon."

"With that fantastic point, let's all hit pause for tonight. We've given ourselves so much to work with," Jessica said.

She was right. They had accomplished a great deal that night, and Leighton was glad she'd come. The Jamie factor was an unanticipated snag, and Jessica would certainly hear from her on it later. But for now, she basked in the knowledge that she and Jamie had done just fine together. In fact, when the group said good-bye in front of the building later, she hung back on the steps for a word with Jamie.

"Again, sorry if my presence caught you off guard," Leighton said.

Jamie, who seemed much more relaxed than when they'd arrived, shrugged. "It's not a big deal. The group gelled really well together tonight. I don't have a problem working with you if you don't have a problem working with me. Just a grown-up school project, right? We don't have to make it personal."

"Right. We don't." The sentiment yanked away the spring in her step because simply exchanging ideas with Jamie tonight, listening to her interact with others, reminded her of the magical time they'd spent together years ago. She saw all the things that had drawn her to Jamie in the first place. "But I'm glad it won't be a problem." Leighton pulled her business card from her bag and handed it to Jamie. "For committee planning purposes."

Jamie studied the card. "Vice President of Community Relations." She looked up. "Congratulations. You've ascended." There was a bite to her tone. Leighton absorbed it.

"Thank you."

"Is that like PR?"

She nodded. "Yes and no. We have a PR arm of the company, but my team is adjacent. A bit more proactive with a strong focus on building relationships with our customers and the communities we're tied to across the country." She shrugged. "The truth? I wanted to spend my time building bridges rather than burning them." A deep breath as regret swarmed, familiar and potent. "I'm learning as I go."

Jamie seemed to be dissecting the implication, and Leighton thought she saw her soften. Finally, she slid the business card into her bag. "Let's build some bridges for these women who need it. Deal?" She held out her hand, a partnership. They were going to work together in spite of what they'd been through.

"Deal." She appreciated the grace Jamie was extending her, another example of how good a person she was. "I appreciate that, Jamie, and I don't take the invitation to work together lightly." For whatever reason, Jamie met her gaze and held on, searching Leighton's eyes. She imagined she was a kind of puzzle to Jamie, and likely not the good kind. She'd brought shock, anger, and sadness into Jamie's life, and Jamie hadn't deserved any of it. She laughed now, thinking back to the moment she'd naively asked if they could hold on to what they'd discovered between them. "Jamie?"

"Yes?"

"Before you go, I need to tell you that back then I had to sell myself on the logic that everything we did as a company was for the greater good. A survival strategy. I know better now, and I have a lot of regret."

"I'm glad you see that." Jamie shrugged beneath the halo of the streetlights. "I guess in the end, we're all just trying to make our way." She gestured up to the building. "Like the women we're trying to help. But I'm glad to hear you're working on yourself. Good night."

It was certainly not forgiveness, but it was an acknowledgment that Leighton needed deep down. Because she *was* a work in progress, but pleased with the changes she'd made in her life. She and Jamie would never be close again, but it was enough to know that Jamie heard her out, knew of her efforts.

Leighton struggled for sleep that night, instead lying there with the cool sheets against her bare body, remembering the feel of the most perfect lips on hers, the skin beneath her fingertips, the sound of Jamie when pleasure washed over her. She shifted her position, uncomfortable, longing for release. She missed Jamie and all she'd made Leighton feel. Their weeks together felt like a distant dream she'd once had, perfect and rare, a glimmer of a time that somehow managed to surpass every other time in her life.

At least she had the memory of *them*, the way they'd fit together so perfectly, laughed so effortlessly. The Jamie memories were hers to keep, tucked away and safe, always and forever.

Chapter Ten

Sometimes, life called, and it was important to stop everything and answer. When Jamie's father died a year and half ago, she'd made changes to her schedule in order to see her mother more often. She'd struggled with how she'd possibly come up with more time as a small business owner, but the change had been a blessing in disguise. Not only did she learn to rely on her team more often, but she and her mother had developed a kind of one-on-one friendship that they'd never had before. It was nice having this new little piece of her life to look forward to. She and her mother hit up the farmers markets on the weekend, met for wine in the bar every other Wednesday evening, and watched dogs play in Washington Square Park while sipping Leo's iced blueberry lattes.

"I just don't know if it's the right choice for me," her mom explained on a park bench, late that afternoon. Nearby, behind the chain-link fence, the dogs of New York wrestled and played. "A dog is such a great responsibility, and I live in an apartment."

"I hear you. It would take some work to keep him or her exercised and happy. But I also know you've mentioned it about eight hundred times, so it's at least worth talking out."

Her mother sat forward and grinned. Her dark hair with the occasional gray streak was pulled into a low bun. "Look at that one." She tapped Jamie's knee about five times in excitement. "Jamie, look. His fur bounces when he runs."

"Looks like a happy fella." The rough-coated mix that ran through the dog park was small in size and probably about what her mom could handle on her own. It was a nice thought, her mom having a friend, and Jamie would be there to help out whenever she could. She worried her mom was lonely now, and a dog was a way to fill the apartment with a little bit of joy. Another soul to cuddle with while she watched TV or read a book. "I think you should do it."

Her mother shook her head adamantly. "It would be unwise." A beat. "But so much fun." Another beat. "The work involved, though." She exhaled. "But look how sweet they are."

Jamie laughed. "You are living the kind of struggle I don't envy." She turned to her mom. "Take your time deciding. There's no rush."

"Have you ever seen a woman so conflicted? I'm like two warring nations in one body. Change the subject. Save us." She waved her hand. "Tell me what new thing happened to you this week."

"Easy. I ran into a woman who once broke my heart with her dishonesty, and I didn't kill her. Surely, that warrants a motherly pat on the head." She presented her head. "Whenever you're ready."

Her mother tilted hers. "Tell me this isn't that awful Laurel. She criticized the Berber rug my mother brought over from Morocco to Saudi Arabia before I was born."

"I know. That's because she's the worst kind of human, Mom. We should avoid people like her at all costs and will. But it wasn't her."

"Then who is this other one? Why are you dating so many unkind people?"

"Leighton was a business exec with Carrington's Department Store when they were trying to take over the block. She was there to scope out Bordeauxnuts for the kill and eventually decided to ask me out without telling me who she was."

"We hate her, then." Her mother nodded once decisively.

"Hate is strong. But yes. She's on the unfavorable list in the imaginary sky." She hesitated. "But we were fine last night, so maybe she can just go on the list in light ink."

"Your heart is too generous, Jamie."

She turned to her mother. "Says the woman who gave her watch to her next-door neighbor because the woman said it was pretty."

"What are possessions if not for sharing? She looked better with it than I did."

"See? Self-deprecating all over the park."

Her mother laughed. "I can't help it if I wasn't gifted a lovely wrist."

"I can't with you. I just can't." Jamie shook her head and laughed along.

"You just be careful around the woman from Carrington's. If she's the one I'm thinking of from back then, you had more than a crush."

"Moot point. I have a girlfriend."

"The bouncing child?"

"She's twenty-nine. There's barely seven years between us. And, yes, she does bounce."

"But what about up here?" Her mother tapped her temple. It was hard to argue. Mo hadn't come off as the most scholarly or mature when they'd had dinner two weeks ago with her mother. In fact, she'd spent the first five minutes of their dinner explaining to Jamie's mom that she'd sworn off Doritos but missed licking the seasoning off her fingers.

"I'm cutting her some slack. She's young. Plenty of potential there."

Originally, Jamie had been drawn to Monique's vivacious energy and excitement about, well, everything. She was this exceptionally cool girl who knew the passwords to all the secret clubs, which, at the time, made Jamie feel cool-adjacent. Now, the realization that they'd have to actually *use* those passwords and race around the city until three a.m. was starting to set in. She was growing weary of talking about social media trends for hours over dinner at only the in restaurants. Sadly, she was going to have to figure out next steps.

As a Jack Russell and a poodle played chase around the perimeter of the dog park, Jamie placed a finger above her lip. "We might not be as compatible as I once hoped. But sometimes you have to grow into each other, right? Did you and Dad have some sorting out to do in the beginning?"

"Are you kidding? We couldn't bear to be apart for more than five minutes. Is that what you feel?"

"Um...no." The extra detail that she refused to formally acknowledge tapped her on the shoulder anyway: Mo and their compatibility issues had been put in startling perspective the second she'd seen Leighton Morrow again. She'd tried not to compare the two women but lost the battle. Leighton moved through the world as a thoughtful adult, capable of deep conversation and with an eye on a world much wider than just *her*. How could Jamie find someone like that without the *willing to screw me over* factor that Leighton came with? It felt like a large ask.

"Jamie, listen to me. I'm old. I know things, and since I lost your dad, I know even more. Grief has to be the most enlightening affliction."

"I'm listening."

"Life is fleeting. Don't waste it on people who don't make you light up the second you see them in the distance."

She thought on Monique and was saddled with an uncomfortable sinking feeling, like she was a lead rock on her way to the bottom of the dark ocean. "I think I have to end it." She took a deep breath. Didn't help. "This is the first girlfriend I've had in a long time." She shook her head and tried to let the adorable dogs cheer her up. "I was actually proud of myself. No longer sad, single Jamie."

Her mom dropped a hand onto her thigh and gave it a pat. "Well, I'm still proud of you. You're assessing what's right for you and taking action, even though it's not easy." She shook her finger. "That's emotional maturity. I saw it on *Good Morning America*." She tossed in a smile to say she was kidding. "What can I do to help? I've got the time. Lots of it."

Jamie laughed. Her mother was pulling fewer hours at the alterations shop and starting to explore life on her own. She wasn't a retiree yet but had one foot in a new, slower approach to her work schedule. "Oh, just shower me with unending love and affection. Gifts are always welcome."

"I know this. You opened all of your father's birthday presents when you were five and ate two bites from his cake before we even had a chance to show it to him."

"And lived with the shame ever since!" They shared a laugh. "Well, I think it's decided. You're getting a dog, and I'm losing a girlfriend. Sigh."

"Well, this has been a very eventful talk with my daughter. We should watch dogs play more often."

"Solve all the world's problem via pug races."

Her mom beamed. It warmed Jamie to see her happy, especially after a dark year threaded with grief. "Terrier therapy. It's all the rage in Washington Square Park."

They shook their heads, laughed, and watched the dogs on the other side of the fence frolic, run, and zoom in the waning sunlight. It really was the best kind of afternoon.

Jamie dropped her head back and turned to the side, meeting her mother's brown-eyed gaze. "I don't say it enough, but I love you, Mom."

"You say it a lot, but I love to hear it." She touched Jamie's cheek on the far side and kissed the one closest to her. "I love you, too, sweet Jamie. I'm very lucky you're my daughter." A pause. "And that you give me free coffee. And wine on Wednesday."

"That's true. You have it good, lady." She folded her arms and watched a Corgi splash around gleefully in the doggy water fountain. It had been an afternoon of taking stock, celebrating the joys she had in her world, and maybe thinking about what she wanted for herself moving forward. If she let things with Monique drop, she'd be on her own again and facing a possible franchise deal with a man who wore flip-flops to business meetings and wondered why she didn't automatically trust him. She sipped the last of her iced latte as the sun made its way lower in the sky. "Life is certainly interesting, isn't it?"

Her mom touched their cups. "And stays that way. I was born in Saudi Arabia and married a white boy from Long Island. Now I'm a widow dreaming of a new dog with my grown daughter, who spoils me." She lifted her shoulders and smiled, showing the many lines around her eyes. "It's up to us to find a way to enjoy the roller coaster, Jamie. Even the scary parts."

"Well, when you put it that way. Maybe I should buy more tickets."

Her mother beamed. "That's my girl."

❖

"Becca, I know you have a couple more certificates you can toss in. We're using the three-night stays in the silent auction, but do you think you could connect us with a seven-night stay in a two-bedroom unit for the live auction? It would be tons of flash for The Jade and Elite Resorts."

Becca sighed in dramatic fashion. "You're gonna owe me one for this, Lay. It's a reach for me."

"But I'm drinking so much of your wife's wine."

"Oh, you just played the right card."

"I thought you'd like that. Also happens to be the truth."

Leighton smiled and sat back in her desk chair. She missed her old college buddy and knew she could count on her for a pretty pricey donation from the wine country resort she managed in Oregon. It just took a little finessing. "The next time I see your face, I'm going to kiss your cheek and stroke your hair like a sweet little puppy."

"You'll have to explain to Joey why you're petting me."

Leighton paused, imagining the conversation with Becca's wife, who was one of the more fun and effervescent people she'd spent time with. "I feel like she'd support it."

Becca laughed, her voice rich and clear. "You got me there. Just know that I'm hooking you up, but I'm the godfather now. I'm tenting my hands. You just can't see them."

"The best looking godfather ever."

"Oh, you flatterer. It's why we get along."

"Well aware, Crawford."

"Take care, Morrow."

They said good-bye, and Leighton tossed a fist in the air. She luxuriated in a good victory and had her friend to thank this time. She wrote down her newest donation to report to the committee later that day. They'd agreed to meet weekly, which Leighton secretly appreciated. The three meetings they'd had so far had given her the chance to naturalize things between her and Jamie in an innocuous environment. No need to talk about their past. A few group pleasantries, then on to the task at hand. Those busy planning sessions where no one was paying attention to anything except the work offered her the chance to steal glances across the conference table. She'd take in the way Jamie held the back of her pen to her cheek when considering a concept and then use it to gesture when it was her turn to speak. Leighton also very much appreciated the way Jamie took in what everyone in the room had to say, turned it over in her mind, and came back with a thoughtful, and often game-changing, answer. She had a unique view of the world, more of a boots-on-the-ground outlook that was immensely helpful. Though she was gregarious and warm in her café, she was the quiet rock star of their little charity team. It made sense. Jamie interacted with a variety of people all day long, spotting habits and trends—and put that knowledge to use when figuring out how to get humans to cough up cash.

"I like your idea of having a success story featured onstage rather than just a video presentation," Leighton said as they strolled from inside the building into the moonlight-kissed evening air. She always left these meetings lighter, more energized. "It shows the donors exactly what their money can do right in front of them. Not just a faraway idea in a produced package."

"Good," Jamie said with relief. "I hoped it wasn't too bold of me to suggest we sidestep the video presentation." She stepped closer to keep their conversation just between them. "Because Toni seemed to have her heart set on a video testimonial and wanted to put the whole thing together herself."

Leighton shrugged. "I think even she had to agree on this one. We can still showcase the organization in a montage. She can flex her muscles all over the project."

"Right. That's true. And good catch about the order of events. I'm glad you saw the catering issue. We need to allow time for the servers to clear at some point."

"I have a cousin who plans events meticulously, and it rubbed off."

"The Carrington daughter, right?"

"She's just Courtney to me and brings the best snacks to twelve-year-old sleepovers."

"My kind of person."

They were riffing like two people who didn't have an awful past. It felt like a much-needed warm bath after an awful day, only the day had been years. God, she'd missed this. At the same time, she didn't want to push her luck.

Leighton tossed her head in the direction of the crosswalk. "I'm this way. See you next time?"

"I'll be here."

The next week's meeting was even better because they were the first two to arrive. With Jessica down the hall on a client call, small talk grew into an actual conversation. Jamie clearly had something on her mind, but Leighton didn't want to push, sticking with topics like her overly talkative Uber driver who simultaneously blasted Olivia Newton-John, making her wonder if she hated him or loved him.

"I see the conundrum." Jamie nodded and stole a giant cookie close to the size of her face. Leighton's brain paused everything just to prepare for her to take a bite. The payout was everything she'd hoped for. Jamie dabbed the tiniest bit of chocolate from the side of her lip, making Leighton quickly flash on removing it for her in a more creative fashion. She ordered her brain to behave. "Pardon my gluttony," Jamie said. "I had a difficult afternoon and need this cookie."

"At work?" Was she allowed to ask that brand of personal question? Jamie had brought it up herself, after all.

"In a way. I have a business proposition on the table and am not sure what to do about it."

Leighton opened her mouth to inquire further just as Eileen arrived looking like the fashionista she was in a lime-green pants suit that she pulled off expertly. "Did I hear you say business proposition? This is catnip to me." She slid into a chair. "What kind?"

Leighton grieved for the one-on-one time she'd just lost, but at least she'd still get the details.

"I've always wanted a second location for Bordeauxnuts. I'm a businesswoman, and I believe in our concept."

"You should do it," Eileen said, leaning in. "Ride the success all the way to the bank and then buy the bank."

"I agree," Leighton said, waiting for the other shoe to drop. "Maybe don't buy a bank."

Jamie sighed. "I wish it was that easy. The funds aren't there. But in waltzes this superslick entrepreneur who wants to open up his own franchise location."

Leighton sat taller. "That's great news. Isn't that great news?"

Jamie slid a strand of hair behind her ear. "I don't know. He's presented an offer that's hard to turn down."

"Why would you want to?" Leighton asked.

Jamie didn't hesitate. "Because the idea of this guy, this particular man, managing, making decisions for, and representing Bordeauxnuts, my brand and baby, is as jarring as it is depressing." She exhaled slowly, as if still taking in the whole concept.

Leighton nodded. "He doesn't get it."

"He doesn't get it." Distress crisscrossed Jamie's features.

Leighton had only seen that look one other time, a memory she didn't trot out often.

Eileen sat back coolly in the leather conference chair and crossed her lime lined legs. She exuded power and decisiveness. "Then you say thank you, but no."

Jamie took notice. "That simple, huh?" She slid a palm onto the table. "But what if another opportunity like this never presents itself again?"

"Then you'll be just fine. Life is too short to sell your soul, Jamie. I read up on your café, and its reputation is stellar. Wait until you can captain this venture yourself, or simply enjoy the fruits of your store."

Jamie offered a grateful smile and seemed to absorb the words. But the wheels in Leighton's head were turning. The idea was far-fetched, and she should probably take some time to work out the details before ever speaking on it. She'd always been someone who planned out each and every move. Today felt a little different, and as the meeting pressed on, she felt her decisiveness crescendo.

"Jamie, do you have a sec?" she asked as the group corralled their belongings after the meeting.

Jamie blinked up at her as she slid her laptop, decorated with a series of sunray stickers, into her messenger bag. "Uh, sure. What's up?"

Leighton scanned the room, waiting for the others, lost in their own conversations, to file out. Jessica tossed a questioning glance over her shoulder but gave them their space. "I had a thought."

"Okay." Her blue eyes sparkled as bright as ever, but they also held curiosity.

"I happen to have money."

"And wanted to brag?" She added a smirk.

Leighton pushed forward. "I love Bordeauxnuts. What if I wanted to invest?"

Jamie frowned, trying to follow the thread. "In what way?"

"That new location you're interested in opening."

"Wait. What?" She quirked her head to the side. "You don't have time for a coffee shop."

"None at all. I would be a completely silent, hands-off partner."

Jamie blinked. "Then what's in it for you?"

Leighton stole a moment to formulate a sensible answer because she wasn't sure she'd organized her thoughts quite yet. "I'm always on the lookout for investments, and I know the bar and enjoy the concept a lot. I like the idea of being a part of something I believe in."

"And you believe in me?"

Leighton swallowed. They held eye contact for what felt like an important moment. "I do."

Jamie seemed nervous. "Um. I don't even know what to say. This is a lot and a little out of left field." She was speaking rapidly, racking focus to the wall and back. "Can I—"

"Definitely, think on it." A beat. "But tell that guy no. It's not the right deal for you."

Jamie nodded a few times, living in the land of absorption. She placed a flustered hand on her hip. "Are you sure? I mean, maybe you want to think on it, too."

Leighton knew her answer. "No. I'm actually good. Want to walk out?"

Jamie eyed her like she wasn't sure what Leighton might do or say next.

She held up her palms. "No ulterior motives. This is not about you and me. Business. That's it."

Jamie exhaled. "I believe you."

"Good." A pause. "Now let's get out of here before Jessica's assistant trots in more planet-sized cookies."

Jamie held up a finger. "See, that's not a good reason to leave."

They shared a laugh in the quiet hallway. But the energy had shifted, and Leighton couldn't help but feel that this was an important moment for her. She believed in fate, signs, and following her intuition, and that was exactly what she was doing.

"I want you to know you can trust me."

Jamie arched a brow, inclined her head, and passed her a look that she damn well deserved.

She closed her eyes, cringing. "I know. I heard it the second I said it. But it's true all the same. You have my word."

Jamie ran a hand through her dark hair, and it fell back to her shoulders in layers, forcing Leighton to look away. She had trouble not noticing Jamie's startling beauty, yet didn't feel it was her place, a devastation that was hers to live with. "Why don't we take tonight and reconvene tomorrow?"

"We can do that."

Jamie looked up at the clear night sky. A fire engine wailed in the distance. "But I don't think I'm going to take the offer for the franchise."

"Thank you. You deserve better than an off-base pseudo replica shop. It would be the Upside Down version of Bordeauxnuts."

She laughed. "You do have a way of putting things."

"I'm serious, Jamie. You'd hate it. You'd walk in and die a little each time. The doughnuts might be cold."

"The blasphemy hurts to think about." She stepped closer. "He was planning to get rid of the chalk menu."

Leighton's mouth fell open. "Not the chalk menu."

"Oh yes."

Leighton sent Jamie a grin. They were on the same page as far as the bar went. Leighton knew what she didn't know, and Jamie was the coffee and doughnut queen of New York. A breeze hit and offered cool relief from the warm city air that clung. Jamie studied her, and Leighton would have given anything to know what thoughts moved through her mind.

"It's intriguing. Your proposal," Jamie said finally. She let her head lean to one side.

"So, you *are* considering it." Leighton nodded, absorbing the information. It was good news, but she wanted to go slow. Do this thing right. Her heart thudded at the idea of this new partnership. Maybe this was her way of making amends for the damage she'd done. It felt fitting, assisting with the bar's growth "I wasn't sure if you were just being polite."

"I feel no pull to be polite to you. At all."

"Understood. And I get it."

Jamie held out a hand. "Let's talk soon."

Leighton took it, closing her hand over Jamie's. Firm handshake. "You're on. Maybe bring some of those tiny sugary doughnuts next time."

"Nope." Jamie tossed a look over her shoulder from down the sidewalk. "Don't press your luck."

"Got it." Leighton nodded and took a minute on her own to ruminate on the very strange, and not unwelcome evening. With her hands on her hips, she took a cleansing breath and let the night wash over her, excited for this new prospect, intrigued with herself for even initiating such an impulsive offer. Also? She was quite pleased that she had.

"Leighton Morrow, something important is churning in that head of yours." She turned to see Jessica strolling her way, still wearing a black and purple dress and heels, relics from the long ago workday. So much had happened since five p.m. Leighton Time.

"You're not wrong."

"Oh?" she asked as her personal town car arrived at the curb.

"It's too soon to talk about, but something interesting might be in the works. Stay tuned, Lennox."

"I love suspense." She winked and slid inside.

"Hugs to Brooklyn," Leighton said through the open window.

"From you maybe. I have a little more to offer tonight." With a four fingered wave, Jessica was carried off into the twinkling lights of the skyline. Leighton smiled after her. Alone and feeling freer than normal, she decided to walk a bit, stretch her calf muscles, and lose herself in thought. She had a few things on her mind worthy of marination. Plus, summer in the city was actually quite beautiful.

Chapter Eleven

"Things are starting to disappear from the list," Clarissa said as she scrolled her wedding registry on her phone. "And did I tell you that RSVPs are starting to roll in."

"Can you even believe it?" Jamie said from her spot on Clarissa's couch. "I can't, and I'm not even you."

"Jamie. I'm going to be a bride. And my mother will be forced to attend a lesbian wedding. That's the best part, honestly. I love watching her pretend to be comfortable."

"She's trying. That's important." Jamie lifted her shoulders to her ears. "Just think of it. You. A married lady."

"I'll need to learn to knit, probably. Don't married people do that on weeknights in front of the TV? I can't have a cold wife. She'll need scarves and gloves."

"I agree. Knitting is a matrimonial requirement. It's your announcement to the world that you've settled down and no one else gets to take your clothes off. I bet Marjorie would teach you."

"Did you know she's a bistichtual?"

Jamie blinked. "That might be my favorite thing you've ever told me. Define this word. My dad would love it."

"Marjorie asked if she could be in our queer club if she was bistichtual, and laughed. Apparently, it means you both knit and crochet. Two kinds of stitching."

"That's amazing."

"She was incredibly proud of herself for that one." Clarissa sat upright on the couch. "Oh, somebody snatched up the PlayStation?

Tara is going to sob with joy. She tossed that on to the registry just for fun."

Jamie shrugged. "People get tired of buying plates and towels. I'm actually kind of sad I missed it."

Clarissa's brown eyes went wide. "You're handling the coffee station and doughnut bar at our reception. I hardly think there needs to be another gift. In fact, I forbid it. No, no, no."

"You're not the boss of me," Jamie said with a grin.

Clarissa then proceeded to lunge for her, WWF style. "You better stop it right now. I'm the bride. The chooser of all things. Say I'm the bride." She had Jamie in an unconvincing headlock that she easily slipped out of.

"This woman was no match for Jamie," the voice-over said.

She toppled Clarissa and pinned her. "You're the bride, but you will never best me in a wrestling match. Do you hear me? I practice alone at night. Rigorous and determined."

"Of course you do."

Jamie released her. "Never know when you're going to meet a criminal in a dark alley. I have to be ready."

"I forgot you believe you're Supergirl."

"Aspiring. Don't be too generous."

Jamie slid back onto her spot on the couch next to Clarissa, looped their arms, and snuggled in. "I can't wrap my brain around the fact that you're about to get hitched. I'm literally going to be the only lesbian in New York unattached."

"You could always race back to Mo. I hear she danced on top of a van in front of a Pinkberry last night."

"That tracks. It's also one of the reasons I likely should not rush back to Monique, but I do admire that carefree vibe. I use that word a lot now."

"I'm impressed."

"The lingo, ya know?" She shook her head. "But you can only cheer for a person on top of a van so many times before you just want to watch *Jeopardy* in leggings at seven p.m. for the rest of your life. Is that too much to ask?"

"No," Clarissa said matter-of-factly. "I registered for a PlayStation and got it. Tara and I may never leave this apartment. You can visit."

She kissed Clarissa's T-shirt clad shoulder. "Sold. You're lucky.

You're in love and careening toward a life of romantic wine sipping and gazing into each other's eyes."

"That's literally all we do. Not a single dish is washed. Just gazing." Clarissa laughed, shaking Jamie's knee. "But I love the way you idealize any and all settled relationships as if they're perfect."

"It's never-ending envy."

"I know. And I am very lucky. I recognize that. Tara lets me double dip and leave my towel on the floor and still tells me I'm the hottest woman alive. She even wants to learn Spanish. My mother is already buying workbooks."

"See? That's what dreams are made of." She collapsed into the cushion. When Jamie was with Clarissa, she was one hundred percent herself, and lamenting her single-again status felt called for today. She was depressed and owning it.

"Your dreams will come true, too. But right now, you're chasing something unattainable because your world was rocked off its axis three years ago and you can't seem to duplicate the experience."

"I'm not chasing anything. I've resolved myself to the fact that what I had with Leighton was fictional, a mirage, because everything about *her* was. You can't chase what never existed."

"Except nothing since has measured up in your eyes. It's your perpetual measuring stick."

Jamie sighed. "Don't point out accurate things. Wisdom and insight have no place in the midst of my self-wallowing." She lifted her empty wineglass. "Dare we have two? Are we those people?"

"If we're not, then I don't want to know us."

Jamie brightened. "Maybe your insight is welcome after all." She scurried into Clarissa's kitchen and returned with the open bottle of French rosé. "I might also be stalling because it's Thursday, and Marlene and Edward always have sex on Thursday nights. It's an event. A loud one."

"The elderly neighbors?" Clarissa covered her mouth, which did nothing to smother the sound of her genuine laughter.

Jamie nodded slowly, communicating her very fragile feelings with her eyes. "There's grunting, Riss. Sometimes happy squealing, and I don't even know how squealing happens. The mattress could also be quieter. It's not even trying."

Clarissa's face was red from silent laughter by this point. She fanned herself to dry the tears of mirth that escaped. "Every Thursday?" she gasped. "Why have you not told me about this? I wonder if there's an alarm that goes off to remind them it's special time."

"I needed the wine to find courage. Plus, I was trying to spare you. Absorb the horror on your behalf. It's me who has to face them in the hall the next morning, and talk about the weather and coffee like I didn't just ride the train to Pleasureville as an unwilling passenger."

Clarissa fell over and covered her face with a pillow, muffling the laughter. "This is the best thing that's ever happened to me. We have to tell my mom."

"We absolutely do not. She already thinks I made you gay by proximity. Next, she'll think I listen in on my neighbors."

"She's a work in progress. She adores you just as much as the rest of the world." A pause. "So, what's it like showing up to those meetings in the same room as Bambi's Mom?"

"No comment."

"Not allowed. When we sit on my couch and drink two glasses of rosé, we share freely and without thought. Now, go. Leighton is the topic. Expound, por favor."

"Pushy as always. Fine." She gave the question her full attention and tried to explain how spending time with Leighton felt. And there were many feelings. Warring ones, even. "It's kind of a mindfuck, to be honest."

"Harsh language from the Jamester. I like it."

"There's no other way to say it." She grappled for the right words. "I see her and think she's the most beautiful person I've ever spoken to, but I also hate her for what she almost did. Then there's the part where she lied straight to my face, literally right after sleeping with me. So, I don't trust her. Never will."

"Does that mean after the charity event, you'll part ways forever and ever?"

This was a test. "Well, there's a development I hadn't mentioned." She'd been too afraid that actually speaking Leighton's proposal into the universe would make it real, and she'd have to come to a decision on what in hell she was going to do about it. The offer was hugely tempting, almost too good to be real, and also the most terrifying thing that had ever happened to Jamie. Was she really prepared to dance with the devil?

"I'll need to hear this development in glorious detail."

"She wants to financially back a new Bordeauxnuts. A silent partner, so to speak. She puts up the money, and I make the decisions for the running of the business."

Clarissa's response was to swat her hard across the arm.

Jamie covered the wound in offense. "Ow! You can't just wallop me!"

"I can so," Clarissa said, bucking up. "This development should have been the first thing uttered when you crossed the threshold, like a goddamn hello. We're approaching two hours in. You can't deliver the goods two hours in."

"I was working up to it."

"And?" Clarissa demanded, ignoring her. "Are you gonna do it?"

Jamie exhaled slowly. "I haven't gotten that far."

"But you turned down the franchise offer, and now I'm thinking it was because you had this little deal on your desk the whole time."

"Only partially the reason. The franchise wasn't right for me."

"I agree. But is Leighton?" Clarissa arched a brow, suggesting her meaning extended beyond simply business.

"No. Most certainly not in the way your face is insinuating. But maybe, just maybe, this is the step up I would need, and it fell into my lap within twenty-four hours of having to deliver my answer to that Michael Stoneking guy." She lifted a shoulder and paused, trying to slow her racing thoughts and rapid-fire speech. She harnessed her zen and pressed on, slower. "I also happen to believe in signs, and the timing was too freaky to fully ignore."

"Do it. Who cares if she lies after sex? She'll want to protect her investment, and she seems to have done well for herself, careerwise."

They held eye contact. "You think I should? Because I value your opinion and am worried I can't see this thing as clearly as I want to."

"I one hundred do. It's like you said, timing wise. There's an arrow draped in destiny pointing boldly to Leighton. Follow it."

"I can't fathom that this might happen. I suppose there's always the chance she'll flake and change her mind." Jamie took a moment. "But I get the feeling she's a driven person."

"Maybe she could drive right into you."

Jamie widened her eyes. "No more rosé for you. Cut off!"

"But I'm the bride."

"You can only play that card for a couple more months."

"Then I'm damn well going to fork it over every chance I get." She slung an arm around Jamie's neck. "This is going to be a good year for us. I can just sense it with my rosé afflicted sensibilities."

"Well, if the rosé says so, it might just be true."

And maybe it would be. Jamie had always been a risk taker, but a conservative one. She measured her chances at success and leapt when they seemed tipped in her favor. This felt beyond that scope, however. On the other hand, maybe she needed a little excitement in her life. Clarissa was getting married, her mother was about to enter retirement and adopt a new friend, and there was Jamie, in the exact same spot as always.

Time to hold her breath, say a prayer, and take a precarious leap with a very beautiful liar.

CHAPTER TWELVE

I own part of a small business.
     Leighton blinked at the fresh ink on the paperwork in front of her. After Jamie had accepted her offer to move forward with a partnership, Leighton could hardly believe it. She woke up the next morning energized about the news, imagining the new Bordeauxnuts, this cozy oasis from the hustle and bustle of the city. Something *she* helped establish.

They'd worked out the details with their attorneys, giving Jamie creative control and controlling ownership. Leighton would finance the lion's share of the project and serve as a consultant on an as-needed basis. They were in this together but, at the same time, not, which was why they had decided to meet the week before the signing.

"I just want to make sure we're both on the same page," Jamie had said at their meeting, looking entirely professional. They'd chosen a hotel restaurant halfway between Leighton's office and Bordeauxnuts to have a serious conversation and go over Jamie's estimates. She'd done her homework and presented her business plan with a few adjustments for the retail space she had her eye on in Hell's Kitchen. Her smile was gone, and her eyebrows were drawn down, making her look like a more serious version of the Jamie she'd known previously.

"We are. You're in charge. I take a back seat."

"I understand that you want to protect your investment. Who wouldn't?" Jamie offered a hint of a smile. "I need to know that you trust me in the grand scheme."

Jamie wasn't taking the meeting or the investment lightly, to her credit. Out of respect, Leighton tried not to notice how pretty she looked or the way she smelled of cotton candy. Yet she'd taken in both details. Jamie had changed out of her work clothes and wore gray slacks and a white dress shirt, looking crisp and sophisticated. That was the thing about Jamie. Just when Leighton thought she had her figured out, Jamie would show off another side of herself, another look, another brand of smile, and completely hook Leighton all over again. And the most surprising part? Jamie didn't even seem to know she was doing it.

"I know you're good at what you do," Leighton said. "That's why I didn't want to miss out on the opportunity when I saw it. I have money to invest, and I'd like to see it go to work on something...that makes life a little brighter." She shrugged, feeling a tad self-conscious. "That's what Bordeauxnuts did for me once upon a time."

That seemed to give Jamie pause. She opened her mouth, closed it, and then opened it again as if she couldn't resist. "Did it really? To this day, I don't know how much from back then was real and how much was part of the act." She looked down at the table. The flash of vulnerability slashed Leighton like a cool blade.

She sighed because she'd been the one to inspire doubt, and it was up to her to undo the damage one section of debris at a time. "Any affection I showed for the bar was one hundred percent genuine. In fact, the research I did for Carrington's made me love it all the more." She added a shaky laugh. "I liked it so much, I'm buying a slice."

Jamie raised her gaze along with a soft smile. "Good point. So, you must like the place." A beat. "Or me." They stared at each other, and Jamie's cheeks slowly shaded red. "I meant as a manager. Of the store." She cleared her throat. "And wine selection. We haven't talked about that. I've always gone where the water is warm. I have a distributor who visits, and we taste. You could always swing by on those days."

"I never turn down a wine tasting."

"Smart woman."

"I like your business plan. I actually spent a lot of time with it last night. You know what you're doing."

"I very much do." Okay, the rock-solid business confidence and the way Jamie eased a strand of hair behind her ear shortly after the statement were both sexy.

She ignored the thought. "Shall I have my attorneys draw up an agreement?"

"Yours are probably better equipped," Jamie said. "But I'd like Hank, my guy, to look it over when they're finished."

"That can be arranged." They'd ordered coffees on arrival, but this felt like an important moment. "Shall we have a drink and celebrate?"

Jamie held up a finger. "No. Drinking with you isn't the best idea."

Oh, now that was a stone Leighton could not leave unturned. "Because…"

"Nothing's changed between us personally."

"Oh." A pause. "Understood."

"And I need to make it clear that just because we have found a way to work well together doesn't mean I've forgiven you." She placed a hand over her heart and the implication was clear.

"Your heart hasn't." She searched Jamie's face. "Do you think it might someday?" It was a bold question, and the state of her own heart hung in the balance.

"No. Leighton, not in the way you're asking. You lied to my face moments after we…"

"I know. It was awful. I panicked that night, and the words were out before I could stop them. I had this grandiose plan that the right moment would come along for me to tell you. In fact, I was hoping to tell you at dinner that night, but when I got to your apartment…"

"I made a move. Didn't matter. You're an adult. You gently stop me and confess."

"I should have."

"Let's focus on the business and the future, okay?" Jamie stood. "We'll talk soon."

"Okay. I look forward to it."

Jamie left the restaurant, and Leighton sat back, heavier than she'd been just a few minutes ago. Through the large front-facing window, she watched Jamie in front of the hotel, studying her phone. The world whipped past her, and when the traffic light changed, she eased her way to the other side of the street and disappeared into the throngs, a metaphor if Leighton had ever seen one.

But today, she celebrated. The contracts were signed, and she and Jamie were officially partners. In just an hour, they had plans to visit several locations Jamie had on her radar for the new storefront. She felt the new shop would thrive in Hell's Kitchen, away from the tourists in Times Square but still adjacent enough to benefit from the overflow.

"I've zeroed in on a ten-block radius north of Forty-Ninth Street and ranked my choices sight unseen. Of course, that could all be upended once we get into the spaces," she told Leighton over the phone. They'd scheduled a brief call to get their ducks in a row before meeting with the agent who would show them the listings.

"I don't want you to sell yourself on anything until you see it in person. I do have a little bit of experience in real estate."

"I've heard that somewhere."

"And after Eduardo sent the listings over, I spent some time writing up an analysis."

Jamie was quiet on the other end of the phone. "I'm impressed." She said the words softly, almost to herself. "And I do want your expert opinion."

"Not a problem. And you can determine functionality and aesthetic once we're in each space."

"Go, team. See you soon?"

Leighton grinned. It was going to be a good day. She could feel it. "You're on."

❖

"Coffee station here. Dining room over there, but there's really not sufficient space for the lounge, so we'd have to get creative." Jamie surveyed the petite spot. Square footage was pricey in this neighborhood, but Hell's Kitchen came with just the right combination of trendy and authentic. She couldn't discard the neighborhood just because she couldn't have everything she'd once hoped.

Her Realtor, Eduardo, quirked his head. "Lounge?" His purple tie had swung onto his shoulder. Jamie fixed it.

"You call it the couch section," Jamie said. "You met your last boyfriend there, if I recall."

"Accurate. But he stole my sister's identity and ruined her credit, so I'm not sure if I should love you for that one."

"You still should because there were free doughnuts along the way. It's a trade-off."

"I'm going to have to think about that one, Jamie. I will do so over more doughnuts, however."

Jamie strolled the space. "Regardless of identity theft, the lounge is great for board games on a rainy night or snuggling close on a couch with the person you came in with." In the corner of the empty retail space, she saw Leighton smother a soft smile. She'd been extra-quiet as they toured potential storefronts, likely trying to walk the walk of the investor/consultant. Admirable, but Jamie did want Leighton's opinion on a decision as large as this one, which was implicitly why she'd asked her to be there. She knew real estate risk. It was actually the mechanism for their initial meeting. "What do you think of this one?"

Leighton peered out the front-facing window. "Lots of natural light, which psychologically draws people in. It's a great street with lots of action. Most of the businesses have been here for years, which speaks to viability. The neighborhood is growing, another selling point, but the square footage doesn't leave you much wiggle room. Literally. How are you going to feel being boxed in three years from now?"

"That being said, we can put in whatever offer you want and adjust for the petite size," Eduardo told them. "But I do think the clock is ticking on all of these properties. When you know what you want, we need to act fast."

"Which we're prepared to do, right?" Leighton turned to her.

"Absolutely." Jamie exhaled, the enormity of this decision sitting square on her shoulders. But she was also thrilled with the entire prospect. "I even had trouble sleeping last night because I'm so unbelievably ready. I had to count cheeseburgers. There were thousands by the time I finally drifted off. Woke up so hungry."

"Cheeseburgers?" Leighton asked, coming to stand next to her. She picked up the faint cotton candy scene of her perfume. Maybe her soap. Why did it bother her that she didn't know which?

"Yes. They're captivating and fit right in your hand. I will eat a cheeseburger any time of the day or night. People don't appreciate them enough."

Leighton raised an eyebrow, signaling intrigue. "I'll never handle a sleepless night the same way again."

"Give it a shot. Burgers often work. Just not recently." Jamie's restlessness had been brutal. The burgers hadn't been able to save her from twisted sheets and constant tossing and turning. The problem was she couldn't remember a time in her life where she'd been as excited for a new venture. Not only was the leap a scary one, but the new arrangement also meant she'd be spending occasional time with

Leighton, which always had a way of affecting her, getting beneath her skin, and not letting go. She'd had a wonderful connection to this woman once upon a time but vowed to never allow herself to go back there. Leopards didn't change their dishonest spots, and her heart couldn't take another breaking at the hands of Leighton. That meant she had to get past the attraction that bubbled now and then. But how? Something about the two of them sharing space made rooms feel smaller and air in scarce supply. Yet she was committed to getting her feelings under control because Leighton was a dead end for her. A no-go. Surely, the more time they spent in each other's presence, the more normalized their interactions would be. She looked forward to the day Leighton was just another boring, everyday part of life. Her brain had zero interest in any extended interaction. Dammit. Now, it was time for her traitorous body to get on board.

"You okay over there?" Eduardo asked. "You went extra quiet." Her gestured to his face with a circular motion. "Serious expression. Eyes searching."

"My brain is a busy place these days, Eduardo, but trust me. This has been a great afternoon."

Leighton straightened, making Jamie very aware of her height. "Agreed. Lots of potential already."

"I'm glad you think so, too." Jamie grinned at the confirmation and looked around, imagining the magic of a second Bordeauxnuts. "All right. On to the next."

As she took in each of the four spaces that day, she visualized tables sprouting up from the floor, customers crisscrossing the space, cabinets sliding closed, and the loud chatter of a busy café at eight a.m.

"Well, I saved your favorite property for last," Eduardo told them, rubbing his hands together. "I wanted you to see the other locations with clear eyes first."

"Smart of you. I appreciate the strategy. But yes, let's go there now because I'm gonna combust."

Eduardo laughed and held open the car door, and Leighton slid in, followed by Jamie.

The afternoon had proven incredibly useful. Jamie had eliminated two of the spaces on sight, and kept the remaining two in the running, even though both would require renovation for service to flow smoothly.

But when they arrived at the fifth property, the one she'd been afraid to hope would be as good as the photos, Jamie blinked and exhaled.

"It's beautiful." Her eyes scanned the room, trying to process all she saw, running through the same imagination exercise, bringing the space to life in her mind. The ceiling towered above them, making the place feel huge. The front windows stretched just as high. Built-in bookshelves, brown and tall, stood watch behind the service counter. They would be gorgeous with pin spotlights directing focus to favored wines and roasts of the month. "I can see it so easily here," she breathed, walking in a circle. Both Leighton and Eduardo hung back, allowing her space to explore on her own. "It's perfect. Slightly out of our price range, but not by much."

"Everything is negotiable," Eduardo told them. "This is the one?"

Jamie nodded. "What do you think?" she asked Leighton.

"I think we should get to know the neighborhood. Do a little immersive mission. If we like it, we put in an offer before close of business."

It wasn't a bad idea. "Go undercover?"

"Sure."

"Your forte."

Leighton went still, almost as if she'd been surprise slapped. The world seemed to stop. Dammit. Jamie couldn't seem to keep her fingers off the bruise. It wasn't helpful if she wanted them to work together in harmony and professionalism. She had to walk that walk.

She covered the distance between them and lightly touched Leighton's wrist. Eduardo, ever intuitive, wandered away, giving them space. "I'm sorry. Sometimes my mouth gets ahead of my brain. I'll work on it."

Leighton nodded, but the edges of her mouth turned down. Jamie wasn't proud of having been the cause, and her skin went cold. "Just out of curiosity, do you think that will ever go away? The tendency to strike whenever the opportunity presents. Or will you always hate me?"

Jamie was thrown and grappled. She didn't have the right words, but she knew she didn't hate Leighton. Not overtly. It wasn't that. She had trouble trusting Leighton fully and thereby refused to let her in. But hate wasn't a part of the equation. "Please know, Leighton, that I don't hate you. I promise."

"Well, that's something." Her brown eyes had lost their sparkle, though.

"Leighton. Don't."

"I'm not. Promise." She somehow managed to find that incredibly attractive smile that had a way of making Jamie's tummy dip. Even still. "There's a diner over there. Want to people watch? Get a sense of the neighborhood's daily vibe."

"You sound like a pro."

"I am." The serenity of her voice really was appealing, soft yet confident.

"I'll follow you."

They snagged a table by the window and ordered giant chef's salads because when a salad is giant, it's glorious and worthy. Leighton seemed to understand that, too.

"The large salad has certainly made a name for itself in the last ten years," Leighton said. "It's true."

Jamie touched her chest. "Thank you. I carry strong opinions about salad size. Don't bring me a side salad and expect any kind of excitement." She held up her most expressive finger. "Lettuce, dressing, and a smattering of croutons are not enough for me to get out of bed." She placed her napkin in her lap.

Leighton grinned. "I think I agree with you without ever having giving it explicit consideration. But yes, a big, plentiful salad is always worth my time. If you add some crunch, a sunflower seed addition, I'm even happier."

"Definitely throw in all the complementary ingredients you have. But nary a tomato in a small lifeless bowl? No thank you. I'll take the fries and pay the metabolism gods later."

"I've always appreciated your take on food." They smiled at each other, and Jamie went against her own rules and allowed herself to enjoy it.

"What else is there to live for?"

Leighton set down her glass of water and seemed to work on swallowing the drink she'd taken. She reached for her napkin and laughed. "You say that with such bravado. Some people might argue that *people* are worth living for. The connections we make to one another. Romance. Excitement. Visiting the Eiffel Tower at sunset after a fantastic bottle of wine."

"Are there big salads in France?" Jamie waved off her own comment. "Ignore me. I recently broke up with my girlfriend, so romance is the farthest thing from my mind."

Leighton's eyes went wide, signaling surprise. Finally, she nodded, absorbing. "I'm sorry."

"I am. And I'm not." Jamie shrugged. "Compatibility is apparently a real and vital thing. She's good people, just not good for me."

"And what's good for you?" Leighton said the words with soft care, but they still put Jamie on alert. She much preferred the salad conversation to anything that might give Leighton a peek inside.

Jamie gestured to the window. "I think we're forgetting ourselves. We're supposed to be scouting the neighborhood."

Leighton sat taller and turned. "Right. We veered. My fault." She gave her head a shake, and Jamie stole a glimpse of the blond hair settling on her shoulders.

She swallowed and ordered her brain to readjust. "Lot of bikers. And beautiful people."

"Actors scurrying from one audition to the next."

Jamie smiled. "If we open up here, we might be able to consider ourselves in show business."

"We can and will."

"Check out the calves on that guy. Yep, definitely a dancer."

"Jessica's cousin is an actress."

"That's right!" Jamie said. "I forgot completely. Does Jessica know we're, you know, in business together?"

"I gave her the drive-by version, but she wants details the next time we have drinks."

"And where will that be? I sell wine, you know. And soon, you will, too."

Leighton's lips parted. "I never really considered that angle. All wine and coffee bars are now my new competition." She set her fork down gently. "To answer your question, we usually go to Puzzles."

At the mention of the spot, Jamie felt the slightest tingle up her spine. She remained still, not giving even a shoulder wiggle in response. "Oh. I haven't been back there since…"

"Really?"

"Nope."

Leighton nodded. "And I go all the more." She sipped her iced water. "A perfect example of how two people can have opposite reactions to the same kind of loss."

"The neighborhood." She gestured to the window. "Remember?"

"Right. But you were the one who asked."

"Ignore me next time." They moved back into the business lane and stayed there for the next hour. As always, they had an easy give-and-take. Neither came with a larger-than-life personality, and there was no wrestling for the floor. It was honestly refreshing. Jamie could admit that.

"So, are you thinking what I'm thinking?" Leighton asked as they stood from the table.

Jamie hugged herself, savoring the certainty of the moment at hand. "It all feels meant to be. I don't know how to describe it other than that. The timing. The committee. What you bring. What I bring. The location."

"I think because it is. Call Eduardo. Let's do it."

Jamie smiled and took out her phone. This was an important moment that felt like the start of a brand-new chapter. There was a lot of work ahead of her but a lot of reward too. She knew one thing for certain—she didn't want to miss a moment.

Chapter Thirteen

The night of the Hope and Help Gala arrived at long last, and it was a stunner. Decorated in all red and purple, the swanky event space at the Javits Center was outfitted with draping that swooped across the tall ceiling from one side of the room to the other. The pillars were lit from the floor with colorful, dramatic lighting shooting up to the sky, and the large round tables boasted towering floral centerpieces that climbed and climbed. Leighton stood in the archway in her pale blue gown with her hair swept up and surveyed the space with pride. They'd really come together to make this event a special one.

Behind her, attendees in their finest caroused in the lobby. Glasses of wine and the evening's signature raspberry cocktail floated by, hand-passed by the servers. Across the room, she caught a glimpse of Jamie's profile. When the couple standing between them moved three feet to the right, Leighton's wineglass went still in her hand. She'd never seen a more beautiful woman or dress, and her accelerated heart rate proved the point. Red was most certainly Jamie's color. Almost as if Jamie could read Leighton's thoughts, she turned and their gazes met. In that moment, she saw a look on Jamie's face that she'd not seen since their last night together *Oh my*. It was unmistakable hunger, and Leighton felt the effects over every inch of her body. Slowly, Jamie lifted her long-stemmed glass in her direction before turning back to her friend.

"You are lost in something," Jessica said quietly in her ear. "Or someone."

Leighton blinked, mourning the end of a moment she'd very much enjoyed. "I'd lie to you, but you'd know."

Jessica, in a floor-length black dress with a slit up to her thigh, followed her gaze. "She looks amazing tonight." Jamie had her hair partially up and softly curled. The dress had one strap, leaving her opposite shoulder bare. A tiny hint of cleavage taunted, captivating Leighton.

"She does. But she could wear a worn-out T-shirt, and I still wouldn't be able to take my eyes off her. I say this only to you, but there's never been someone with the ability to strip me of my free will." She shook her head, still mystified by the power of Jamie. "When she's in the room, I'll always know exactly where. My life sentence."

"She's also your new business partner. Lots of opportunity for together time."

Leighton shook her head. "I don't want to take advantage. The bar is her world, too sacred to leverage. I wouldn't."

Jessica looked at her coolly, a small smile tugging. "Oh, if it was me, I'd leverage the hell out of that opportunity. When destiny opens a door, Leighton, you walk through it with purpose." It was such a Jessica thing to say.

"And what door opened?" Brooklyn asked, appearing at Jessica's side with a grin. Jessica's wife was always a warm ball of sunshine, cheering up every space she entered. Tonight, her blond hair was loose with the exception of a diamond clip on one side. She wore a gold-sequined dress that looked like it had been tailored perfectly to her body, and it damn well might have been. "Hi," Brooklyn said, giving Leighton's hand a squeeze. "You look stunning."

"Thank you. But you two are the most beautiful couple ever."

"Did you hear that?" Brooklyn said, quietly. "We won."

"Thanks to you," Jessica said softly.

"Am I intruding upon a moment?" Leighton asked. She hooked a thumb behind her. "I can go chase down more wine. I'm not scheduled to speak tonight and can just get sloshed in the shadows."

"Probably don't do that," Jessica said, but she was still making eyes at Brooklyn. Finally, she pulled her gaze back to Leighton. "But the moment has concluded, so you should stay." She took Brooklyn's hand in a sweet gesture. "Our schedules have been a little intense these days, so it's nice to—"

"Get to feel fancy together," Brooklyn supplied and kissed Jessica's hand. "And for a moment you two will have to feel fancy without me because I see a client across the room that I should schmooze for five minutes."

She slipped away, walking with purpose toward a woman in the corner. Jessica snagged a Raspberry Riptide off a tray floating by. "I've been looking forward to one of these."

"They're gorgeous. I love the candy garnish. Where did we get them again?"

"One of our friends is an amazing mixologist. She developed the recipe and donated all the alcohol and ingredients."

Jessica offered her a sip and Leighton savored the flavors, agreeing with the praise. "Oh, wow. The raspberry starts you off, but it's lemony and refreshing on the finish."

"That's exactly how she described it."

She shot a look across the room. "I wonder if Jamie's tried this." Of course she wondered. All roads these days.

"We should all have dinner some night." Jessica paused. "Unless that would feel out of bounds."

"We'll see," Leighton said, knowing full well that would feel like a date with another couple, thereby making Jamie uncomfortable. No-go. She wouldn't put her in that position.

The chimes sounded, signaling dinner, and the group moved inside for the event, which truly went off without a hitch. The surf and turf dazzled, the stand-up comedian they'd hired to emcee was entertaining, yet sensitive. The special speaker was a woman who'd spent time in jail for a crime she'd committed when she was young. With the organization's help, she now owned a successful lingerie shop and was set to open several more regionally. Her story made Leighton realize what a difference the money raised could make. Everyone needed a hand now and then.

Jamie was seated across the twelve-person table, but they hadn't had a chance to speak. A shame. But after dessert, while the attendees mingled and perused the silent auction, she felt a soft tug on her elbow. She turned to find Jamie not just smiling at her but beaming. "They accepted our offer."

"Honestly? Just like that. Not even a counter?" They'd been waiting days for a response.

"Nope. Eduardo said the owner is on to a new project and wants a quick close. Because we were agreeable, it's mine. *Ours*. Sorry."

"Don't be. It's your baby."

"Well, just know that I'm going to do everything in my power to make sure you don't regret your investment. I will make you proud."

"You already do."

The words earned a smile that was quickly pulled back as if shown to her in error. "You can't say nice things to me tonight, okay?"

"Why not?"

Jamie placed a hand on a nearby cocktail table. "I was too nervous to eat because I don't do this kind of thing often, and now the wine has gone to my head, and I just want to talk to you." She'd blurted the last part but hadn't looked away or tried to pull it back in.

Leighton could have been knocked over with a feather. "Oh." Her skin went warm, and an intense tingle danced across its surface. "I think, um…" She glanced at the masses headed for the dance floor as the DJ kicked off the party with a Beyoncé hit. Her brain was short-circuiting. There were imaginary lines of caution tape around their whole relationship, but in the dim lighting of the vibrant room with alcohol coating her judgment and Jamie looking at her like that? She was ready to step right over it. "Let's dance."

Leighton didn't wait for an answer. She took Jamie's hand and pulled her along to the sound of quiet laughter from behind.

"Wait. Dancing?" Jamie called over the music.

"Yes, have you heard of it?"

But they were already in the middle of the dance floor and moving. Gelled lights flipped and dipped, and in that moment, Leighton's inhibitions vanished. They'd raised more money that night than any of them had expected. Why not cut loose? They'd worked hard. Leighton danced with anyone and everyone to the fast-paced music, the DJ overlapping one song with another. The moments of eye contact she and Jamie exchanged turned into brief touches. Harmless. But not. Leighton was tipsy rather than drunk, but definitely leaning into it. Leighton pressed her back against Jamie's shoulder and flipped around. Jamie took her hand and pulled her in before dancing away. Whatever game this was, Leighton couldn't stop playing. Across the dance floor with white light silhouetting her from behind, Jamie took her hair down and gave it a shake. Leighton had to remember to keep dancing when all she wanted to do was make sure that exact moment was emblazoned in her memory for always.

The event eventually began to wind down with guests taking their leave one by one. Tables were quietly cleared and stripped as the last few attendees enjoyed themselves. The dance floor was down to half, and Jamie gave her wrist a squeeze.

"I think I should go," Jamie said. "There's a business to run tomorrow."

"Are you sure? Because this was fun," Leighton said in her ear, heart pounding and not from dancing. Tonight felt like a dream she didn't want to wake up from.

"You know, it really was. Walk me out?"

"Of course," Leighton said quietly, locating her discarded heels and clutch. "I should head home, too."

"Come home with me."

❖

"Come home with you?"

"Not like that." Jamie closed her eyes and took a breath. She tried again. "It's an important day. Eduardo said he had the papers messengered over. Let's have a signing drink and celebrate. I have one of those half bottles of bubbly and would feel sad opening it alone." Jamie did a lot alone. She didn't want to tonight. Wisdom be damned.

"I'd love to have a glass of celebratory bubbly with you. Sure."

It took Jamie a moment to compose a response. She'd lost herself. Leighton had no business being so beautiful. Her end of the evening look, heels in hand, stole the air from the room.

"Great. Let's say our farewells, and I'll meet you in the lobby."

"The ride's on me. I hired a car service for tonight."

Jamie paused. Leighton did everything in style. "I think I just upgraded."

Jamie crossed the room, kissed Jessica's cheek, and thanked her for the opportunity. Afterward, she made the rounds to the other committee members, said good night, and headed to the front with tingling palms and a shiver of anticipation. Jamie had no clue what she was doing, prolonging their evening together. But in the moment, she didn't care about repercussions. She was walking out onto the ice and hoping it would be fine. Their offer had been accepted. The event had been a smash hit. Clarissa was getting married and achieving happily ever after status. And for once, Jamie wanted to take something for herself. She wanted to enjoy a little crumb of happiness all her own, even if it was just for an hour or so.

"Just over here," Leighton said, leading the way down the steps to the waiting black town car. She moved with such confidence and grace. All part of the drug that was Leighton, thrust into her life because a department store had an eye on expansion. The world was strange.

Her senses fired in overdrive as they made their way through the city to her place. The driver had the windows down as he navigated the streets of downtown, which offered a nice summer breeze. The radio played on low, and Jamie was wildly aware of the fact that the side of her hand was lightly touching Leighton's. Had she realized it, too? Jamie turned to look at her, studying her profile as the wind blew her hair and the streetlights caressed her features. Jamie was struck when Leighton turned her head and met her gaze. A soft, sincere smile appeared, and for a minute it was just the two of them in this world. The spell was broken when the car came to a stop and the driver turned down the music. Right. They had arrived and were idling in front of Jamie's building.

"Oh. This is me."

Leighton peered out the window. "You haven't moved. Still close to work."

"The best part."

They bid their driver, who Leighton called Robin, good night and made their way to the elevator. "No doorman," Jamie said, feeling the need to point out her working class lifestyle.

"Most buildings don't have doormen."

"Yours surely does."

Leighton leaned back against the side of the elevator as it ascended. "Does that matter?"

"No." She placed a hand over her heart. "I love my place." The elevator dinged. "And here we are."

She scooped up the envelope leaning against the door, let them in, and watched Leighton's face as she took in what Jamie always thought of as a homey space. "Jamie. It's the same place, but not really at all." She pointed to the wall that showcased a series of framed photos of landmarks from around the city. "I love this series."

"Thanks. I bought them right off the wall of the café. I love what the photographer did with light and shadow." She grinned, her heart squeezing pleasantly that Leighton had noticed them. Details mattered. The deep violet throw pillows on the lime green couch with the sculpted back. A large bookshelf, filled to the brim with the stories she'd lost herself in over the years. A few framed and matted classic rock albums that reminded her of the music she'd grown up with. To make up for the square footage, the ceilings were high, which was one of the reasons she'd snatched the apartment up years ago. The last time Leighton was here, she'd not taken the time to see it through her eyes. It was fun doing so now.

Leighton strolled through the short entryway into the living space. "I'd live here."

Jamie took joy in the compliment. "Thank you. I really like it here." A beat. "Not that I wouldn't trade for the lap of luxury. Is that kind of your speed uptown?"

Leighton laughed and took a seat on the far side of the couch grabbing a glimpse of the view which offered a sliver of the river if you looked to the far right. She wasn't sure Leighton had. But something about her making herself at home pleased Jamie very much, stripping away any element of formality. They were no longer guest and host but just a couple of business partners having a drink. Sigh. And maybe friends? She honestly couldn't keep her head and heart from mingling. It was a problem.

"My apartment is too big. I've always thought so," Leighton said.

"Then why hold on to it? I imagine you could move into most any place you wanted."

Leighton tilted her head, searching for the words. "I was hoping it wouldn't just be me there one day. I guess I'm holding on for *that*."

"Oh." Jamie imagined Leighton hand in hand with a girlfriend, a fiancé, a husband or a wife, and immediately set the image aside. It wasn't one she cared for. She also refused to imagine herself in that role at all, making the overt reaction confusing. Something to examine another time. "How about that drink? Got the papers right here."

Leighton beamed and followed Jamie into the kitchen just off the living area. She easily found the bottle of prosecco she'd purchased recently for this very occasion and went to work on the cork. She could feel Leighton watching her.

"I'm impressed with how easily you're maneuvering that thing."

"I work at a wine bar. It's all about finger placement."

Leighton's eyes went wide and Jamie heard her words, cueing the laughter. Both hers and Leighton's. "Yeah, I just said that out loud." Her face had to be going red as so much heat hit her cheeks. The cork popped, and they laughed even harder, tears pooling in Jamie's eyes. "Oh my God. Too many metaphors here. I just can't." She wiped the tears.

"The timing on that cork…" Leighton wheezed.

"The best." Jamie shook her head, wrestling for control again. They took a minute to compose themselves, and Jamie poured two flutes of bubbly.

"Now the reason for our assembly." She produced a bundle of paperwork. In reality there would be many more signatures in a formal setting, but the last page felt like a big deal. With a flourish she applied her signature, to which Leighton applauded and raised her glass.

"A toast to the future of Bordeauxnuts in New York City. Hell's Kitchen has no idea how lucky they're about to be."

"I'll drink to that," Jamie said and touched her glass to Leighton's with a soft clink. They sipped their prosecco and grinned. Now what? Jamie was suddenly hit with a shot of nerves and turned to her counter, where she found her Bluetooth speaker. Music, something to cover the silent tension in the room, was needed because all she could concentrate on now was Leighton's big Bambi eyes, Leighton barefoot in that dress, Leighton standing in Jamie's kitchen like a Christmas present to unwrap. Maybe this hadn't been a good idea after all.

She found a station on her phone that was essentially mellow soft rock, turned, and knocked over her own drink. "Dammit." Little tipsier than she'd thought.

"I got it," Leighton said, quickly retrieving a roll of paper towels in the same moment Jamie grabbed a dish towel to soak up the stray liquid. They met at the counter and worked together in an overlap to clean up the spill.

"Do you think this is a bad omen?" Jamie asked. "Spilling the celebration bubbly can't bode well."

"I don't know," Leighton said, meeting Jamie's gaze from merely inches away. "It doesn't seem so bad right now." The implication was clear.

"No." There she went, telling the truth. In the moment, she didn't have the capacity not to. The room was a little swirly, and Leighton smelled amazing. Beachy and sweet. Her eyes were soft, and Jamie so vividly remembered what they looked like right before she was kissed. Yes, kind of like that, she thought as she leaned in, pressing her lips to Leighton's. Good God. Better than she'd even remembered. She sank into a heavenly oblivion and didn't want to return. Leighton parted her lips to receive the kiss, and perfection ensued. She was transported in time back to that night in this very apartment. Desperate to live in the feeling for a little while longer, she stepped closer, clinging to the euphoria, to Leighton. She went up on her toes and cradled Leighton's face just as her tongue slipped into Jamie's mouth. Satisfaction. Yet Jamie was desperate for more while savoring the pace of the kiss. Leighton angled her head, and their lips clung, made to fit. Heat descended like a lightning bolt, and the blur that was real life seemed a distant distraction. She didn't care. Leighton's tongue explored her mouth, and the center of the universe shifted. How had she gone so long without feeling what she was in this very moment?

Leighton pulled her mouth away and their gazes connected. "Jamie," she murmured softly, running a thumb over Jamie's lower lip before her focus shifted to it, too.

This was Leighton's way of checking in. Her answer? She crushed her mouth to Leighton's and there was nothing slow about them anymore. That was good because there was also nothing she needed on Earth right now except Leighton beneath her fingertips, her mouth, her tongue.

"Is that a yes?" Leighton said with a breathy quality to her voice. Not only was that new but sexy as hell.

Jamie nodded. "This way," she murmured against Leighton's lips, backing up and turning. Holding Leighton's wrist, she guided them down the hallway to her bedroom. She flipped on her overhead light and thought better, flipping it off again. The blue illumination from the semifull moon draped the room in both light and shadow.

With her arms tightly around Jamie's waist, Leighton's lips pressed to her neck, kissing along its column as Jamie pulled in air. Her center ached, but she yearned to turn the tables. The unquenchable hunger overtook her, and she allowed herself to be walked to the bed and turned around. Her zipper. Down. The red cocktail dress she'd shopped for over the course of several weeks was slid to her elbows.

Leighton reached from behind and cupped both of her breasts softly, pushing them back against her body with more force. *Holy fuck.* She was instantly wet. There was a soft moan that she recognized as her own. The dress fell farther down her arms, and she stepped out of it, leaving only the red underwear she'd matched to her dress just for fun. No one was supposed to see it. She turned, and Leighton went still, taking her in. Leighton lightly traced the curve of Jamie's breast with one finger, sending a shiver. Soft touches seemed designed to torture her tonight. She stepped closer and slid her hand into Leighton's hair to hold her there as she kissed with the kind of abandon she'd fantasized about. The startling part was that the reality surpassed the memory. As she deepened the kiss, Leighton offered a soft hum of pleasure that shot Jamie's arousal through the roof. She'd done that. She'd inspired that hum.

She was quickly placed on the bed, left to watch as Leighton's moonlight-kissed body was revealed with the removal of each piece of clothing. The smooth skin and subtle curves were everything. "I want to touch you," she whispered, reverently. "I've always loved this body."

"Good," Leighton said, eyes dark and determined. Naked and gorgeous, she slid on top of Jamie and paused, holding eye contact for a moment and sliding a strand of hair behind Jamie's ear. The feel of their bare skin pressed together brought a rush of longing. With one hand, Leighton tugged Jamie's underwear down her legs and settled her hips between them. She pressed against Jamie, rubbed, inspiring a shot of something so intense she heard herself cry out. She'd never been so sensitive before, so ready.

"God, your legs," Leighton said, running a hand up the outside of her thighs. Jamie nodded, rocking her hips, searching for relief and hoping Leighton didn't tour every inch of her body before offering any, while at the same time kind of hoping she did. Leighton leaned down and kissed that thigh, moving from the outside to the sensitive interior. Jamie sucked in a breath just as her mouth neared—Nope. In a traitorous move, Leighton crawled up her body, refocusing.

"That was cruel," Jamie said with a shaky laugh. "You're cruel tonight."

"I'm thorough," Leighton corrected, just before her mouth covered Jamie's nipple. Jamie reveled in the pinpricks of sensation that shot like arrows from her breasts downward to between her legs. She couldn't get enough of Leighton and pressed her hips upward. When she heard Leighton's breath hitch, it made her realize that Leighton wanted her every bit as much.

"I want you inside," Jamie whispered. "Now."

Leighton nodded and slipped a hand between them, touching Jamie intimately. *God, send help.* She almost rose up off the sheets. How many times had Jamie dreamed of Leighton back in her bed? How many fantasies had she cut short? The reality was so much more potent. She pressed herself closer, shutting her eyes and reveling in the feel of Leighton's hand between her legs. When it was replaced with the soft, tentative touches of Leighton's mouth, it was almost Jamie's undoing.

"Outrageous."

"Outrageous?" Leighton lifted her head, but that paused the action. No good.

"Yes. Outrageous. That you can. Do this," she hurried to say.

Her only answer was a quiet laugh from Leighton who was back to using her tongue to expert extremes. She had a gift, clearly, and Jamie was benefitting in the moment. Lazy circles, then tighter ones. She grabbed a section of her sheet and squeezed. The need was nearly too much, yet she never wanted this magnificent torture to end. She rocked her hips against Leighton's mouth, seeing stars and aching desperately to tumble over the edge. She slid her fingers into that gorgeous blond hair and held on. One stroke of Leighton's tongue. Another. She was climbing to startling heights, and just as Leighton pushed inside, she broke, careening off the edge in a burst of pleasure, strong and unending. She savored the ride and heard herself swear out loud. When the last remaining shockwaves subsided, she reveled in the feeling of Leighton, still inside her, watching Jamie with a reverent smile.

"You doing okay?"

Jamie tried to slow her breathing. "I'm recovering nicely. Thank you."

"Anytime," Leighton said quietly. As she withdrew, Jamie felt the loss acutely. But her gaze was already roaming Leighton's naked body, her smooth skin, and the breasts she longed to touch, hold, and squeeze gently. As Leighton crawled up the bed over her, Jamie caught both of her breasts in her hands and held on as Leighton lowered herself with an appreciative murmur. Her hair had fallen all to one side and rested on her right shoulder. *So fucking sexy.*

Jamie caught her lips and clung, pushing her tongue inside as she massaged Leighton's breasts and pressed in close. "I need you now," she said in her ear and kissed the column of Leighton's neck and she eased her onto her back. She stared down in awe at the masterpiece of a body beneath her fingertips. She shoved aside any trepidation and allowed herself to enjoy the moment. Leighton cradled her face and pulled her down for a searching kiss, bruising her lips until they came up for air. Breathing ragged. Hearts hammering. "Whoa," Jamie said, steadying herself from the dizzying need to make Leighton feel. But only for a moment, because this was her show now. Placing open-mouthed kisses down Leighton's neck to her chest led her to the breasts she'd missed. She pulled a nipple into her mouth and sucked, enjoying the sounds Leighton made in response. Jamie longed for more of those sounds and wanted to be the reason for them more than anything. Eagerly, she licked the pebbling of the other nipple, moving her tongue in a circular motion as Leighton desperately searched for something to grip. The pillow seemed to be her choice. With a smile, Jamie continued kissing her way down Leighton's body, taking time to enjoy each curve, linger on each sensitive spot. She reminded herself which areas made Leighton moan and then worked to make her moan again. She basked in each new discovery, in the back of her mind, knowing the gravity of this experience. There would be recriminations, but she refused to think about them now, slamming the door on reason. This night was theirs, and the rest of the world could wait outside.

"Jamie." Leighton's voice was softer, not her own.

"Mm-hmm?" She kissed the inside of Leighton's thigh and lingered. She licked it. Another kiss. Leighton's hips were rocking, searching. Jamie was entranced and loving every second of it.

"I don't know if I can wait much longer. Please?"

"Not true. You can." She kissed the other thigh and trailed a finger lightly over Leighton's center, listening as she hissed in a breath. She caressed her folds using feather touches that caused Leighton to buck her hips. "So sensitive."

Her only answer was a half whimper, half sigh.

Jamie lifted her head and took in the scene. What she saw made her go still. Leighton's hair splayed out on her pillow, her skin touched by the light of the moon. She'd been in a cocktail dress Jamie couldn't take her eyes off merely an hour earlier, and now here she was, naked in Jamie's bed. With the image burned into her memory, she went back to the moment at hand, parting Leighton's thighs and tasting her. She wanted to go slow, honestly she did, but the hunger took over, and she was a woman with a mission. She placed an open-mouthed kiss at Leighton's center and let her tongue explore until Leighton was whimpering and pulling aggressively at the sheets. She laid her body halfway across Leighton's, slid her fingers inside, and was enveloped by warmth. Swearing quietly to herself, she began to move, savoring the motion, and this very gratifying rhythm. Leighton's hands went to Jamie's hair, gripping softly, a request. Jamie nodded and directed her attention where Leighton needed her most. She increased her speed and pulled Leighton fully into her mouth until she exploded in a cry. Her eyes were closed, her head tossed back, and her lips were parted. The moment was everything.

She stayed inside as Leighton rode out the waning shockwaves of pleasure and smiled up at her in amazement.

"Come up here," Leighton said. She kissed Jamie's lips softly and swept a strand of hair from her forehead. They shared a smile, a new boundary between them torn down. They didn't say much more than that. The night could speak for itself. It was late, they were exhausted, and before Jamie knew it, she was drifting off in Leighton's arms, which—it turned out—was a pretty awesome place to be.

CHAPTER FOURTEEN

*U*h-oh. Something was off.

Jamie blinked and looked around the room, distinctly aware of a warm presence at her side, but she couldn't quite make sense of anything through the hazy alarm bells sounding. The deep sleep she'd just been pulled from hung on like a cloud, impeding her brain from properly processing. As she searched for orientation, the warm presence moved, and a hand was placed on the small of Jamie's back. That did it. The night before rushed back to her like a movie on fast forward. The party, the cocktail dress, the prosecco, the kissing, the mind-altering sex. Leighton. Sigh. They'd had sex. She'd had sex with Leighton Morrow, which was not wise or okay with the sober version of herself. What now?

She turned and saw a beautiful woman gazing up at her sleepily. *Do not give in to this.* A small smile played on Leighton's lips. Before Jamie could speak, Leighton held up a finger. "Don't freak out. Everything is okay."

"It is?" Jamie asked, but even she could hear the shaky voice behind the word. "No. I mean, it is. It's fine." She didn't have to disclose that inside her brain, by the light of day, she was experiencing a full-on freak-out. It was surely apparent.

Leighton sat up, bringing the bedsheet with her. "This doesn't have to mean anything if you don't want it to."

"Of course not," Jamie said. "We had a night. People have nights. Adults do all the time." A really, really good night, she was realizing, flashing back to how well they'd brought each other to the edge. The heat level they'd achieved without trying. No awkward fumbling or relearning their way around each other. They were an anomaly. Special. But hadn't she already known that?

"So, you're okay? Because your fists are clenched and your eyebrows are pulled low."

"Who? Me?" She immediately relaxed her hands and bounced her brows. "I think I'm just absorbing. Right? You probably are, too. This was unexpected."

"It most certainly was." Leighton nodded. "But I don't have any regrets."

"Good," Jamie said, scurrying to make this moment feel as relaxed as possible when she was anything but. "No one wants regrets, right?" The early morning sunlight slanted in through the window and highlighted the brown in Leighton's eyes. She was certainly extra pretty in the morning, even with rumpled hair. Jamie nervously checked the clock. "I do need to get to the coffee bar. Luckily, I didn't have to open. Planned it that way on purpose." A pause. She played that back. "Not because of this. I could never have guessed that we'd...The charity event. Was the reason for the scheduling. Because I knew I'd be out later than my usual."

"Say no more. Let's get you on your way." Leighton scanned the room. "I will get out of your hair, but I'd rather not wear a cocktail dress home. Do you happen to—"

"I have clothes. Of course. I'll just—" Jamie walked quickly to the white terry cloth robe on the back of her door, covering herself in a move that felt silly given all they'd done just hours ago. Somehow, by the light of day, things felt different. She did, and she didn't want to share any more of herself with Leighton.

"Thank you. I know you're in a hurry, but can I just say that I had a really nice time last night."

Jamie forced herself to slow down and calm her racing thoughts, because she had, too. It wasn't Leighton's fault that she'd made a self-indulgent and reckless decision last night. "Sorry. I didn't mean to gloss over what happened. I, um"—she circled a strand of hair behind her ear—"had fun." A slow exhale. "I'm just wondering if it was wise. It's the wisdom factor that's tapping on my shoulder. Because there's not a future here, because I don't think I can get past what happened, and—"

"Ah. Okay. I understand." Leighton nodded but seemed to deflate.

"Well. We can just put things between us back as they were. Business partners."

"And friends," Jamie said sincerely. She came and sat on the edge of her bed. Something in her had shifted, and she'd love for that to be a goal. Leighton was a factor in her life now, and it was time to stop running from the past. "I'd like to try for that."

"Good. Because that makes two of us."

For a moment, the morning slowed down. They held eye contact in the small space they occupied in the world, complicated and laced with regret about what could have been. "Once upon a time, right?" She heard the wistful quality in her voice.

Leighton nodded, a conservative smile appearing. "Right. Once upon a time."

Jamie glanced behind her toward the closet off the bathroom. "I'll get you some clothes. And there's coffee in the kitchen. On a timer."

"That's okay. I'll grab some on the way home."

Their good-bye was friendly, but shrouded in words unsaid. For the best. The rest of the day was uneventful by comparison. But honestly, anything would be after that caliber of night. It was a weekend, which meant the regulars were off duty, and a new band of Saturday customers sat in their chairs instead, like understudies in a play. Saturdays tended to be lower key. Customers were more laid back, interested in making small talk for longer periods of time. The day always felt a little longer but lazy at the same time.

"Have you ever done something that you wish you could undo?"

Jamie blinked at the young woman in front of her register. Nose ring, jet-black hair, insistent stare. "Who sent you?" Jamie asked suspiciously.

"My brother. He wants an iced coffee and said he'd buy mine if I did the run."

"Right. Never mind then. You're merely an innocent."

"Sorry I blurted that question. I just had one hell of a twenty-four hours, and I'm dying like roadkill."

Jamie leaned in. "Me, too. An ex?"

"No, I bought an iguana and my apartment is a matchbox. His aquarium takes up half of it. And I can't, like, give him back now. He thinks he's home." Her brown eyes went wide. "But I never should have done this. Like, ever."

"Right." Jamie straightened. "I think it's going to be okay. You have a nice roommate now. Next year, you'll wonder what you ever did without..."

"Fernando."

"Great name."

"Thanks. My brother doesn't think so."

"Screw him. Tell you what." Jamie placed a hand on her hip. "Since we're both struggling with our poor decisions, your two coffees are on the house."

"Oh no." The girl gasped. "Did you buy one, too? The pet fair in the West Village, right? They're so fucking persuasive."

"No. But there is a kind of parallel."

"Score. I'll take two larges, then."

Leo, who was weekend subbing for Bart, who had his sister's dance recital that morning, filled the order with a question mark practically painted on his handsome face. When the girl left with coffees in hand, he turned to her. "What'd ya do?" he asked in an even voice. It was his gift, acting like he didn't care much to get people to feel like the stakes were low. She was on to him.

"Nothing important."

"Know you pretty well." He sat on the back counter and regarded her thoughtfully with folded arms, a scientist deciding if his chemicals were mixing correctly. "Can't remember seeing you so jittery on a Saturday morning."

"Stop assessing."

"Fine." He turned around casually and went to work restocking the sugar dusters.

"I do have news, though. We got the awesome storefront in Hell's Kitchen I was telling you about. I want you to come over there with me some afternoon and make sure my light renovation plans will provide the function we're used to. See if I'm missing anything."

"That's awesome. You got it." He flipped back around. Jamie felt like things were unfinished. Clarissa would have dragged it out of her. Why were men so easy to move on from a conversation?

"It was Leighton Morrow," she whispered. She did still have a bar with several customers nearby. Two in the midst of a very rowdy chess game in the lounge area.

He turned around, victorious grin on his face. "You get it, boss? Last night?"

She nodded. "Apparently, I lost my logic. I get dressed up, fed a little wine, and I go back on the most important promise I've made to myself."

He bagged an order of doughnuts and placed them in the warmer. "But how'd it go? You have fun?"

"Yes, it was mind-blowing and awesome, but there are larger complications. She's my business partner and a damned liar. She's not someone I want my heart mixed up with."

"Enjoy it for what it was, at least. A nice way to end your Friday."

"Don't let me off the hook."

He shrugged. "Life is here to live, James. You can't police yourself into playing it so safe you suffocate. We all screw up. We move forward. You will, too."

"It sounds good in theory. Feels a little terrifying when the aftermath is literally upon you."

"Like she was." He offered a steady wink and went back to the sugars.

"You're lucky we don't have an HR department."

"I'm also lucky I don't have an iguana from the West Village."

"Aren't we all, though?"

"Besides, I wasn't talking to Jamie my boss, I was talking to my friend."

For some reason, every time she realized she had one of those, she went warm and grateful. It's not that she'd been unpopular as a kid or dealt with any kind of true trauma, but sometimes she had to remind herself that people she respected could and *did* genuinely care for her. *Why do I assume it's a one-way street?* She impulsively hugged Leo's bicep and didn't let go.

"What's that for? You're mauling me."

"For, I don't know, life and stuff."

He freed his arm and wrapped it around her. "Well. Life and stuff to you, too. It's gonna be okay. Promise. Just ride that wave and don't look back."

She popped her chin up and regarded him. "Do you surf?"

"Course I surf." She should have known. There was nothing Leo couldn't do. "Now get out of here. We got this under control. It's close to wine time."

"Wine o'clock in fifteen," she said to the dining room. "We're about to try hard for sophistication. Get ready."

Before heading home, Jamie sat with a glass by the window and watched the sun touch the tops of the buildings, her favorite moment of each afternoon. The peaceful winding down of the day helped her harness her thoughts and rein in her worries. She and Leighton had stepped out of bounds, and as two consenting adults, that was okay. They'd regroup and refocus on the business and all they had in front of them. And maybe, just maybe, they'd find a way to build upon that friendship they'd discussed. Jamie was working on letting go of the past, and believing that people truly could change. Leighton wasn't a bad person, she decided, sipping her merlot. She just couldn't be *Jamie's* person. So, maybe that meant Jamie didn't have to fight the draw, but instead, channel it. She could do that. In fact, she wanted to. "A new friend," she murmured to herself. She caught the breathtaking last sliver of the pink and orange sunset. There was a parallel there. A new shop. A new partner. A new version of her and Leighton. The ending of one thing and the beginning of another. Poetic and perfect.

Jamie decided not to be afraid of what was ahead.

She sipped her wine and exhaled.

Chapter Fifteen

L eighton clicked off the call with the representative from the Hope and Help organization. The event had been a smash success, but she knew that Carrington's could do more and had personally arranged for the department store to partner with the group to outfit the women with the clothes they would need once ready to seek employment. The phone meeting had been beneficial and productive, and now she was ready to fall on the floor of her office and end what had been a long day.

She'd been going hard lately on purpose.

"Who's working late and why?" Leighton spun around in her chair at the sound of a very familiar voice. She laughed at the silly face her cousin pulled. "Ta-da."

"Courtney. What? You didn't tell me you were coming."

"And miss out on the look on your face right now? Never. I asked Mindy to clear your calendar and keep my secret. I was on a store visit and took a few meetings. Surprise!" Courtney in her high heels and gorgeous tan business suit scurried toward her, arms outstretched. Leighton stood and moved immediately into them, relishing the embrace, thrilled to see Courtney. In this moment, she realized just how much she missed the concept of family, having a tether. With her mom gone, Courtney served as an important link.

"It's really good to see you, Court." The emotion rose up in her throat.

"We have waited too long to cross the country this time." She grabbed Leighton's chin the way she used to when they were kids. "I love it when you're caught off guard. It goes against your very serene, thoughtful nature."

"I'm turning into a sap is what's happening."

"Nothing wrong with that. It looks good on you. How's the new coffee investment coming along?" Courtney leaned her chin in her hand from the chair across from Leighton's desk.

"Amazingly well. I stay in the background, just checking in here and there, but they were scheduled to paint today. Jamie is supervising."

"*The* Jamie." Courtney bounced her eyebrows. "Back in your life."

"It's not exactly like that." Leighton let her head drop. "I probably shouldn't have told you about the night of the charity event. I just needed to confide in someone, and you're my person for that kind of thing."

"Are you kidding? Of course you should have. I'm just sorry there weren't more juicy details provided. Did I ever tell you what I once did in the middle of a strawberry farm?" She offered a wink.

"No, but you've certainly sung the praises of life in small towns. Now I know why."

"I'm just saying that if you can find yourself a small town girl, I highly recommend it."

"Oh, I'm not giving up on the city quite yet."

"And we all know why," Courtney said with knowing eyes. On cue, she fluttered her lashes.

"We've actually turned over a new leaf, and it's going well. We're working on an actual friendship, and it feels really good."

"You prefer a friendship to happily ever after?"

Leighton raised a finger. "You should have been a lawyer. You ask the hard questions."

"Are you going to answer? Either way, I was hoping to take you to dinner. I have reservations at Four Charles."

"Well, well. It really pays to have the Carrington last name, doesn't it?"

"Fancy cheeseburgers will be my downfall." Courtney's blue eyes held regret. "Answer the question."

"There was a time when I wanted more with Jamie. Yes. For a long time. But I think working on our friendship is the right move. For everyone."

"Objection. Nonresponsive."

"The cheeseburger attorney is just gonna have to live with that answer because I do." Leighton grabbed her bag and came around the desk. Courtney gave her hand a squeeze.

"Just don't lose that hope entirely. There's always someday."

"No. I can't do that." Leighton squeezed back and let go. She touched her heart briefly. "Too dangerous to think that way. I'll be crushed by a semi if I stand in that road." The night she and Jamie spent together all those weeks ago still hadn't left her brain. She'd had trouble moving on from the feelings it had so intensely ignited, even when her head knew better. Leighton had spent the following week daydreaming about holding Jamie close, kissing her, and so much more. Turning off those thoughts when they sprang up had been her only recourse. At this point, she was actually getting quite good at keeping Jamie in the friendship box. They'd gotten drinks a couple of times since. Dinner once. It had been really nice. She had no intention of blowing the chance she had. Jamie was too important, and in light of the fact that Jamie didn't want more, she planned to protect what they did have.

Courtney nodded, serious now. "Standing in that road. I know exactly what you mean. Been there myself once."

"I remember. Earned you a marriage that never should have happened."

Courtney sighed. "Don't remind me." A pause. "I love you, you know. And you're going to be okay."

"I believe that, too. I also love you back. Shall we go get those really expensive cheeseburgers?"

"God, yes. I've been counting the hours."

"Ever count cheeseburgers? To get to sleep, I mean."

"What?" Courtney asked, whirling back.

"Nothing," Leighton said with a laugh.

Thirty minutes later as they waited for their food—the double Wagyu cheeseburger for Courtney and the honey peppered king salmon for Leighton—she exhaled in happiness. "I'm so excited you're here." In actuality it was more than that. Until laying eyes on Courtney, Leighton hadn't understood how alone she'd felt lately. This was a startling spotlight. She had friends here and there in the city. Mindy was great, but she had a family of her own. Jamie fit the bill, but they weren't exactly in that spot. She'd needed to see Courtney, her own family, badly. "How are things? How's Maggie?"

"Tearing up the small town real estate world with her charm. We've been thinking about a family."

Leighton's heart squeezed. "Soon?"

"It's looking that way. I think I'll carry, and take a little time off. The rest of you can run this little company, right? At least until I'm back."

"I'll do whatever you need me to do as long as I get to hold that little baby for as long as I like."

Courtney's cheeks went pink, a sign that the topic made her both nervous and excited. It was incredibly sweet.

"Enough about my hopes and dreams. Tell me your updates. I need any and all Leighton news."

She had one distinct one that she hadn't planned on telling anyone. Until this very moment, when she felt the need to release a bit of that burden. "I'm thinking of reaching out to my father. Sending a letter."

"Oh, wow." Courtney's eyes went wide and she sat back in her chair, absorbing. "That's a big move for you."

"I'm a little surprised myself." She'd actually written the letter five different times, throwing the first four away. The fifth, well, the fifth she'd actually addressed and placed in a drawer until she officially decided whether she wanted to send it. "Ever since I moved to New York, I notice myself searching for his face in the crowd. I get angry and wonder if maybe that's the whole reason I moved here, to prove some kind of point. I just don't know. Maybe I need some closure on that front."

Courtney reached for the bread basket. "The last time we touched on the topic of your father, you said you had no interest. Given, that was years ago." She tilted her head. "What do you think changed?"

"My mom died. Something shifted on that front. I was all of a sudden parentless. Yet I'm not. He's here, living his life, celebrating birthdays with his kids, his real family."

"He does know about you, right?"

"Oh, he knows everything. My mother tried to get him to meet me many times when I was young. He refused."

"He sounds wonderful," Courtney said wryly. "Are you sure you want to do this? Sounds like a can of worms you might want to think hard about opening."

Leighton tapped her chin and took a sip of the wine they'd ordered. Courtney's treat. "I know. I haven't fully decided if I'm going to send it yet."

Courtney looked thoughtful. "My dad was an asshole. You saw firsthand. There's a part of me that wished he'd been missing from my life. Maybe yours did you a favor."

"Either way. I'd like him to answer a few questions for me. Acknowledge my existence for five seconds." She set down her glass with purpose. "He's lived what looks to be a fantastic life. Success in politics, a happy little family of four, and then there's me, his dirty little secret. Fuck him."

"Fuck him," Courtney said with fire in her eyes. "You deserve more."

"And so did you, by the way. At least yours set us all up financially. Left you an empire to run."

"Let's not give him too much credit." She watched Leighton with concern slashed across her features. "Whatever happens, I hope it helps rather than hurts."

Leighton thought on the sentiment. "I don't think he can make things any worse, but we'll see."

"Dads." Courtney shook her head and leaned in. "We might need another glass."

❖

Bordeauxnuts Too, as Jamie had officially named the new place, was nearly ready to meet the public. She liked that the sign in front let folks know that this location was a sequel, maybe prompt them to check out the original if they were ever in the neighborhood. The countdown was on, and the excitement was brimming. After two months of mild remodeling, heavy decorating, a new coat of paint, equipment delivery, intermittent staff training, and lots of her own sweat and love, she couldn't have been happier with the result. The space with all its dark wood and high ceilings was exactly what she wanted. Cozy. Happy. Somewhere you want to stay awhile while you read a book of poetry or knit a scarf, like Marjorie. She surveyed the dining area, complete with matching light brown and dark brown tables, imagining who the new Marjorie might be and how long it would take for new regulars to assemble.

"I don't want there to be a new Marjorie," Marjorie had said earlier that morning with a pout. Most of the other regulars, except for Marvin in his corner, had packed up and headed off in different directions, but Marjorie hung back until after lunchtime, which signaled she had something on her mind. "What if she's cooler than me? She probably cut a good five inches off her hair and has taken up swimming in the evenings. She looks like a million bucks now. She might have a secret lover. I can't keep up with new Marjorie. I give up." She sat back in a frustrated huff. These days, she'd swapped knitting for crossword puzzles. Her pencil rolled to the edge of the table and plummeted, much like Marjorie's mood.

"Nope. No new Marjorie. I checked under all the chairs," Jamie said from behind the drink station as she wiped down the equipment during the midafternoon lull, a routine. "You'll have to represent all Marjories."

She didn't seem placated. Marjorie rested her chin in her hands. "I'm afraid once the new shop opens, you're going to spend more time there and forget all about us. We'll be the also-rans. I depend on this place, Jamie, and you're part of that."

Jamie frowned and came around in front of the counter. "It's impossible that I would ditch any of you. This bar is my first baby. I just have two children to keep track of now. I don't love either one more than the other."

"Listen. Hell's Kitchen is no Chelsea. She'll be here more than there," Marvin said with a shrug. "Who wouldn't be? The sheer number of people uptown gives me palpitations."

But Jamie had to admit that change was part of life in the hospitality business. The crew of regulars also had an ever-changing status, which was par for the café course. People moved into the group, and others moved out. Lives, plans, and trajectories changed. She only glimpsed Lisa and Chun once every couple of weeks now that they'd focused their flipping efforts on Brooklyn properties. But Naomi, a student at NYU, had taken to using a table near the front of the dining area for studying. After a few weeks of audition, the others had readily added her to their routine conversation. She was the quietest one in the group, but when she did contribute, her words were always valuable.

Naomi looked up from a bioscience textbook with a serene smile. "Bordeauxnuts is not going anywhere. It's spreading its wings and so is Jamie. I'm here for it."

Jamie pointed at her. "This is why we're keeping you. No new Naomis."

And now here she stood in the new bar, days from the soft opening, with butterflies dancing in her stomach and excitement radiating from every pore.

"Will your parents be swinging by for your big opening?" Leighton asked, watching Jamie test out the new doughnut maker on the back counter. She'd sprung for the newer model and was impressed with its speed.

"You can say *ours*. It's okay. Want to try one?"

Leighton closed her eyes. "You know I can't say no to these things. I keep waiting for you to disclose their doughy narcotic center."

Jamie dusted cinnamon sugar onto the doughnut and passed Leighton the napkin. "No drugs involved."

She smiled at her new doughnut friend "*Our* opening, then. I feel important all of a sudden, and kind of guilty because all I did was put up cash."

"We aren't here without cash. And we will most assuredly see my mother. Couldn't keep her away, even with the promise of a dozen puppies. Not that I'd want to."

"I remember you telling me once upon a time that your dad used to swing by daily for an Americano. Not anymore? What happened?"

"A lot actually, and rather quickly." Jamie smiled, mid-counter wipe down. "I would give anything for him to swing by, but he passed a year and a half ago."

"Oh no. That day on the bench. The test results?"

The space went silent. "Yeah, it wasn't good for a long time after that. Then we lost him."

Leighton shook her head in shock. "I'm so sorry for your loss." The sincere sorrow that crossed her features tugged at Jamie's heart. "I feel awful for asking."

"It's okay." She walked over and gave Leighton's hand a squeeze, which actually softened the room noticeably. "My dad's still with me. I feel him every day, arguing with me about whether to take ten minutes for Wordle or get to work without having to rush."

"Was he a word guy?"

Jamie let go and returned to the doughnut machine which she just might call Mark, as it was the brother of Mike. Her dad would get a kick out of that. She grinned. "Obsessed. The *Times* crossword was his first love, back in the day. But he moved on to Wordle when it burst on to the scene. These days, I do it every morning and think of him, our own little time together. One of us is just a little more physically present than the other."

Leighton leaned a hip against the counter. "Thank you for telling me. That's the best way to honor him, you know that?" She looked around. "You could always hang a framed photo."

"Hmm. You think?" Jamie took a moment and considered the suggestion. It felt right, like a puzzle piece in the decor. "I like that idea. My mom would, too. He'll get to be a part of this place, even though he never got to see it in life."

"What about over there?" Leighton motioned to the side wall overlooking the cash register.

Jamie followed her gaze to the dark paneled surface. It was perfect. "Done. Reserved." She turned back, but Leighton had moved closer toward the wall, leaving them in each other's space. She could have taken it somewhere tension charged but didn't. That's not what this was. She stepped around Leighton, happy with the new addition to the store. "Thanks."

Leighton hadn't moved. "Yeah. Anytime."

CHAPTER SIXTEEN

I want to put little Santa hats on the doughnuts."
Leighton paused from her spot on the top rung of the ladder, a string of holiday lights in hand. Jamie had invited her to help decorate Bordeauxnuts Too and dangled free merlot like a carrot on a wine bottle. "That sentence is hard to decode. Do you mean literally? That sounds intense. You'd need small hands."

Jamie placed one of hers on her hip, looking adorable in *her* Santa hat. Christmas was exactly one month away, and she'd been actively bouncing all her holiday ideas off Leighton via text. In fact, they talked most of the day lately. Every time she had a break in the course of her workday, she checked her phone for Jamie, getting a little hit of dopamine when there was a message waiting.

The week before she'd glanced at her phone to find, *Marlene told me that Edward might be moving in.*

Leighton typed back, smile on her face, *Oh, so that means...*

I need to invest in an industrial sized box of ear plugs or go to Sexyland with them on nights beyond just Thursday.

Leighton laughed loudly, and Mindy appeared in the doorway of her office. "Someone's got your attention. It's Jamie, isn't it? You don't even have to say. No one makes you laugh like that."

"It's a whole thing with her neighbor."

"It's a whole thing, all right," Mindy had said with confidence.

She'd gone back to work that day, but lighter. Each moment of connection with Jamie seemed to do that for her, and she was wildly aware of how lucky she was to have Jamie back in her life.

"A little to the right on those lights," Jamie said, hands on hips at the base of the ladder.

"Like this?" Leighton pulled the lights a tad tighter.

"You might have to stretch onto your tippy toes. Use that height of yours."

"Bossy down there. Where's that wine I was promised? I might have to strike."

Jamie laughed quietly. "Coming right up. I actually set this bottle aside because I thought you'd like it."

"In that case, I take back the bossy comment."

"Wise."

"More like opportunistic." Leighton enjoyed the give-and-take, their lighthearted quips. They'd developed a *them* over the past few months. Guards were coming down, and they'd found a comfortable, safe rhythm.

Leighton finished the lights and descended the ladder to an over-sized wineglass, filled with Jamie's wine pick. "What are we toasting to?"

"The new season." It had a double meaning, and they both knew it.

Leighton lifted her glass. "To the new season." She swirled, inhaled, and tasted. "First of all, I love the new oversized glasses."

"Yeah? The customers seem to, as well. Marjorie is jealous. No idea how she heard about them. I'm convinced she has underground channels."

"Never underestimate a retired schoolteacher. They've developed resources we can only dream about." She held up the glass. "This is really good. It's got legs, too."

Jamie grinned. "Told you it was up your alley. Fruity on the front, dry finish."

"My jam." She cradled her glass. "You can one hundred percent say no, but I have an extra ticket to *The Nutcracker* at Lincoln Center next week. I have no clue if it's your thing at all, but I wouldn't mind the company." For the first time, she didn't feel the need to explain that the invitation was platonic in nature. They'd seen enough of each other lately that the understanding coated everything. "I think the tickets are for next Tuesday at—"

"I'm in. I love the ballet. I've been a handful of times and can't wrap my mind around how those dancers manage to make me feel what they do."

Leighton's heart went soft. "Yeah. That's the perfect way to describe it." She should have known Jamie would appreciate the art form. "I'm always so moved by the artistry, and *The Nutcracker* has become a holiday tradition for me. I took Courtney last year, but she's not in town this go-round. I was hoping to not go alone."

"You're not, but only on the condition that you let me buy dinner. I'm sure you know more uptown haunts."

"Wait. Not a single reference to money or snobbery?"

Jamie touched her chest in offense. "Me? I would never. Not to the person who just offered me a ticket."

"Wise."

She flashed a dazzling smile that made Leighton's heart sing. "Or just opportunistic."

Leighton hired Robin that next Tuesday night and pulled up to Jamie's building just as she exited in a beautiful turquoise sweater dress and heels. Her hair was up, showing off the column of her neck and the diamond studded hoop earrings she wore. She touched them as she slid into the car. "My entire inheritance from my grandmother."

"They look fantastic."

"You do, too," Jamie said, beaming. "We're fancy people tonight." A pause. "You're fancy all the time, but tonight, me too."

"Stick with me, kid." She offered a wink to convey the light-heartedness of her comment, and they were off. An hour later, with champagne flutes in hand, they watched as the New York City Ballet transported them to a magical world of nutcrackers, sugarplum fairies, mouse kings, all seen through the eyes of a child. Midway through the performance, Jamie snuggled up to Leighton's arm and passed her a smile. It was a moment between them that she would treasure.

Leighton had been able to snag them reservations after the show at Bad Roman, and from the corner of the restaurant, they excitedly talked over their impressions of the show.

Jamie rested her chin in her hand. "What's interesting to me is that you're in tune to all the little details. The set, the costumes, the choreography, and I lose myself in the emotion, the story."

"I love that, though, because I get to hear about the experience from your perspective and enjoy the show in this whole new sense."

"We might just be compatible theatergoers." Jamie glanced behind her. "I don't mean to interrupt our flow, but there's a woman who keeps shooting glances your way, and she's on her way over."

"What does she look like?"

"Tall. Dark curly hair. Black. Gorgeous. Wow."

"Helen," Leighton said, following Jamie's gaze to see Helen Sloane approaching. Two dates, a few follow-up texts, and then they'd kind of drifted. Helen was nice enough, though. Leighton just hadn't been in a place to take it any farther. She smiled as Helen got close, stood, and offered her a hug. "Helen. Good to see you."

"I thought that was you, but I didn't want to interrupt. It looked like a fantastic conversation." Helen smiled at Jamie. "Helen Sloane. Leighton's a friend." It was kind of Helen to not announce they'd dated, given she didn't know Jamie or their status. She got points for that.

"Jamie Tolliver. Hi. We were tossing around our impressions of *The Nutcracker*. We just came from the show."

"Jamie just opened a coffee and wine bar in Hell's Kitchen, and I invested in her talent and know-how."

Helen nodded enthusiastically. "Sold. I love both."

"My kind of customer."

"Anyway. I was happy to see you and wanted to say hello. Glad you enjoyed the show. I remember those days all too well. Stiff ankles to show for it. Enjoy your night."

"And who is she exactly?" Jamie asked, as they settled back into their chairs just as dessert menus were delivered.

"Helen and I met through a mutual friend. Coincidentally, she used to dance with the New York City Ballet."

"Impressive."

"She's great."

Jamie studied the small menu for a few moments. "Lesbian?"

"I'm not sure how she identifies, but she does date women. We went out a couple of times. Nothing came of it." Was this weird? Leighton couldn't tell. There was a strange energy bouncing between them, but Jamie did still have a smile on her face. That was something.

"Been there. There was no T-shirt." She peeked out from behind the menu. "That saying is a lie, by the way. There are never shirts to accompany a bad experience. There should be. Can you imagine? One would say *I ate bad shrimp last week*. Another, *My girlfriend likes to dance on vans*."

"Wait. What?" Leighton said, laughing. "That's too specific to not be true."

"It is. Status report. You dated elegant Helen over there, and my ex, Monique, was a party girl who liked to van dance. Now we know everything." She sipped her wine. "This friendship continues to grow. Are we doing dessert? Please say, *Yes, of course, Jamie*."

"One of my favorite things about you is your undying commitment to food and beverages. We're alike in that way."

"No. I think I win, but you can be a distant second." Her eyes sparkled, and that made Leighton surrender. "I will give you that."

They sipped in silence for a few moments before their server returned and took their order for the lemon cheesecake that came in the shape of two realistic-looking lemons. "We need a photo. This is too impressive." Jamie held up the dish and indicated Leighton should slide closer. With cheesecake lemons in front of them, they smiled for Jamie's phone. Like clockwork, Leighton felt the warm tingle that being close to Jamie always brought on. She bit her lip to correct her body's reaction and signaled the server for the bill. There was one problem. She didn't want the night to end. It had been the best she'd had in a while.

After they'd killed the wonderfully creative cheesecake, she took the leap. "My place is near here. Want to swing by and see the view? It's breathtaking at night."

Jamie turned her head and side-eyed Leighton. "Is this—"

"No. Nope. Not a come-on. A boring, everyday request to show off."

Jamie handed her credit card to the server, upholding her promise to buy. "In that case, I'd love to see it."

❖

Jamie walked around Leighton's twenty-second-story apartment with a view of Central Park on one side of the living space and a view of the twinkling city lights on the other. "You shouldn't get to have both. Now, that's just not fair." Jamie'd said it with a grin. "I only say that because I'm jealous."

Leighton found them a couple of bottled waters from what looked to be a huge fridge. "You have an in with the owner. I bet she'd let you swing by now and then."

Jamie made a point to light up, catching the water Leighton tossed her. "That's right. I know a girl." She walked the perimeter of the overly large apartment that only one person lived in. Surreal. She had a feeling three or four of her apartment could fit in this space. "You could set up a little jogging track in here. Have you ever considered that?" Leighton in spandex was an image she set aside. Peeling her out of it was, too.

"It's only large by New York City standards."

Jamie nearly choked on her water. "You have liquid gold coursing through your veins if you think that. Where is that silver spoon you were born with? Do you keep it in the kitchen or the bedroom?" She passed Leighton a sweet smile so she didn't get tackled in a high-rise.

"I'm going to take that as a compliment regardless of how you meant it." She made an exaggerated grandiose gesture. "Please make yourself comfortable."

"Too good an offer. Don't mind if I do. Gonna see how the other half lives. We should call Clarissa. This room would make for a fantastic sleepover."

"Hmm. Maybe not tonight."

"Fine." Jamie took a seat on the softest leather couch she'd ever encountered. She was about to remark on it when a magazine open to an article featuring Logan Morrow caught her attention. She picked it up and gestured. "Are you related to the Congress guy? Just occurred to me that you have the same last name." Maybe Leighton had a politician uncle in the city. She wouldn't put it past her.

"He's my father," she said dully.

"Oh." The playfulness evaporated from the room. Jamie turned around, absorbing. "Really? I had no idea. He's pretty famous in this state." She shook her head because the pieces didn't fit. An uncle might have gone unmentioned, but not her father. She'd only ever said she didn't know her dad.

Leighton leaned back on the granite countertop in the open concept kitchen. "Really."

"You've talked about your mom. The Carringtons. Courtney. But you've never talked much about him."

"Right." She took a moment. "I've just never actually met the guy."

"Wow." Jamie went still. Her heart ached as she began to understand. "Okay. So he and your mom weren't…"

"He had a wife and a family when they met at a campaign stop back in the day. The Carringtons were donors. He wanted nothing to do with her once he heard the news about me. I think he sent some money on occasion. Obviously, with Carrington stock, she didn't need it. What she needed was a father for her kid."

Jamie downshifted, imagining the little girl with those big brown eyes that this man turned his back on and ignored for her entire life. What a contrast to the warmth her own father had shown her. Hugs each morning. Stories before bedtime. He'd taught her how to solve a Rubik's Cube before she turned seven. Suddenly, the large apartment felt chilly and lonely in a whole new sense. Leighton had lost her mother a few years back, had never known her father or her half-siblings. She was, in a sense, on her own up in this tower. "I'm very sorry he did that to you. That wasn't fair." She felt the anger rise in her chest on Leighton's behalf. Her nails dug into her palm.

"Thank you for saying that." Leighton came to the sofa and took a seat, staring off into the night through the large window in front of them. The mood had definitely shifted, a weight hanging over them now. "I wrote him a letter." She held up a finger to correct the statement. "I've actually written him many, many letters over the years, but this was the first one that I've mailed."

"What did it say?" Jamie asked quietly, gazing at Leighton's profile.

"I was sincere. Most of the others I've written were angry in tone. Not this time. I asked some questions about my family history, about his other children, and why he made the choices that he had regarding me and my mom."

"Have you heard back?"

Leighton turned to look at Jamie, vulnerability and disappointment all over her face. "Nope." She exhaled. "And here's the thing that gets me. I wish I didn't keep checking the damn mail every evening with a nervous stomach, but I do. I wish I didn't imagine a parallel universe where he was actually my dad and a part of my life, but I do that, too. I hate that I give him that kind of power." She reached over and flipped the magazine closed, hiding her father's face as if she couldn't stand it another second. It made complete sense.

"I don't think you should beat yourself up for being vulnerable. That makes you human."

Leighton nodded but said nothing.

Jamie, in solidarity, took her hand and slid closer on the couch. Together, they looked out over the twinkling rooftops of the city, still alive, always pulsing with energy. "It's going to be okay," Jamie said softly a few minutes later.

"Thank you," Leighton said, and though Jamie wasn't sure, it looked like she wiped away a stray tear. Out of respect, she pretended not to notice, which didn't mean that her heart wasn't aching.

They stayed up late that night. Sitting quietly. Talking some. They even found their way back to laughter. In the end, it had been a truly nice evening together, and Jamie took pride in the strength of this newfound bond. Leighton mattered to her. And maybe all that happened between them was meant to bring them to this very moment. To each other.

❖

There was one key difference between Bordeauxnuts in Chelsea and the new one, and that was the outdoor seating Jamie had been thrilled to add to the front of Bordeauxnuts Too. Well, that and the red and white awning that made her feel happy whenever she saw it. The property offered just enough outside space for four tables, two on either side of the door, and they already had seen a ton of use.

"Can I bring you a parasol, madame?" Jamie asked her mother as she placed a bowl of water in front of Pronto, the cutest looking little Chewbacca of a dog. Pronto was her mother's new shadow and cuddle bug. He'd been groomed that week and had the most adorable fluffy hair and bangs.

"No, but can I have another one of whatever this thing is?" her mother asked, shaking the ice in her disposable cup. "And is it almost wine time? That's my favorite time here."

"It's everyone's favorite time. You know I'll serve it whenever a customer asks, right?" Jamie placed a hand on her hip.

"No, I know that. But I like to wait until the café transforms, like a boring human morphing into a superhero."

"Did you just call the coffee side of the bar boring?"

"What? No. I love the coffee side. That's why I want another of this thingy." Another ice rattle. "What is it again?"

"That's a Holiday Spiced Iced Latte. I'll get you another one."

"I love this place. Don't you?" her mother remarked to Pronto. "The service is just so good."

Jamie laughed. "Not surprised. You're literally the only human who gets table service."

"I know. That's why I come here." She gestured to her dog, who now had one paw on top of her shoe. "Pronto approves, too. He likes the sun patches you so generously offer."

"I snatched up this location just for him." She scratched the dog's head. "You're a supermodel, Pronto. I dare anyone to argue."

"Is Leighton coming by?" her mom asked. They'd run into each twice now at the café and had hit it off right away. "I want to tell her about the geraniums on my terrace. I brought a photo."

"You've spent a collective two hours together and are best friends?"

"We're birds of a feather."

Jamie laughed. "A hardworking immigrant and a trust-fund baby. I see the parallels." She was being a tad snarky and wasn't sure why. But Jamie was aware that she constructed an invisible fence around Leighton. She loved spending time together, but she only let herself get so close. The trust just wasn't there, and probably never would be to a full extent. Leighton's bond with her mother felt a little like an encroachment on that barrier, making her squirm. Somehow, she would breathe her way through it. No harm, right?

"You're just jealous that we bond over flowers and you struggle to keep yours alive. You should listen to our conversation sometimes. You might pick up a tip or two."

"I killed two plants. Well, three, and now I'm a registered plant killer?"

"Yes." She grabbed Jamie's hand and placed a kiss on the back. "Is there any chance she might be my future daughter-in-law? That could be fun. We could go to gardening shows. I have friends I could introduce her to."

"No. Sorry. Not in the cards."

"And why is that? You have a good give-and-take between the two of you. You smile so much more when she's in the room." Her mom tapped her temple. "I notice."

"Because we've moved beyond that part of our relationship. There are some people you're simply meant to be friends with. Plus, we have this past that I can't just erase."

"You're holding a grudge."

"I most certainly am not, or I wouldn't have agreed to her investment. I wouldn't spend so much time hanging out with her." But underneath it all, she knew her mother was right. There was a grudge dangling between them, and Jamie was beginning to feel like it was time to let it go. Leighton had shown herself to be dependable and forthright. Now it was up to Jamie to take note and do the work.

"Who are you spending so much time hanging with?"

Oh damn. Jamie whirled around at the sound of the familiar voice. Leighton. Her cheeks flamed. "We were not talking about you. At all. Want a drink? You likely had a long day."

"It's not wine time yet," her mother said, consulting her watch. Leighton was already kneeling down in her navy pants and pink top, making eyes at Pronto. They might have been a stock photo, she thought, staring at them. She could imagine the search terms now: *beautiful business woman bonds with adorable pup.*

"It is now," Jamie said to an amused stare from Leighton. "You're off early today."

Leighton had developed a habit of swinging by after work most days of the week. The ones she skipped always left Jamie feeling a little adrift. It was nice having someone to bounce ideas off of, and generally just spend time with. She and Leighton had something unique. She could admit to that.

"I wrapped a project and decided not to leap into the next one until tomorrow. What are we drinking?"

"Yes, what?" her mother asked. "Leighton, you can sit with me if you'd like."

"Best invitation I've had all day." She looked over at Jamie. "But I don't mind getting the drinks. Just tell me what you want and—"

She patted Leighton's shoulder. "Nah. You just got here. Be right back with a couple of glasses of this new blend we just got. California."

"Ooh la la," her mother said. She was certainly enjoying herself more these days, and after the difficult time she'd been through with the loss of Jamie's father, it was a relief to see a small bit of joy return.

Jamie moved inside, soaking up a bit of warmth, as she went about assembling their drinks and a couple of orders of warm doughnuts with extra seasoning and a chocolate dipping sauce she was trying out.

Since the opening of the second store, she'd gotten into a good rhythm with the two locations, spending the mornings in Chelsea and the afternoons and early evenings in Hell's Kitchen. She had Leo and George managing each location respectively, overseeing the schedules and employees. She was finding that delegating more of those responsibilities freed her up to focus on big-picture issues and make sure her customers received extra attention. She worked the counter, moved through the dining areas, even played an occasional game or two of chess with the customers. She liked being as present as possible, getting to know her guests without being pressed to make up every order personally, like in the early days. Yes, the hours were long, but the reward was worth it. She loved her job, her brand, and everything that came with coffee and wine, even the occasional drunk person she had to call a cab for.

"You're getting pretty good at this whole two-store tango," Leighton said as Jamie slid an oversized oval wineglass in front of her. "You seem less stressed. Dare I say, serene?"

"Dare to. Because I am." She sent Leighton a soft smile and received one back. Part of her serenity definitely had to do with the company. That part, she didn't share. Leighton surely knew their friendship was becoming more and more important to Jamie. They spent tons of time together these days, sometimes under the pretext of going over numbers or buys for the store, but inevitably those meetings turned into dinners out or a movie at one of their places.

"You're slumming tonight," Jamie said, handing Leighton a large metal bowl full of popcorn popped in coconut oil, Jamie's secret recipe.

"No, I'm not. This apartment is expensive. I used to work in corporate real estate, remember? I learned a lot about this neighborhood."

"Did you pick a movie?"

"I can't."

Jamie grabbed two beers and headed over. "You must. It's your turn, and I made you watch that cop movie you hated."

Leighton slid her feet beneath her on Jamie's couch, staring intently at the screen. "There are too many to choose from. I'm overwhelmed."

"What does your heart tell you?" Jamie asked.

Leighton's eyes went wide and she paused. "About what?"

"Just what kind of movie you'd like to watch." She felt the smile fade from her face, understanding that there might have been something to that answer she didn't want to dive into. Her stomach went tight and she moved right out of it. She had to quit doing that. She and Leighton needed to have the ever important talk and define what they were becoming. The only problem was, she tended to lose her courage whenever the moment presented itself.

"Oh. Something that doesn't make me think. Let's start there."

Jamie quickly used the remote to point out several films that might fit that bill, realizing that most of them were romantic comedies that would make them laugh and feel, which felt about perfect.

Leighton pointed at the screen. "Serendipity. I remember seeing that when it first came out. Wanna?"

"I'm in."

Leighton smiled. She had her hair pulled up in what could only be described as a messy twist with wisps of escaped strands framing her face. Her makeup from the day had faded, and she looked so incredibly cozy wearing a navy Pepperdine sweatshirt on Jamie's couch. The entirety of the scene made Jamie incredibly warm and happy. She slid onto the couch directly alongside Leighton since it was a must for popcorn sharing. The unplanned warmth from their proximity was also nice on such a chilly December evening.

"Oh, see, this movie is perfect because it starts out during the holiday season," Leighton said with the biggest smile. The thing about Leighton was that she smiled a lot. But her smiles were typically composed, conservative. Tonight's brand of smile was different, and it had a way of filling Jamie's cup clear to the brim.

"I'd forgotten about that. And it's in the city."

"Our own concrete backyard."

As the film played on and the couple in the story continued to dance around each other over time, Jamie noticed that they'd eased closer together on the couch, her body resting partially on Leighton's. How had that happened? She could have slid back over into her own space, once she'd realized, but didn't. This was just them. The inarguable connection she had to Leighton was something she was learning to accept and maybe even rely upon.

As the credits played, Leighton turned to her and offered a soft smile. "I really liked that one."

"Yeah, me, too."

Nights like that one, where nothing important actually happened, yet everything had, were their norm. She was growing to look forward to her Leighton time, and she was working on leaning in to that more. Thinking less. She treasured their times together, their conversations, their ability to understand each other from a glance across the room. She'd finally come to the conclusion that it was simply a matter of accepting that she might have to allow herself to be vulnerable to Leighton if they were ever going to get to the next step.

From her cherished spot in front of the café, her mother explained to Leighton that her geraniums would keep wasps and mosquitos away, and Leighton pointed out that the petals of the geranium were actually edible, to which they both remarked how amazing nature was. She watched, smothering a grin before returning inside to prepare for the great coffee-wine swap. The blackboard would need to be changed out, she'd dim the lighting scheme to something a little more romantic, and couples and groups would rotate into the wine bar as the laptop dwellers packed up. The transition was one of her favorite parts of her workday.

"This was fantastic wine," Leighton said, carrying in the two glasses from outside.

Jamie leaned her chin in her hand on the tall counter from which orders were picked up. "Want a top-off? I might be able to make that happen."

Leighton widened her eyes. "You're generous." She extended her glass and bounced it. Jamie filled a third of a pour, checked in with Leighton, and upped it to a half. "Now we're talkin'. What time do you hang up your boss hat tonight?"

She stopped and stared at the wall. "Well, now I need a boss hat."

Leighton sipped her wine and took a look at the glass. "This is really fantastic. We should order more."

"Two cases on their way already. Why are you asking about my night?" She was half ready to collapse on her couch, and half ready to go on any adventure Leighton laid down.

"Was hoping for a little company. It's been a weird day." Leighton's expression had changed on that last sentence. The smile was forced.

"Why don't we grab a bite? Let me finish up a few things here, and we can go. I think my mom—"

"She sent me in to say that she has Bunco group in an hour and would like a hug and a kiss before she goes."

"On it." As she passed Leighton, she gave her hand a squeeze. "Don't go anywhere."

"Not a chance. I'll be right here."

The words sang comfortably in Jamie's chest as she moved through the bar, happier than just a few minutes before. Dinner with Leighton was on the agenda. She'd needed someone today, and she'd chosen Jamie. She tapped her lips and closed her eyes, wondering if maybe this was the night she'd tell Leighton that she was ready to take a chance on them. It was a big step, but Jamie felt her courage assembling. "It's go-time."

CHAPTER SEVENTEEN

The two of them touched a lot. Leighton had noticed it more and more in the past couple of weeks. Little squeezes, like the one Jamie had just given her hand, or the trailing of fingertips on a shoulder as one of them passed the other. She loved their interactions, but the more time she spent with Jamie, the more she craved…well, *more*. It was a problem, and she knew in her heart that she couldn't stand still waiting any longer. She'd been careful not to step outside the friendship box Jamie had carefully drawn. She had wanted that move to come from Jamie. And yet it hadn't. She had to accept that it likely never would.

Regardless, she'd had a difficult day and needed to talk through her swirling thoughts with someone, and there was really no one better than Jamie.

"What's going on with you?" Jamie asked and popped a bite of bread. They'd chosen the little tapas place a few blocks up from the café because Jamie lived for their patatas bravas. "You're vacillating between breezy and haunted, and that's not normal."

She took a deep breath and thumbed her napkin. "The letter came back. The one I sent my father, and it's messed with my head."

Jamie's knife went still near the butter. She set it down. "Bastard." A pause. "Lay, I'm so sorry."

"I told myself under no circumstances would I let his response get to me. Now his lack of one has made me feel like I've been rejected all over again." She sat back in her chair and rolled her lips in, gazing on the back wall in refuge. "When I opened the mailbox and found that letter, the air left the room. I'd been punched and literally sat in the lobby of my building like a shell for half an hour." She took a sip of her iced water. "Sometimes I feel like such a loser. Why did I have to send that letter? I set myself up for this."

Jamie leaned in. "Because you're a person just like all the rest of us. You have every right to have feelings and thoughts and wants in regard to how other people treat you."

"Yeah, I guess so. I just have expectations for myself and who I let in. I should never have tried to open that door because now I feel like a nobody."

Jamie leaned to her right, interrupting Leighton's session with the wall. "Look at me and listen up." Leighton took a moment but shifted her focus begrudgingly. Facing Jamie while in the emotional trenches left her feeling exposed. She didn't like it. At the same time, it was Jamie, and she couldn't look away.

"In a sea of millions, you shine the brightest, okay? And you know that after all we've been through that I have trouble giving you that kind of credit, which means it has to be true. You're an amazing person."

Leighton blinked, surprised by the compliment.

Jamie wasn't done. "Everyone notices you when you walk through a door, and they want to get to know you even more after speaking to you for a few minutes. You leave an impact." The intensity with which Jamie said that last sentence resonated, because at one point she'd left a horrible one on Jamie.

"I didn't mean it that way," Jamie said, covering Leighton's hand. She clearly understood where Leighton's mind had drifted. "What I said is a compliment. It means you matter to people. Me included."

"You matter to me, too." She tried to smile, but the emotion forbade it. "And thank you."

"And that guy? Your father. We won't say *dad* because he's never been that. But what he doesn't realize is that he's dimmed his own life experience by leaving you out. He'll never know the light you bring, okay?" Jamie sat back in her chair, and Leighton couldn't take her eyes off her. The way she'd tossed her hair with such authority as if telling someone off in that perfect way everyone dreamed of. Her eyes blazed blue, and Leighton's skin lit up with tingles. She was something, this woman. The kindest spitfire you'd ever meet.

"I'm buying you dinner," Leighton said quietly. "Because that was a good speech."

"And tomorrow, too?"

"Don't push it, okay?"

"I could write another speech."

"We'll see."

Jamie had been the perfect person to turn to after the bad day she'd had. She always came with the right combination of insight, vim, and kindness. They spent the rest of the evening bouncing between topics, never an uncomfortable lull. The more time she spent with Jamie, the more she grew to love *them*. They were a good duo. Jamie brought Leighton's sillier side out in a way no one else ever had, with the exception of Courtney back in junior high.

"What are you laughing at now?" Jamie asked around her bite of truffle mac and cheese. She had every right to ask. Leighton had found Jamie's stories highly amusing that evening. Not that it was anything new. Her job put her in the path of some interesting individuals and exchanges.

"I'm thinking back to that guy talking on the phone through his AirPods and you thinking he was talking to you the whole time."

Jamie shook her head. "So apparently I wasn't the hottest chick he'd ever seen dance on a pole."

"There's always next time."

Jamie nodded. "Guess I have to practice more." She grasped an imaginary pole and flung her hair to the side, which was the best. More laughter. Jamie was going out of her way to cheer her up, and Leighton happily accepted the effort.

"There won't be poles, but there's one of those holiday street fairs in my neighborhood this weekend, if you want to swing around uptown."

"Rich people like the holidays, too?"

"I've heard rich people love any opportunity to throw money around, but I wouldn't know anything about that."

"*Pshh.* Not like you randomly bought a coffee and wine bar on a whim."

"Who does that?" They shared a laugh.

"So, if you're up for it, there's something I want to speak with you about. Just some thoughts that have been percolating. Little coffee analogy."

Leighton nodded. "Sure. I'm definitely up for it. What's going on?"

"Okay, let me figure out the right words." Was it just Leighton or did Jamie look nervous?

"Okay, this is getting weird." Leighton looked up to see Helen standing a few feet away in a green and white striped sweater dress, a Chanel bag on her arm.

Helen put both palms in the air. "I promise I'm not stalking you." She gestured to the woman next to her. "My sister and I were just grabbing a quick dinner."

Jamie's gaze moved from Helen to Leighton and back again.

"I guess we just have really great taste in restaurants," Leighton said and introduced herself to Helen's sister, whose name was apparently Tamara.

"And this is Jamie, right?" Helen said, filling in the gaps for everyone. "Jamie is Leighton's business partner."

"Yes, so good to see you again," Jamie said.

Tamara pointed at Leighton. "Is this the woman you're seeing?"

Helen's eyes went wide. "Sorry. She has no filter. We've gone out a few times. Yes."

"Not a problem at all," Leighton said. "Your sister's great," Leighton told Tamara. "And it's wonderful to meet you." She and Helen held eye contact for an extended moment. She really was a sweet person.

"I'll give you a call soon."

"I'd love it," Leighton said, feeling the warmth hit her cheeks. Was it awkward that Jamie had just witnessed that entire exchange? She quickly decided that it wasn't. Jamie was now a supportive friend who'd made her intentions crystal clear.

"I can't promise I won't see you at another restaurant first. You two enjoy your evening, and I need to come by and see the coffee-wine place soon."

"I'll save you a seat," Jamie said with a four fingered wave. As soon as Helen was out of earshot, Jamie leaned in. "I think the sister thinks the two of you are still dating."

Leighton stared in Helen's direction as she exited the restaurant. "We are. We went out a couple of nights ago, and it went really well."

Jamie's mouth formed the shape of an *oh* before her voice caught up and said the word. "I had no idea."

"I was planning to tell you, but the thing with the letter happened. Is it weird to talk about dating, given our past?"

"No, not at all."

"Good."

"Well, she's beautiful."

"She is."

"I get a warm vibe from her."

"I do as well."

"So, I vote yes."

Leighton nodded and sipped her water, wishing quietly that Jamie had expressed just the opposite. "You know what? I think it might turn into something, and I credit running into her after the ballet."

"Cheers to happy coincidences," Jamie said and touched her glass to Leighton's.

"Now can we get back to what you wanted to talk to me about?"

Jamie regarded the tablecloth for a moment before returning her gaze to Leighton's. "I wanted to know what you thought of adding sparkling wine to our lineup. You know, expanding our offerings."

"I love that idea. Gives people a choice for celebrations."

"Great. We're on the same page."

"Always," Leighton said.

As she lay in bed in search of sleep that night, Leighton played through the events of the day. The returned letter. She flipped onto her back. Telling Jamie about her date with Helen. Back onto her side. Jamie practically tossing her into Helen's arms. She threw the covers off her body and pulled them back on. Her green silk nightshirt felt like it was strangling her, so she tossed it onto the floor, opting to sleep in the nude. Maybe this was a sign she needed to pay attention to, the universe telling her to stop dwelling on the past with her future dangling right there in front of her.

Helen was nice and sweet and smart and attractive.

She also helped take her mind off Jamie Tolliver and all she couldn't have.

Chapter Eighteen

"Five, four, three, two, one! Happy New Year!" Leighton called, champagne glass in the air. She hugged Elise, who had invited her to the New Year's party, and waited for Jamie to finish her jumping-in-the-air hug with Clarissa before claiming one for herself.

"It's going to be a fantastic year," she whispered in Jamie's ear. "Just you wait."

"It already is," Jamie said back and kissed her cheek. "Two cafés, a new dog brother, and some really amazing friends. I'm blessed."

Leighton pulled back, thoughtful. "Me, too. But only one bar and no dog brother, but I got a new doorman who offers me chocolate when I get home, so I'm equally blessed."

"I keep waiting for my doorman to materialize. Pretty sure his name is Gerard and he has appeared in multiple cologne ads. He's going to report to work any day now."

Leighton laughed. "I will hope you get your New Year's wish."

Jamie fisted a handful of Leighton's sweater. "I knew I could count on you. Now, I need to go find a giant brownie and consume it without help."

It had been a fun evening at Elise and Jeremy's apartment. About twenty of them had gathered around in the living room as the time had neared midnight, keeping things to a decent sound level since their one-year-old was passed out in her crib down the hall. Leighton was three glasses in and feeling grateful for the year behind her, and hopeful for the one ahead. She'd been on a handful of dates with Helen, who was currently in London for a long-planned family vacation. She had Jamie, who made every day better, her job, which she'd been able to turn into a truly rewarding position, and Courtney, who offered her a family tether.

Jeremy arrived next to her as Jamie departed. It was nice to see the guy again. It had been a while since they'd gotten together. She remembered fondly how it had been his engagement party with Elise where she'd first encountered Jamie outside of the bar. She owed him for that. He stared at her. Hard.

"What is that look?"

He leaned in. "So, you and Jamie. Are you a thing?" he asked in a quiet voice.

"No. Why?"

"Just a vibe Elise picked up on. She said there's chemistry there and sent me on a mission to find out. It's part of being married. You get sent on missions. Yesterday, it was to find rosemary scented soap. A bar. Not the liquid form. Today, it's about the love lives of two of our party guests."

"Marriage is missions. Who knew?"

He shook his head and passed her a rueful look. "You have no idea."

"Good to know. I'll file that away." She touched her temple. "But I am seeing someone, and it's not Jamie."

"Whatever you tell me, I'm going to have to tell Elise." His eyes went wide with warning. "Gossip is her currency."

"Understood, and thank you for the heads-up. Elise is welcome to intel on my very mundane life."

He narrowed his gaze. "You're a Carrington. There's nothing boring about you to us. We chat about diaper counts and drooling bibs."

She laughed. "Got it. Well, her name is Helen, and this is our second time giving things a shot. A few dates in and so far, so good." She gave her phone a little shake. "She actually woke up early in London so she could send me a Happy New Year text."

"That's fucking romantic. Not a drool cloth mentioned." He smiled to let her know he was kidding. She was well aware of the fact that Jeremy loved his wife and daughter beyond all measure. His sense of humor, however, remained intact. She was glad for it.

"I want that, too, you know. The family. The middle of the night feedings. All of it."

He nodded. "I wasn't sure you did. You seem so happy."

She nodded. "I tend to do that. Everyone always thinks every-thing's wonderful in my world. That makes sense. It's what I put out."

"You should have been in PR like Elise."

They clinked glasses. "Missed opportunity."

"I see the snacks could use refilling, and my wife is shooting me a look with about seventy-five different meanings."

What Jeremy had alluded to tracked. She put on a brave face more often than she probably should. It was something she wanted to work on, however. She didn't have to seem okay all the time. In fact, in the coming year, Leighton wanted to make sure that she didn't sacrifice calm waters for authenticity. The next time someone asked how she was, maybe she'd just answer plainly, and say that she felt a little lonely these days, but things were looking up. She saw what Jeremy and Elise and millions just like them had and experienced a burst of envy. She wanted a partner and a family, people to come home to, a life bigger than the one she was currently leading. She stared across the room at a beautiful brunette in the midst of a conversation with her best friend, giant brownie in hand, and smothered the shot of longing that descended like clockwork. She smiled down at her phone, at the text message from Helen with the blowing-a-kiss emoji.

Life was waiting for her, and it was time she stopped dragging her feet. *I can't wait until you're home*, she typed back. *Hurry.*

❖

"Holy hell, I need help," Jamie called into the phone she had on speaker. She turned to the next customer in line. "Hi, I'll be right with you. We're having a bit of crisis, so I'm on a limited menu."

"Um, okay," the stern-looking woman said. She glanced at her watch, which made Jamie feel extra pressure. Not helpful.

"What's going on?" Leighton asked. She sounded concerned, but there was laughter in the background. Under the impatient gaze of the customer, Jamie clicked off speakerphone and stepped away from the register. More laughter. "Hold on a sec, okay?" Leighton said. What was happening on the other end of that line? Didn't matter. There were bigger fish. "I'm back. Tell me what's wrong."

"The water's been turned off at Too." Their shorthand for the second bar. "I called the maintenance man to turn it back on. He came right away, but there's apparently a lock on the meter. The management company didn't pay, and now I'm dead in the water, except there is none. No water, I mean. See? That saying doesn't even work!"

"*Okay*," Leighton said, dragging the word out. She was apparently following the trail for the larger implications.

Jamie could help speed up the process. "It means I can't make coffee. I can't do dishes. I don't have a restroom. I'm panicking. I think we have to close, and that's a lot of lost revenue."

Leighton didn't hesitate. "What did the office say when you called?"

"The receptionist laughed, said she was sorry I was having a bad day and that she'd pass on the message."

"No. That's not going to be good enough. You're going to document each and every potential lost sale as it compares with a similar day—pull an average number from last week. Then you're going to let the management company know that you'll need a rent credit in that amount and that you'll be keeping a tally of lost income until the moment the water is back on. That should light a fire."

Jamie blinked because it was the perfect response. "I would kiss you eight times if you were here right now." She heard the words and corrected. "All over your perfect uptown cheeks. Gotta go."

"Jamie, wait."

"Yeah?"

"Do you have a lot on your hands? I could help." It was Saturday, so Leighton wasn't at the office. It wasn't a bad offer. She had a sink full of dishes and a growing line of customers she was going to have to apologize to. They'd make as many drinks as they could for the existing line, sans water, and then close early. Having Leighton around would give them an extra pair of hands, and—let's be honest—also steady Jamie's ship.

"I mean, I would love help, if you're offering. A hundred times yes."

"Done. Let me throw on some clothes. See you soon."

It was thirty minutes later when Leighton, wearing a soft forest-green sweater, dark blue jeans, and tall brown boots arrived at the café. She loved winter Leighton and the way she put an outfit together. "Hi," Leighton said as she pushed through the glass door.

Jamie had two customers left to assist and was happy to see—

"I brought help."

From behind Leighton, Helen popped her head out. "Surprise!" She pulled off her gloves and rubbed her hands together. "Put me to work. I hear there are dishes."

Jamie's spirits plummeted for reasons she couldn't explain, but she forced herself into a wide smile anyway. "You're the nicest, but you don't have to do dishes. Can I have Ally make you a drink?" She smiled over at her part-timer, who was fast on the espresso machine but didn't say a whole lot.

"Absolutely not. I'm here to help, not take." Without waiting, Helen pulled her dark curls into a tieback and headed behind the counter. She grinned at Jamie. "You're gonna be really impressed with me. I'm a dish monster."

"If you're sure you're okay with—"

"I am," Helen said. "You've got more important things to handle."

Jamie turned back to Leighton, who was watching Helen with a hint of pride, and something about it made Jamie tense up all over. Not the time. She handed out complimentary bags of doughnuts to the three customers waiting on their drinks and the two still in line. She'd switched the sign from Open to Closed and gulped down some air.

All was under control. "We're gonna get the water back on and all of this sorted out," Leighton said, offering her a side hug. "Why don't you get started on the documentation of loss, and I'll help out here, speak to anyone who shows up wanting to know why we're closed."

"Yeah, that sounds great. I'm sorry that all I have are the jugs of water for you to work with. The maintenance guy was nice enough to have a bunch delivered."

Leighton shrugged. "Not a problem we can't handle."

Jamie exhaled slowly. Her thoughts had slowed down, and the adrenaline seemed to be receding. She excused herself to the small office in the back and composed a rough draft of an email. But Leighton was better at this sort of thing, so before sending it off, with laptop in hand, she headed back into the café for a second opinion. Maybe Leighton could give it a scan and make a suggestion or two. She paused, stopping in her tracks. Leighton and Helen stood in front of the back sink, very close together and speaking quietly, ridiculously happy smiles on their faces. She shouldn't be watching this private moment. Yet she couldn't seem to pull her gaze away. When Helen leaned in and brushed Leighton's lips with hers, Jamie felt sick. Her hands trembled, so she set the laptop on a nearby table and returned to her office where she closed her door, pressed her back against it, and took a few shaky breaths.

"Stop it," she whispered to herself with ferocity. She had zero right to have any kind of reaction to Leighton and Helen and their blossoming relationship. In fact, it was a wonderful thing. Leighton deserved to find her happiness. She whirled around and walked right back into the dining area of the bar, bright smile on her face. She would not be that person.

"You two are adorable," she said cheerfully and grabbed a dishrag to wipe down a table.

"You think?" Helen said, turning around, threading her fingers through Leighton's. Jamie briefly made eye contact with Leighton, who smiled back. *Just look at her. She's practically glowing.*

"Definitely, and it's really nice to see." She'd done well, but it wasn't a moment she could live in for too long. At least not yet. The longer Helen hung around, the easier this whole thing would get, right? It made sense. She'd never seen Leighton with a girlfriend before, so of course it would take some getting used to. She'd get there. She touched her chest absently in the spot it ached.

"Jamie, did you hear me?" Leighton asked.

She lifted her gaze. "Hmm?"

"You're clutching your chest. Are you okay? You're scaring me."

"I'm fine," she said. "Promise. I think I'm just gonna go send this email before I get distracted."

Leighton stared at her, perplexed. Worry creased her forehead.

Jamie laughed. "What? Why are you so serious over there? I'm perfectly fine." She touched her shoulder. "Just a really awful day is all."

"You were there for me when I had a bad day not too long ago. What can I do?"

Jamie gestured to Leighton, to Helen. "You're already doing it. You're the best, Lay. I mean it."

CHAPTER NINETEEN

L eighton had been up since two in the morning. She wasn't sure why. All was right with the world, and she should be sleeping like a baby. Helen had stayed over but would be getting up soon to teach a class at the School of Ballet. With her favorite tan silk robe around her, Leighton looked out at the city slowly waking, the pink and orange of the sun making their first appearance. She hugged herself at the warm glow emerging from behind a tall building in the distance.

Exhausted from very little sleep, but with a soft smile to greet the day, she turned back to the bed. Helen slept peacefully on her stomach, sheet pulled to her waist. Tranquil and calm. They were good together, she told herself. They laughed, got competitive when it came to the best method to pop popcorn, and never seemed to get on each other's nerves. She had an interesting job and a kind heart. Leighton was blessed. She didn't let herself examine the section of her heart that hadn't joined the party. She'd get there with a little time. But overall, she was happy, content, and very much looking forward to more. They usually stayed at her place, so her once cold and lonely apartment was now alive with banter in the morning and soft touches at night. She really could get used to this.

"Morning," Helen said, bleary-eyed. "Are you watching me sleep?"

Leighton let her crossed arms fall. She moved to the bed and sat alongside Helen. "Yes. You were saying the most wild stuff. A double agent in charge of celery auctions. Is there a secret life we should talk about?" Leighton asked with a stern expression.

Helen rolled onto her back with a soft laugh. "Celery auctions? You're creative this morning. Time?"

"A little after six."

"I gotta get going. Full schedule of classes. I have that thing tonight, too."

"What thing?"

"The donor thing. Did I not tell you?"

She watched Helen grab her overnight bag and head into the bathroom. Maybe they should talk about a drawer for her sometime soon. It seemed like a big step, but at the same time, it was spring, and they'd been dating several months. "No. I don't think you mentioned it."

"Logan Morrow's campaign. I'm on their donor list and guessing they want more."

Leighton went still. Took a moment to steady herself. "I didn't know you were into politics."

Helen came back in the room wearing one of Leighton's robes, the shower heating up behind her. "Social issues matter to me, and I want to see the right candidate in office." She shrugged. "Plus, there's an amazing amount of good champagne at those events. Who'd say no? Wanna come?"

Leighton didn't hesitate. "No. I need some downtime. Is that okay?"

"Of course. I'll take Audrey. I think she has the night off from that experimental piece with the strobe lights. I don't know how she doesn't come home with a headache."

She'd met Helen's best friend briefly. Bubbly and fun. Another dancer. Maybe Audrey would donate to Logan's campaign as well. She should say something. This was the perfect opening. With a nervous stomach, she turned. "Do you think we could talk about something kind of important?"

Helen's eyes went wide. "Now?" She glanced at the shower.

"I know. I can be quick, but it's going to bother me if I don't get it out."

"Tell me while I shower?" Helen didn't wait for a response and instead stepped inside beneath the water. Leighton closed her eyes, wishing Helen had given her a moment. Didn't matter. She'd learned her lesson about holding back information years ago and would not make the same mistake again. Ever.

"Here's the thing about Logan Morrow. He—"

"I did catch he has your same last name. Now my brain's in overdrive. Don't you dare tell me he's your long-lost relative." She added a laugh.

"No. He is."

Helen poked her head around the corner of the shower wall. "Stop. Are you kidding me?"

"He's my father."

Helen's eyes went wide. "Why in the world wouldn't you have said so? This is awesome."

"Not exactly. We don't speak. We've never had a relationship."

"I can't believe that. You're in the same city."

"I know." Leighton swallowed, uncomfortable, but knowing this was an important conversation. She hadn't planned on getting into Logan, but given the fundraiser, it was the right move.

"Come with me tonight. We can change the narrative." Helen popped back into the shower with an amazed look on her face. "I'm literally flabbergasted to hear that he's your dad. I mean, *Logan Morrow*. He's got a lot of great ideas about how to get this state back on track. I love his calm demeanor, as well. Never gets riled up when the other side stoops low."

Leighton blinked. Helen had skated past her feelings. She could tell it wasn't overt. In all honesty, she was probably still processing. But underneath it all, Leighton wished Helen had paid at least a little bit of attention to how this whole thing affected her. A contrast from the support she'd felt from Jamie.

"If it's okay with you, I think I'm still going to skip the fundraiser."

"I don't have to go either," Helen said. That was something, at least.

"You don't have to miss it on my account." Secretly, though, she hoped Helen would.

"Yeah? Because personal feelings aside, I think he can make a real difference. He's pushing some fantastic programs for the arts. We need him."

"Totally understand," Leighton said, swallowing the disappoint-ment. Helen was a good person who cared about her. She didn't need to let this difference in perspective affect their relationship. Politics mat-tered to Helen more than she'd anticipated, perhaps.

"Wait," Jamie said the next day when Leighton swung by Too after work. She'd stayed a little late for a West Coast meeting, which meant they were well into wine bar hours when she arrived. She scanned the space, amazed at the number of red wine and hot doughnut pairings. People were really taking to the combo, which she understood entirely as she bit into a warm cinnamon sugar. "What do you mean she went to the fundraising event? After you told her he was your absent asshole father, she still went?"

"She already had the invite and was so excited. I think her friend Audrey was going as well, so there was a social component."

"Did you tell her about the letter you wrote and how it came back? Or the way he treated your mom?"

"No."

Jamie paused mid-bottle open. "Leighton." Her voice was quiet. "This thing with Logan is a big deal for you, and she needs to honor that. Loyalty is a real and true thing." She poured the glass of merlot and delivered it to the waiting table by the window, brightening as she went.

Leighton watched her progress and the warmth that radiated off her as she interacted with the customer. Jamie had recently cut a couple of inches off her hair. It just brushed her shoulders now. Leighton loved the new look. Plus, she felt better after just talking to Jamie about the fundraiser scenario, which of course she knew would be the case. It always was. Jamie just seemed to understand so much about Leighton and what she needed. It was nice to feel truly seen by another person. "I hear you, and if the opportunity presents itself, I'll tell her how it made me feel," she said when Jamie returned.

"I want more than that for you. Do you want me to talk to her?" There was a fire behind those blue eyes. "I will have no problem explaining how her actions could affect you."

Leighton laughed. "No. Absolutely not. The day my friends have to communicate to my girlfriend on my behalf would be a sad one. I can do it."

"If you say so. I know Helen means well, but this was not cool."

"I'll handle it. You've given me the kick in the ass I needed."

Jamie nodded, the fire dimming. "Girlfriend, huh? I knew you two were official, but this is the first time I've heard you use the word. It's a big step."

She had to agree, but that's what Helen was. "I know. I haven't had an actual girlfriend in a long time. It feels really nice, aside from the hiccups, which I imagine are to be expected."

Jamie nodded. "You two are good together. I mean that."

"It's not weird for you, given our…" She trailed off on purpose and raised an exaggerated brow. "You know."

Jamie laughed. "Maybe for the first five minutes." She grabbed a rag and sprayed down the counters. "But now you're just Leighton and Helen. It looks good on you."

"Thank you. What about your love life? Anything on the horizon?"

She paused and looked up. "I have a date on Thursday."

Leighton finished her sip of wine. "Well, well." There was a time when that news would have slashed her in half. But she'd worked extra hard to head off romantic thoughts about Jamie and appreciated the other aspects of their relationship. "Who is this woman?"

"Another setup. Marjorie swears she's met the perfect woman for me, so she brought her into the bar, and it turns out she's really pretty and sweet. So, we're going to a Broadway play together. A comedy about a play going wrong."

Leighton gasped. "Jealous! I want to see that one."

Jamie winked. "I'll let you know if it's any good."

"Look at us. Such adults." Leighton raised her glass and took a sip.

"Right? Who'd have thought?" Jamie said with a shake of her head. A pause. "If this goes well, maybe we could all get together sometime. A double date."

"Hmm. Interesting idea." Leighton refused to let her mind imagine that scenario in its entirety, but she'd work on warming up to the idea. The mature thing to do. Plus, Jamie apparently thought it would be great to go on a double date. With other people. The implication hit with a dull thud. Jamie was so far over them it was ridiculous. Why was Leighton holding on to this tiny thread of hope? No more. She set her glass down on the counter and straightened. "Yeah, okay. I think we'd love that. Helen and I." Jamie's suggestion was the last little nudge

Leighton needed to let go once and for all. She'd give a hundred and fifty percent effort in her relationship with Helen. Whatever small part of her had been clinging to the hope that there was a one day for her and Jamie snapped in half. Nothing holding her back now.

"Well, let me get through Thursday night first."

"Not a problem," Leighton said, eyes on the window. She needed some air.

She felt Jamie's gaze on her. "You okay?"

"Never better."

Chapter Twenty

Jamie was fine. Everything was fine. The evening before, her mother left a voicemail that she missed Jamie's father more than she could stand, which led to a forty-minute cry-fest for the both of them. After that, she picked herself up and managed to go on a date with a very nice woman named Tegan, who had romantic potential, but who also probably saw her puffy eyes and clearly emotional demeanor as a red flag. And then, of course, Leo was sick this morning, and the part-timer they'd recently hired was apparently afraid of working near heat, so Jamie was riding the espresso machine train while still trying to run the place.

"I think it's the idea of steam near my face that bothers me," Brent told her through a squint. He came from California and his skater kid persona colored his speech.

"Yet you applied for a job as a barista?" she asked him as gently as she could.

"Sounded fun, bro, and like there might be free iced coffee." He nodded. "Emphasis on iced." He nodded again. "Should I just hand in my apron? I'm thinking best for all involved, bro."

"Yeah, bro, probably."

That left Jamie to cover the Chelsea bar on her own. Wasn't the first time and wouldn't be the last. It just meant she had to move fast and multitask like a squirrel preparing for winter. In between customers, a text from Leighton snagged her attention. *Time for lunch?*

She typed quickly in squirrel mode. *On my own in Chelsea so no time for anything.*

I have an easy day. Coming to you.

She couldn't smother the burst of energy that hit. Of course Leighton would come. She'd become Jamie's cheerleader. Her person. As she prepared a pumpkin chai latte, she reflected on the first day she'd seen Leighton in her line just a few feet away from where Jamie was standing now. She never would have imagined the ups and downs they would have ahead of them to wind up here. Her life had been changed forever that day. She wasn't the same person, which meant maybe all that heartbreak was worth it, given where they'd landed.

"Teach me the machine," Leighton said half an hour later, wearing a tan apron with a bottle of wine, a cup of coffee, and a doughnut on the front. Jamie had had them specially made for the staff. She'd never imagined them looking this good on any of them, however.

"You're wearing a business suit under that apron. I don't think this is the day."

"Yes, it is. I'm ready." She was adorable, was what she was, and it wasn't fair she was Helen's. Leighton lifted her heels, resulting in a small bouncing motion that made Jamie laugh.

"Fine." She came over to the drink station and stood next to Leighton. "We have to be quick because Dino Dan needs his dry cap."

"How did he get that name?" Leighton asked quietly. Dan was standing a few feet away, but their proximity to each other allowed the private conversation. It also made Jamie highly aware of Leighton's arm touching hers. *Here we go again.* Her body shot to attention. She'd had sex on the brain lately, and every fantasy starred Leighton.

"He has this green shirt with an outline of a brachiosaurus on the pocket. Well, at least he used to."

"One shirt and you're dino branded for life."

"I don't make the rules, Leighton."

"At least I'm not Bambi's Mother anymore."

Jamie paused. "How do you know you're not?"

"Less flirting, more coffee," Genevieve called playfully from behind her laptop.

"No! We're not—" Jamie rushed to explain, hooking a thumb at Leighton. "She has someone. A girlfriend. We're just having a lesson." Her cheeks were flaming. Fantastic.

Genevieve raised a brow. "Is that what they call it now? There's more steam over there than the steaming wand could ever provide."

"You behave," Leighton told Genevieve.

Genevieve gasped. "Admonished by Bambi's Mother."

"See?" Jamie said. "Still a thing."

What had started off as a difficult day had blossomed into a truly fun afternoon. After a proper lesson, Jamie even let Leighton make a few supervised drinks. To her credit, she was a fast study, biting her bottom lip in concentration, which Jamie found hard to look away from.

A lightbulb seemed to pop on over Leighton's head. "Hey, you didn't tell me about the date last night."

"Right. That." Marjorie was visiting her sister in Connecticut, which gave Jamie the leeway to speak freely without the report getting directly back to Tegan. "I like her. A lot. But I had a rough day before our date, which might have shown through. I wouldn't be surprised if she was put off by my red-rimmed eyes and lack of full focus."

"Uh-uh." She shook her head. "None of that matters. She'll get to see the real you next time."

"How do you know there'll be one? She might be done with me."

Leighton leaned back against the counter. "No one is turning down a second date with you, Jamie," she said quietly. "Trust me." She straightened and went immediately back to the drink station, leaving Jamie standing there with a comment that made her arms and legs feel like Jell-O.

"Thank you," she murmured, unsure whether anyone heard her. She turned and watched Leighton quietly wipe down the machine, just the way Jamie had taught her. Her heart squeezed, she closed her eyes, and right on cue that burst of longing that always accompanied thoughts of Leighton nearly toppled her. She gave her head a shake, changing the direction of her thoughts, purposefully running from the dead-end feelings. *Distract. Distract. Distract.* She reached for the waxed paper bags and went about packaging the newest batch of doughnuts.

Later that night, she sat on Clarissa's couch, letting the hectic day fall off her as her friend worked on her laptop, updating the monthly inventory for De Colores.

"*Aaand* done!" She set the laptop aside. "Did you kiss?"

Jamie popped her head up. "More specific."

"On your date, weirdo. I just finished work, and I'd love to be rewarded with a sexy detail about the best first date ever. Was it that?"

"Not quite. No kissing. There was Thai food and get-to-know-you conversation. I'd like to go out again, but the ball's in her court. My mom and I were crying over Dad just before, and it carried over. I was a scattered little mess."

Clarissa took her hand. "Grief never really fades for too long, does it?"

"No. It's the worst. I still wait for him to call and ask me over for his famous chicken noodle soup. It's strange." She shrugged, feeling the emotion well again. "Anyway. Tegan was great. She loves animals and wine. Two of my favorites."

"Right. Well, that's something." A pause. "And why haven't you just been honest with yourself about what else might be holding you back from giving the date your all?"

"I already told you what it was." Jamie sat up. "Where is this headed?" She narrowed her gaze.

"I think it might be time to admit there's a beautiful elephant in the room who you will never be able to let go of."

"Ah. This is a Leighton lecture. Again. Too many of these."

"Sure. Call it that. Even Tara said you two are amazing whenever she sees you together, and she's oblivious to spotting sparks."

"I heard that!" Tara yelled from their bedroom where she was lost in *Mario Kart*. "But it's true," she said, quieter this time.

"Thank you, mi amor," Clarissa called back. Her expression darkened. "Now back to you."

Jamie glanced at the bedroom door behind her. "Why does she get the sweet voice?"

"Because she's not the one I'm talking sense into."

"Is this the principal's office all of a sudden?"

"Yes, it is. If you want Tegan, by all means pursue her. But you'd be missing out."

Jamie closed her eyes. "Leighton's taken. I waited too long, and now I can't make waves in her life."

Clarissa squinted. "Maybe she'd want the waves. Maybe she'd run off with you if only she knew what you were feeling for her."

"It's too *much*. What if she chose Helen? What then?"

"Then you're no worse off. What if she chose you, Jamie? What if?"

"I can't do it." The idea of putting herself out there, declaring herself, in the midst of Leighton's bliss, sucked the air out of the room.

"I'd feel like I'm at the top of the tallest roller coaster imaginable, looking over the edge about to drop."

"And you don't like rides. You're the only person I know who goes to Coney Island for the food alone."

Jamie nodded. "Well, the corn dogs are superior."

"Jamiecita, what I'm hearing is you're afraid of putting yourself out there. It's an age-old problem. Sometimes you have to make yourself uncomfortable." A pause. "Or lead a mediocre little life. Which is better?"

"Mediocre," Jamie said without hesitation. "Marlene has sexy time on Thursday. She knows what to expect. I need the Marlene plan. How do I sign up for that?"

"You're on it already, my friend. Is that really what you want?"

Jamie hesitated. Because she wasn't being honest. She wanted it all. She craved butterflies and excitement and all the good things that came with being in love. In fact, she treasured those feelings. Wait. She blinked, turning over a realization in her mind. She nodded, raised her gaze to Clarissa, and exhaled. "I'm already in love with her, aren't I?"

Clarissa nodded. "For a while now, I think."

Jamie tore her gaze away, needing a moment. She focused on a watercolor painting on Clarissa's wall of a boat in choppy seas and sank into the comfort of the couch as this new realization washed over her one inch at a time. What was she supposed to do with this information? She was in love with a woman she'd pushed away blatantly, who was now in a relationship with someone else. Maybe even in love. Wasn't this wonderful?

"It was not wonderful," the voice-over said.

"Shut up," Jamie murmured. She sat up and faced Clarissa, refusing to be defeated. "Now what am I supposed to do?"

"Nothing. Not until you're ready."

❖

Leighton was close to sleep when Helen's arms went around her waist from behind. It had been a more serious night for them, but it had been worth it to go there, to open up and hash out what had happened with the fundraiser. She felt all the closer to Helen for it.

"I'm really sorry," Helen said again.

"I know, and I forgive you. You don't have to keep apologizing. Unless of course it gets me something amazing, like free pizza for a year." She put her arms on Helen's. "You heard what I had to say and truly listened." She gave Helen a squeeze. "It's all I could ask for."

"I'd take my donation right out of his hands if I could." The moonlight caught her eyes, and Leighton saw the sincerity. Helen was a good person. They didn't always see eye to eye right away, but she cared enough to try. That counted for a lot.

"No need." It had taken over a week, but earlier that night, she'd sat Helen down and explained to her how Logan Morrow had ignored her for her entire life. She'd not held back from Helen the way that had made her feel as a child, knowing one of her parents refused to acknowledge her, while he paraded his other children around for the whole world to see. She'd let Helen know how he'd treated her mom. How he'd not returned calls, even been cruel when she did get him on the phone. All of it, excluding only the letter she'd written and had returned. The rejection was too fresh, and she couldn't quite bring herself to share that detail with anyone. Well, except Jamie. That was different.

"Leighton, can I ask you a question?"

Leighton turned fully to face Helen, propping her head up on her hand. "Of course."

"Do you see a future with me?"

Silence. She did. She could. Helen checked the boxes. Things were easy with Helen. Their interactions were fun and simple. Who wouldn't want to be with her? A smart and pretty ballet dancer. "I do. Yes."

"Marry me."

"What? Helen." Leighton sat up in bed. "I can't tell if you're kidding."

"I am absolutely not kidding." Her dark eyes flashed with determination. "Listen to me. I'm thirty-two years old, and I know what I want. I don't need to spend a year dating you, kicking the tires, when you're right here in front of me. Leighton, you're gorgeous. You're successful. You make me smile, and when we walk in a room together, heads turn. I'm proud to be with you. Let's do this thing fully."

Leighton believed her, but it felt like a leap. They were surely skipping a few very important steps. At the same time, she wanted to settle down, didn't she? It's all she'd been hoping for. "Can I think about it?"

The wind seemed stolen from Helen's sails. "If you need to. Of course." Her voice sounded a touch higher in pitch. "Take as long as you need." She went back to her side of the bed, though, leaving Leighton wide awake and consumed with this new development.

The next morning, she hadn't been in her office more than five minutes before she called Jessica. "I don't know what you're doing, but I need a sounding board."

"You got it. Hang on just a sec." The connection went muffled. "Bentley, can you stall for a few? Take the client on a tour of the office. I'm back."

"Remember Helen the ballet dancer?"

"I do. You two still seeing each other?"

"She proposed."

The call went quiet. "I'm confused. Is this a hyperbolic version of a U-Haul moment?"

"I get the confusion. I was floored myself, but the more I think about it, the more it sounds like a really nice thing. I'm not a kid anymore. I don't need years to go by in this relationship before knowing what I want." She heard herself echoing the very sentiment Helen had expressed to her during the proposal, but the concept resonated. What were they waiting for?

Another pause. Jessica's skepticism was okay. In fact, it's why she'd chosen her to call. Courtney was a forever optimist who would unquestioningly support her in the name of love. Jessica, however, would tell her like it is. "I'm worried you're rushing into this in the very early stages. Are you sure that she's your person? The one person put on this Earth that fits with you more than any other person? Because that's what Brooklyn is to me. I had zero doubts."

"You sound like one of those rom-com couples come to life. I don't think your relationship is a realistic goal for the rest of us."

"Well, it should be," Jessica said flat out. "Anything less is settling, and that's sad. You've never been the type who shied away from putting in the work, doing things the right way. Why are you settling?"

"You think I'm settling." A kernel of indignation sneaked in and coated the sentence. *Don't get defensive.* A deep breath helped.

"Well. Are you head over heels in love?"

Oh, really? Jessica was bringing out the big guns now. What was love anyway? A subjective feeling people assigned based on their own set of standards.

"I could get there."

"Not good enough. You asked for my opinion, and I'm giving it, despite how angry I might be making you. In fact, yes, get angry at me. I can take it. What does Jamie think?"

"Jamie? I haven't asked her yet."

"You two have been inseparable this past year. I thought she'd be your first stop."

Leighton tried to assemble an answer that would make sense to both of them. "I just trust your wisdom and wanted your take sooner rather than later." She nodded, turning over all Jessica had said. "You've given me lots to think about."

"Good. And, Lay? I'll be happy for you no matter what you decide. Know that."

"I do. Bye, Jess. And thank you. Hi to Brooks for me."

When she clicked off the call, Leighton's stomach dropped. She'd lost some of her momentum and understood that she'd have some soul-searching to do before arriving at an answer to Helen's very important question.

Strangely, the day played on like any other day. Meetings, calls, and schmoozing on behalf of Carrington's. Didn't the universe know that her future hung in the balance? As she packed up for the day, her phone buzzed with an incoming call. Helen.

She slid on. "Leighton Morrow. Exhausted human."

"Ran into Jamie and she tossed out the idea of dinner tonight. She's dating someone and thought we'd want to come. A double. Yes?" That was the thing about Helen and the phone. She didn't hesitate before launching in and unloading everything that was happening in her orbit. Leighton kinda wished they'd take a minute with each other. Regardless, she replayed the ambush of information. Jamie. A double date. She closed her eyes. She couldn't think straight. "Sure, whatever you want."

"Thought you'd say that, which is why I already said yes. Ruffiano's at seven. It's near Too, and I'm told they have amazing bread service."

"Our first double date." Her stomach flip-flopped. It would be fine, though. A chance for both her and Jamie to grow in this new capacity of having partners. Very mature of them, if she did say so herself.

"Let's meet there," Helen said. "I want to swing by a sample sale on the Upper East Side first. I know the designer, and they're pulling some strings to get me in early." Helen had a tendency to collect important people. Seek them out. It wasn't a flaw. Just something to note. Distantly, Leighton wondered if she was, in a small way, a showpiece for Helen, who often wanted to bring people up to the apartment to show off the view. Let them know Leighton was actually a Carrington. It was wrong of Leighton to suspect such a thing. Helen was awesome. End of story.

"What is wrong with you?" she murmured and checked the clock. She'd have just enough time to swing by the apartment for something a little more casual for dinner. And it would be a great dinner. It was Jamie, after all, and they'd laugh and eat and likely have the absolute best time ever. Nothing to stress about.

CHAPTER TWENTY-ONE

Ruffiano's was known for the best handmade pasta in the neighborhood. It was also an adorable little place just outside the theater district, with about twelve tables with white tablecloths, a small bar, and aromas from the kitchen that could send a girl to church. Jamie used all of these details to distract her from the awkward feelings that descended on her the minute she arrived with Tegan to find Leighton seated at the table alone, a customary glass of red wine in front of her. She waved as they approached and blossomed into a beautiful smile that took over the room. Jamie felt the blush infuse her face.

She swallowed and smiled over at Tegan, giving her hand a squeeze. This was their fourth date, and things between them were progressing at an appropriate pace. Two good night kisses, one a little longer than the other. They'd passed a handful of texts between dates. Friendly and flirty in the right combination. Tegan was proving to be a really nice woman.

But she wasn't Leighton.

Underneath it all, Jamie knew that was the headline in her heart. And it was a problem.

With every day that passed, it became more and more apparent to Jamie that no one would ever be Leighton. Instead, whoever she was with would live forever in the shadow of the woman Jamie had, somewhere along the way, fallen in love with. She had to find a way to get her feelings in order and on the shelf. Leighton was happy with Helen, and Jamie had been offered every opportunity to tell Leighton how she felt. That ship had sailed.

"I hope you don't mind that I started early." Leighton gestured to the wine and stood as they approached. She focused on Tegan first. "Hi. Leighton Morrow. Really nice to meet you. Jamie says great things."

Tegan accepted Leighton's hand and gave it a hearty shake. Points for enthusiasm. She had her dark hair pulled back in a low ponytail and wore a green military jacket with black jeans and a braided bracelet. "Tegan Murphy. I've heard all about you, too."

Leighton looked down at their hands with wide eyes. "You have a good grip, Tegan Murphy. Impressive." She shifted her focus and softened. Jamie's heart squeezed at the change. *Dammit.* "Hi, Jamie," she said, leaned in, and kissed her cheek. "You look great." The soft scent of her lotion enveloped Jamie and whisked her to memories far tucked away.

"Hi. You, too." Leighton wore a red jersey dress, both chic and soft. "I'm happy we're doing this," Jamie said. "Helen's coming, right?"

"Yes, but you see, there was a sample sale that led to some sort of private reception, and Helen has trouble saying no to those."

Helen was sure dialed into the elite New York social scene. Jamie had seen as much for herself. Helen chased parties and always glowed when she scored an invitation. Quite the contrast to Leighton, who was happy at home with good company. Maybe Helen brought out her extrovert side. Quietly, Jamie wasn't sure she liked anyone changing Leighton. "Well, if she can't make it, we'll have to do this again," Tegan said. Jamie smiled at her.

"Tegan, are you a big fan of wine and coffee?"

Tegan laughed and leaned to the side. "I do enjoy a good glass of wine, but coffee is kind of my least favorite beverage." She passed Jamie a look. "I've already let Jamie know, so she can ignore my calls if she chooses."

"It is her life's work," Leighton said with an added wince.

Hmm. Defensiveness flared and Jamie patted Tegan's hand. "We forgive them for what they don't know they're missing out on, right?"

"If you say so." Leighton sipped her wine. That comment was not like her. Jamie let it go, and they spent the next few moments perusing the menu and hearing about the specials from their server, Aldo.

"What about a bottle of pinot grigio?" Tegan asked, eyes on the menu.

"Jamie likes merlot," Leighton said evenly.

"Oh." Tegan's gaze shot up. "We can certainly have merlot."

"Actually, I'd prefer white tonight," Jamie said, her eyes never leaving Leighton's. She tried to shoot daggers. She wasn't sure if it was working. What was Leighton trying to do with these subtle comments? Why did she have to wear that jersey dress that showed off her amazing arms?

"Great. Pinot grigio it is." Tegan looked from Jamie to Leighton. "Leighton, you're welcome to join us."

"I'm good. I'll stick with red," Leighton said with an overly friendly smile. She then looked to Jamie as if to say *See, I can be super nice.*

"This woman and her red. Inseparable," Helen said, coming up behind Leighton and placing a hand on each shoulder. "Hi, Baby Bear." Leighton smiled up at Helen and accepted a kiss on the lips. *Splendid.* This whole thing was turning out to be just a fantastic idea. Jamie could tell by the way her stomach turned uncomfortably. She forced herself to beam at the happy couple, well aware of Tegan's puzzled look as she watched Jamie's profile. Maybe Jamie was beaming too brightly. She adjusted to medium-beam, as Helen with her dark curls, dancer body, and beautiful eyelashes slid into the chair across from her. "Hello there, you two. Glad we're doing this." She and Tegan exchanged introductions, wine arrived, and they were off and rolling.

"So this sneak peek of Hyland Wade's new season was beyond. Fantastic sample sale, too. Hyland is a gem." Helen declined the bread that Leighton offered. "Too many carbs." Back to Jamie. "Do you know him?"

"Hyland? No. I don't know *Hyland,*" Jamie said, exaggerating his name. How many sips of wine had she consumed? She glanced at her glass. It irked her to a level that it shouldn't have that Helen was dropping names after two minutes at their table. It honestly was a mild offense.

"Oh," Helen said quieter. "That's okay. It was a nice afternoon, though." Jamie saw Leighton cover her hand and give it a squeeze.

Then Leighton refocused. "So, Jamie, how's your mom?"

She dabbed her mouth with her napkin. "She's thinking of taking up knitting because that's what she hears retired people do. She wants to donate little knitted creatures to the hospital, so I've set her up with Genevieve."

"I knit," Tegan said, which was surprising because Jamie never would have imagined that. She didn't seem the type. Though knitting *was* making a fairly large cultural comeback. The cool kids knitted these days. She'd seen it firsthand in both cafés. "I'd be happy to lend a hand in teaching her."

"Oh, are you to that point yet?" Leighton asked. "Meeting the parents is pretty serious."

"I think my mom would love to meet Tegan." She turned to Tegan. "She's a fantastic cook. I have a feeling you'd love her chicken noodle soup. It was my dad's recipe."

Leighton folded her arms. "I can vouch. She's made me a take-home batch."

Jamie flicked an annoyed gaze to Leighton. "It's true."

"She sounds great," Helen said. She turned to Leighton. "I wish I'd gotten to meet your mom."

"But you got to meet her dad, though, didn't you?" Jamie took a bite of bread. Warm and amazing.

Helen swiveled to Jamie in surprise and then back to Leighton. The look of betrayal that crossed her features spoke volumes. She clearly wasn't aware that Leighton had confided in Jamie about the fundraiser debacle. Leighton then turned to Jamie with a *look*. Icicles prickled Jamie's veins.

"Yes. I'd known him from before. Of him."

"Right. Of course," Jamie said. Another sip of wine. She should have left it there but couldn't seem to. "But I thought she'd told you about him before the fundraiser. Unless I have that backward. Ignore me."

"Yeah," Leighton said flatly. "Let's do that."

"Are we ready to order?" Aldo asked. No one answered for a moment.

"I'll take the lasagna special," Tegan said.

Jamie nodded. "Me, too."

"And I have a headache that I can't shake. I think we'll just take the check," Leighton said, checking in with Helen who nodded that was okay. "Please forgive me," she said specifically to Tegan, leaving Jamie out of the conversation pointedly.

"Not a problem at all," Tegan rushed to say. "Maybe another time."

"I'd love it."

"I'll take care of the bill," Jamie said.

"Wonderful. Then we'll sneak away," Leighton said, still not looking Jamie in the eye.

Well, this certainly hadn't gone well. Shell-shocked and horrified at her own behavior, Jamie tried to rally, but found herself flailing.

Once they were alone, she turned to Tegan. "I'm so sorry about all that."

"It's really okay. But can I ask you a question?"

"Anything."

"How long ago did the two of you date?"

Jamie hooked a thumb to the door. "Leighton and I? We've not really…"

"Okay. Then when did you fall in love with her?"

Jamie, stunned, opened her mouth and found no words. She closed it again. "I'm sorry. I'm still figuring all this out myself."

Tegan shrugged. "It's truly okay. I like you a lot, but I think you have enough on your plate with that little situation. So my proposal is that we eat this amazing food, enjoy the company, and maybe you'll call me again if the circumstances change."

Jamie deflated. She'd wanted things to work out with Tegan, had carried such hope, imagining that the swirling feelings for Leighton would dissolve over time. Tonight made her feel differently. Maybe she'd been naive to think she could handle something this big by simply not addressing it. She'd never been in love before, not in this true a fashion. "I completely understand." She met Tegan's green eyes. "I want you to know that I didn't see this coming, or I wouldn't have agreed to you and me…"

"I get it. But now you have to figure out what you're going to do because she's taken."

"Right. So I'm going to respect that."

"There's only one problem."

"And what's that?" Jamie asked.

"She's just as in love with you."

Everything in the restaurant seemed to go quiet and still. Jamie's attention hyperfocused on one thing and one thing only. Leighton's feelings for her might not be dead after all. She'd seen the jealous behavior firsthand, and apparently, so had Tegan. Maybe it meant there was still something there. Then real life hit. "Do you really think I'd have any kind of shot against beautiful dancer Helen?"

Tegan looked at the door and back to Jamie. "Um, I know you do."

Jamie nodded, trying to absorb, organize, and find her courage. If she was going to do this thing right, she couldn't hold back. That meant she had to be entirely honest with Leighton, putting everything on the line and opening up. That left her vulnerable…and scared as hell.

❖

It started to rain on the drive home from the restaurant. Through the streaked window of the cab, Leighton watched the city fly by as her feelings swarmed and tangled. The dinner had been a catastrophe and made her want to run screaming. She chalked it up to stress around work and the proposal and the conversation with Jessica all sneaking up on her in a thorny jumble. But the whole experience had done one thing for her. It had given her the extra shove she needed to take the leap. What was she waiting for?

She leaned her cheek against the seat and sent Helen a smile. "Remember the question you asked me?"

"Of course I do."

She took a pause and threaded their fingers. "The answer is yes."

Helen sat up straight. "Are you sure?"

Leighton nodded. "Let's do it. And the sooner the better. I'm more than ready."

"I wonder if we can get *Out Magazine* to cover the ceremony," Helen said automatically. "I'm going to call my friend Mark and see if he can make the connection." She took out her phone and immediately started texting.

Leighton celebrated quietly on her own. This was exciting. A whole new chapter to look forward to. She had to tell Courtney. She needed to update Jessica. Maybe tomorrow. Today was for basking, right?

Helen tapped her knee. "You can call Jamie if you want. She's probably still at the restaurant. They can toast us!"

"I'll get around to that. I just want to enjoy this moment with you."

Helen's phone buzzed. "Mark, I'm engaged and need you." She laughed. "No, her name is Leighton Morrow, and she's everything. You're gonna love her. She's also a Carrington, so *Out Magazine* might want in on this."

Leighton focused on the mellow music in the cab, the romance of the rain falling on the city just beyond the window, and completely shut out every other feeling screaming to her from the depths. This was the right decision for her. It would be. Now was the time to be happy.

CHAPTER TWENTY-TWO

Jamie's week had been weird. She hadn't been able to find her groove, and bouncing between bars, a practice that normally had her energized, had instead left her feeling unsettled and off—almost as if she'd left a stove on somewhere but couldn't quite remember where.

"You seem like you're in a fog and trying to fight your way out."

Jamie blinked. "Thanks, Marvin." She quirked her head at him sitting in his traditional left corner of the room, only it was the wrong room. "Hey! What are you doing in Hell's Kitchen? You're a Chelsea regular." Tom and Aurora, two of her Hell's Kitchen regulars, looked over at him with suspicion. An infiltrator.

Marvin shrugged. "There are times in life when you have to step out of your comfort zone. So here I am." He adjusted his bow tie. "Sowing my wild oats."

Well, if that wasn't the perfect parallel to her own life right now. She'd waited for several days for Leighton to come into the store. Her nerves danced each time she thought it might happen. She'd gone over the words she wanted to impart, heartfelt and honest. Her hope was that they could steal away someplace quiet. Maybe have a glass of merlot on the couch in the next room, even after the bar closed if Leighton was up for it. It didn't matter what her response was—Jamie had to at least be forthcoming about her feelings.

But Leighton hadn't come by.

When Jamie inquired about her absence lately, she received a short text about work being killer. But somehow, Marvin's arrival in a new spot served as an arrow sign blinking brightly. It meant that she was on the right path, pushing herself to walk out onto the most terrifying ledge in the name of something bigger than just herself: love.

It was close to seven when Leighton arrived at the bar, and Jamie was glad she'd stuck around a little later than usual. Leighton's hair was down, and the windy day had left it looking like it had been blown out at a salon. Hers would never. "You're here," Jamie said, sending her a nervous grin. Her heart thrummed loud and fast. They'd not seen each other since the dinner from hell, and she wondered if Leighton would still be upset with her.

"I'm sorry. My schedule has been so weird."

"Totally okay." Jamie moved behind the bar. "What can I make you?"

"You don't have to. I can make—"

"I want to."

A pause. "Okay, ma'am. Your finest red."

Jamie nodded. "I have a new one. Bourbon-barrel aged. Are you up for it?" She watched Leighton's face, the way her features came together when she took in information. Her brows slightly raised in interest. Her lips softly pursed. Jamie's stomach dipped. She wanted to take that face in her hands and—

"Now we're talking."

She blinked herself back into the flow of reality. "Do you want to sit?" Jamie gestured to the next room. The lighting was dimmer, and the couches made things feel less formal, perfect for a more intimate conversation. She was nervous now. Her mouth was dry and her palms tingled. Ignoring all that, she focused on the one person that mattered, Leighton.

"Lead the way."

Jamie did, taking her spot on the comfy gray couch that seemed to be everyone's favorite. Leighton had helped pick it out one afternoon after they'd grabbed a quick sushi lunch. The sun had been shining brightly, making Leighton's skin glow and her eyes sparkle. Jamie had known in that moment that they were special, so why had she waited? Fear. The same fear that practically toppled her in this moment and nearly made her lose her courage. "I'll start. I didn't like how things went at our dinner with Tegan and Helen. I'm sorry."

"I'm sure the wine didn't help. But it was every bit as much me at fault as you. I apologize, too."

"Something just took over, and I'm not proud of some of the comments I made."

"I'm sure it was simply echoes from our history, right? The last gasps." Leighton looked off into the distance, seemingly searching for the right words. "We're unique. We're important to each other, right?"

"Yes, we are. On that note…" A flare of nerves struck and Jamie's hand shook. "Just need a minute." She reached forward to set her glass of wine on the coffee table in front of them.

"Because you're important to me," Leighton said, filling the silence, "I wanted to come here today and tell you that I'm getting married."

Jamie's body stiffened, she missed the surface of the table, and the glass went over, sloshing wine onto the floor. The glass rolled on its side, and Leighton caught it just before it hit the floor. The whole scene played out in horrifying slow-motion because the words were too awful to absorb in real time.

"What did you say?" Jamie asked. She didn't make a move for a towel. She couldn't even acknowledge the spill because her heart was in a vise, and she wasn't sure what to say or do. The edges of the world faded around her, and she wanted to scream.

"I know it sounds sudden, but Helen asked and I said yes. I'm actually really happy about it. Do you want me to get something for the—"

"Congratulations," was the word that flew from her lips before she could process. That's what people said, right? She was trying to be a normal human, but her world had just been flipped upside down like the flying pieces of a board game. She wanted to shout *No. Wait. Not yet. Please.* But none of those words seemed okay any longer. Had she really missed her window by five seconds?

"Are you surprised? You look it."

"Yes and no," Jamie said, coming to her senses and moving quickly back to the counter for a couple of towels for the spill. "Back in just a sec."

"I know it might seem kind of sudden."

"Only a little." She dropped to her knees and went to work. Wiping up that wine felt like the clearing away of all she'd hoped for as tears sprang into her eyes. She blinked quickly, focusing on the task for longer than she needed to so Leighton wouldn't spot the emotion. "You both seem really happy. I'm happy, too. For you and her." *Deep breath*. She dashed back to the main room, behind the counter, and stood a moment, gathering as much air as possible and scrambling to think of anything else. She needed to silence her emotion and rise to this occasion. Goofy, silly puppies. Clarissa making ridiculous faces. Her regulars talking so loud in the café she had to ask them to hold it down.

"You need any help?" Leighton asked.

"No. All good." She turned around, mustering a smile she prayed looked authentic. "So, who proposed? Did you say that part already?" Her brain wasn't working. And did she honestly want these details? No, but too late now.

"Helen asked me, and a few days ago I said yes."

"Perfect. Was it over dinner? A ring in a champagne flute?" She put her hands on the back of her hips because she suddenly didn't know what to do with them.

"We're pretty informal. No." A long pause. That was weird.

"Do you not want to tell me?"

"We were actually in my room."

A horrible sinking feeling hit. "In bed. She proposed in bed. I see." It wasn't until this very moment that Jamie realized she'd never once thought of them having any kind of sexual relationship, which made sense when you applied the whole self-preservation method.

Leighton laughed. "Yeah, I probably should come up with a more public-friendly story. Not one I plan to pass around at the office."

"Right?" Jamie joined her in laughter, but everything about it, the sound, the echo, the force, came off hollow. She flashed on what it felt like to be held in those arms, to lie on top of Leighton, feel her body beneath, and look down into those soulful brown eyes. "So, are you thinking later this year? Next?" She'd have to sit through a ceremony, watch a first dance, and then witness the life they'd lead together, Leighton and Helen, happily ever after. All her own fault. All of it. It was a pill she'd have to learn to swallow.

"Neither of us want to wait. So it'll be soon. Helen is working on choosing a date with *Out Magazine*. They're interested in covering the event, so we're apparently working around their schedule."

Jamie raised a brow. "But it's your wedding. Lay." Jamie quirked her head, setting her own feelings aside and thinking about Leighton's. Defenses flared.

"I feel the same way, and couldn't care less about a magazine, but it's important to Helen, so…It's what we do."

"Right. Yeah. I get it." She shifted her weight as silence covered everything. "A married woman," she said quietly, wistfully. "Surreal."

Leighton didn't speak for a moment. "It is. I just wanted to make sure to tell you personally."

Jamie nodded, gutted, imagining what this moment was supposed to be. Her important confession died with Leighton's announcement, and now it would be hers and hers alone forever and always. "I'm glad you did."

The universe felt weird. They did, and there would be no fix this time. Their easy back-and-forth had vanished. Leighton had half a glass of wine left and practically gulped it down. "I should probably get home, check in with Helen about the plans. She has a premiere to attend for…something. I can't keep track."

Jamie nodded. "Have a nice night, Leighton," she said softly. "Enjoy this time." She actually meant it. Her heart was broken, and she was battling a massive army of self-recrimination, but none of that took away from the fact that she wanted Leighton to have everything she ever wanted.

Leighton stood in the doorway, glass door ajar, and sent Jamie a great big smile. "Right? You know what? I really think I'm gonna. Love you. See you soon."

Jamie held up a hand and waved good-bye to Leighton Morrow in more ways than one. She went through the motions for another hour at the bar, simply because she needed the distraction. Dishes. Took stock of supplies. Poured wine. Smiled. And repeat. She handed off closing to Ally, who'd done a lot to impress her already.

"Have a good night, Jamie. I got this."

"That's why I'm keeping you."

She stood outside the bar, looking up at the Bordeauxnuts sign, lit up now, a beacon to those in the area, and remembered the path that led here. Leighton arriving at her register years ago. Their time together. The betrayal. The run-in at the night club. The committee meetings. The business deal. The friendship. All of it swirled in a jumble like a cyclone raging around her.

Her heart was heavy when she hopped the A train, placed her earbuds in her ears, and lost herself in a haze of music and memories.

Tomorrow, she would find a way to pick herself back up and put one foot in front of the other, but for tonight, she let her emotions drown her, tears streaking her cheeks as strangers passed her curious stares across the train. Aching and not caring, she gripped her bag and kept her eyes down for the rest of the ride.

❖

There were moments that stood out in Leighton's memory, rising above all others in their importance. The wine tumbling, spilling all over the floor, the moment she told Jamie she was marrying Helen had now become one of them. She could remember every detail with acute precision. The temperature of the room and the way Jamie had been looking away from her just before the words left her lips. Maybe that's why she'd said it just then, the tactic of a coward. In retrospect, the moment now felt like a metaphor, a period at the end of a sentence. Theirs. The empty glass. The mess. No putting the wine back in.

"What are you thinking about over there?" Helen asked from across the table. They'd decided to treat themselves to brunch before meeting with the wedding planner. Helen hadn't done much but move her stuffed French toast around the plate. Why was she so off today?

"Oh." She gestured to her head and smiled, rejoining the moment. "Just how much we have to do over the next four weeks." They'd scheduled the wedding—along with all the interested parties—for just over a month away, which at first had seemed very doable in Leighton's mind. She imagined a simple ceremony, elegant and beautiful. It was not to be. The event Helen was pulling together required so much more work. The guest list was huge, the concepts more grandiose. There were apparently decisions to be made hourly, from the tiny flowers in the bouquets that no one would even really see down to which fork style they wanted for dessert at the reception. In many ways, it felt like she and Helen were just secondary characters and the event itself had taken over the narrative. She swallowed the sentiment and smiled instead.

"Susan-Jane has it all under control, don't you worry. Megan says she's the best and we have nothing to worry about." Helen's cousin Megan was a highly esteemed event planner herself in Texas and was thrilled to recommend someone in New York who would do a stellar job for them. Susan-Jane didn't disappoint. She was organized, friendly, and terrifying in how aggressively she was putting this thing together. She was a wedding drill sergeant on a mission to plan.

Later that morning, she tapped a photo of Helen's sister on the oversized screen on the wall that mirrored her laptop's display. "Tamara. Stunning. Am I right?" A pause. "Are we sure we want her in peach? What about this shade?" Susan-Jane produced another photo of what looked to be the same color. Leighton blinked.

"Isn't that peach?"

"Peach colored," Susan-Jane said with a nod.

"Peach colored," Helen said at nearly the same time.

Leighton went with it, accepting her color shortcomings. Who knew? "Right. Okay. Go ahead."

Helen scooted to the edge of her chair listening intently. Susan-Jane pressed on, using a long black pointer to showcase her example up on the screen. "It's a tad more vibrant but with your sister's dark hair, she'll radiate."

"I see your point," Helen said. "Well, that's what I want. Total radiation on my wedding day." She looked to Leighton, who sat up straight.

"Always a fan of radiating. Yes." In all honesty, any dress would be fine. Any venue. Any song. Wasn't this more about them and making sure the day was a fantastic one, full of love and fun and memories? Peach was peach.

But the rest of the day was much like that, and by midafternoon, Leighton caught herself checking her phone every few minutes, wondering why she hadn't heard from Jamie in a couple of days. Normally, they texted back and forth throughout the day, and the silence had her scratching her head. Was Jamie still hung up on the dinner-gone-wrong? She seemed a little off the other night at Too when she'd spilled the wine. The more Leighton thought about it, the more she couldn't stop. The wheels on the rest of their day turned at an excruciatingly slow pace, and at the end of it, Leighton needed answers.

"I haven't heard from Jamie in a while," she said to Helen on the stoop in front of Susan-Jane's suite of offices. "I want to swing by and make sure she's okay. Is that all right?"

"Totally fine. I'm gonna meet Audrey and Natalie for drinks, in that case."

"Have the best time."

"Tell Jamie I said hello. And the girlfriend, too, if she's there." Helen headed off in one direction and Leighton in the other.

Maybe that was it. Leighton paused on the sidewalk. It was possible Jamie was so caught up in her new relationship that she simply had to hit pause on the other aspects of her life, including Leighton. She hated the thought but also knew that she had to be mature about the situation. Jamie was entitled to have her own happily ever after, and Leighton would support her no matter how it made her feel, which was, quite honestly, confused.

Instead of texting and waiting the few hours it had been taking Jamie to get back to her these days, she went straight to her place. She wouldn't be working late on Saturday most likely, as she'd been handing off more weekend responsibility to her staff. When she landed in front of Jamie's building, she smiled when she saw Jamie's mother, Sama, descend the steps.

"Leighton. Have you seen the weather report?"

She blinked, searching her brain. "I haven't."

"It's scheduled to rain soon. Would you like my umbrella?"

Sama extended the only umbrella she carried, ready to hand it over and face the rain unarmed. The kindness and thoughtfulness spoke volumes. This was the woman who had raised Jamie, made her into the ray of sunshine that she was. It struck her then just how selfless their whole family was. "No, no. I'll be just fine. You hold on to that." She glanced behind her. "Would you like me to grab you a cab?"

Sama held up her phone. "I've got a car on the way. One of those Ubers. Jamie showed me how to summon them. It's quite magical."

"I've always thought so."

She gave Leighton's wrist a squeeze on the way down the steps. "Let's have wine at the second little bar soon."

She grinned. Everyone had their own nickname for Bordeauxnuts Too. She liked it that way. "I'd love it."

"And Leighton?"

"Yes?" She looked down the stairs to Sama, whose forehead was now creased in concern.

Her demeanor had shifted. She took a moment to formulate the right words. "She's not herself. Maybe you can help."

Leighton looked up at the building with a pit in her stomach. That didn't sound good. "I'll see what I can do."

She knocked on the door only to have Jamie swing it open almost immediately. "Did you forget some—" The words died when she saw Leighton standing there. Her head tilted. "Hi."

"Hi. Where have you been?"

Jamie squinted. "Um, here. Work. Then other work. Then here again." She touched her forehead, brushing away a strand of hair. Hers was up today and she wore a slightly oversized pair of pale blue sweats that made her look cuddly and adorable. "I'm confused by the question."

Leighton swallowed. "I haven't heard from you, which is out of the ordinary these days." What was also weird was the way Jamie was blocking the doorway with her body as if choosing to keep Leighton in the hallway, at a distance. She didn't like it. Where had their informality gone? Why couldn't they just be *them*? "Can I come in?"

Jamie looked behind. She was *deciding*? Something was definitely going on, and the best thing she could be to Jamie, this woman who mattered so much to her, was a friend. "Sure. Come on in."

She followed Jamie inside, but the vibe between them didn't change. Jamie was unusually quiet, her usual words of welcome followed by snack peddling also oddly absent.

Leighton decided to take the reins. "I miss you, and I'm worried about you. There."

There was a hint of a soften behind Jamie's eyes. "I miss you, too. But I promise, nothing to worry about. I just needed some time for me. To get a handle on all the new changes."

Leighton searched for meaning, absently clicking a pen she found on the counter. "What changes? The new bar?"

"Sure. I bet that stress is part of it."

She stared Jamie in the face and saw right through the white lie. "Jamie." With hands on the back of her hips, Jamie looked at her fully, the first time since she'd arrived. The look on her face spoke volumes and everything in Leighton trembled. With that look, she knew. "This is about the engagement. This is about me."

For a long stretch of time, Jamie didn't say anything, and Leighton waited, afraid to move. Finally, Jamie nodded, tears touching her eyes.

The world tilted. Disorientation descended, while Leighton gave her head a shake. This wasn't fair. Leighton was happy. For the first time in a long while, she had something to look forward to, and for Jamie to step in now, for Jamie to—

"I'm in love with you."

"No."

A beat. "No?" Jamie's brows drew in, and she wiped away a stray tear. "I think only I get to decide."

"No, as in it's not okay for you to do this now. There's Helen. Absolutely not." Of all the things she expected she might hear from Jamie today, this was not one of them. She needed to unhear the words. Go back in time two minutes.

Jamie held up a hand. "I know. I get that. And I'm not trying to ruin anything." Jamie came around the island in the kitchen that had been a barrier between them. "I didn't come knocking on your door. You came knocking on mine."

"Then why?"

"Because it's the truth?"

Leighton threw a questioning arm out. "Why is it *now* the truth? Why wasn't it the truth six weeks ago, six months ago, any other time?"

"Maybe it was. That's what I'm working through, but a lot happened between us over the years, and sometimes one emotion topples another until it doesn't anymore. I was scared, Leighton, so incredibly terrified of you, of how you made me feel, of what you were capable of taking away from me." She touched her forehead. "And you're so far out of my league that it's laughable."

"Don't you ever say that." Leighton took a commanding, angry step forward. "Don't you ever—" But she didn't finish that sentence. Instead she stepped forward and kissed Jamie with all the intense emotion this conversation had inspired. She kissed her because she didn't know how not to, knowing what she knew now. She kissed her because Jamie needed to know how amazing Leighton thought she was, even if also a little infuriating. She kissed her because, even in sweats, she was the most beautiful, sexy woman Leighton had ever seen. And most of all, she kissed Jamie because she loved her back. And none of it was fair. As her lips moved over Jamie's, she sank into the most wonderful familiarity. She'd missed this feeling, this exhilaration and wonder, and couldn't get enough of it in this moment. Her memory had even undersold how well they fit together, and just for a few lingering moments, she let herself feel like she was home.

But that was all she was allowed.

She pulled her lips away and gave her head a shake. "Shouldn't have done that."

"I know." Jamie nodded. "It's okay."

"It's not. Nothing about any of this is okay." She'd been meeting with a wedding planner that very day. Her fiancée was out for drinks with friends. She couldn't allow herself to reach for what her heart was already reaching for. "I'm awful for this."

"This was my fault. I should never have said those words."

Leighton shrugged. "But you did." She looked behind her, confused and not sure what to do with herself. She had to get away, though. That much was clear. "I'm just gonna…yeah." She turned and walked straight out the door. Not a good-bye. Not even a look back. She needed air, clarity, and some time alone. What was she supposed to do now with this new information, which, quite frankly, shattered her, given the situation. She spent the next two hours walking in the rain, intermittent showers that would ease until they started again. She wasn't sure where she was going, but the movement and the raindrops stripped her bare and helped loosen up her thoughts. Her head ached just as much as her heart did.

She was mad at the world, she was incredulous, and she knew now, with sore feet and wrung dry emotions, that she needed to talk to Helen.

"Why are you wet?" Helen asked when Leighton opened the door to her apartment. "Did you walk in this rain?"

Leighton nodded. "I wasn't sure you'd be back from drinks yet. I'm glad you are."

Helen regarded her for another curious beat. "Audrey started flirting with some guy, and I know we used to scope out guys together, but I just can't anymore. I watched for as long as I could, but I wanted to get back here and go over some of the plans from today."

"I need to talk to you about something important."

Helen looked up from her laptop. "Yeah. I'm listening." Except she'd gone right back to the screen.

Leighton sat down on the couch nearby and waited. Noticing, Helen sighed and set the laptop aside. "You have my full attention."

"When I was at Jamie's apartment earlier, something happened."

"Was it bad?"

"I kissed her." She shook her head. "I'm so very sorry, and I never should have done that."

Helen blinked slowly. "Okay. I'm processing."

"Totally fair. I want to explain everything and will. I think we need to talk about the implications and why and—"

Helen held up a hand to silence Leighton. "Hang on. Let's not go there. You kissed. Are you planning to kiss again?"

"No."

"Good. Then let's shelve it."

"But there's more to the story, and I think it matters."

"Do you know what matters, Leighton? We have two hundred and sixty invitations on their way to be printed. Each one represents a person coming to our wedding, which is coming together so nicely. So let's not do this if we don't have to, okay?"

Leighton had known what she had to do before arriving home, but Helen's reaction, her hyperfocus on the optics and lack of attention on them, what really mattered, had never been more clear. With both hands flat on the cold countertop, Leighton gathered her wits and courage. She turned around to Helen, typing away. "I think you're a really good person, Helen. But I don't think we should get married."

"Seriously?" Helen asked, mouth agape. "Over a misinformed kiss?"

"We're not right for each other, and I think it's better we come to that realization now than a few years down the line, after we've robbed each other of precious time and have a lot more of our lives to untangle."

"There's no such thing as a perfect fit, Leighton. If that's what you're searching for, you're going to be at it for a fucking long time." She stood, closed her laptop, and exhaled. "You know, I predicted this."

"I'm really sorry."

Helen didn't so much as pause. "I said to myself, she's going through the motions."

That snagged Leighton's attention. "Weren't we both, though?" she asked gently. "Forgive me if I'm off base, but you seemed more focused on what our life would be than you did on us. We're not in love, Helen."

"Love is overrated," she said quietly, slipping her laptop into its case, picking up her bag, and heading for the door. "I'm keeping the key so I can get my stuff. I'll let Susan-Jane know." She paused in the doorway. "We could have been really good together, Leighton."

"You would have hated me one day."

"I guess we'll never know."

YOU HAD ME AT MERLOT

CHAPTER TWENTY-THREE

Honesty was a tricky thing. Jamie didn't regret her confession to Leighton because no truer words had ever been spoken, no sentence more from her heart. But she did regret her timing. She'd put Leighton in a difficult position, and the anguish on her face after the kiss they'd shared had been seared into Jamie's mind for all time. She'd put that look there. She was the responsible party, and she hated herself for it.

She went about her week like an automaton programmed to go through the motions, bringing coffee and wine to the masses with a plastic smile and a hollow existence. Customers came and went. Her regulars at the Chelsea bar joked and laughed as always. She stayed on the periphery, missing Leighton, wondering how she was, where she was, what she was thinking.

"Hi, I'll take a shapely mocha, please. Medium sized."

"I'll be happy to get that for you. Can you tell me what you'd like us to do to make it shapely?"

"It's shaming to call a drink skinny just because it has low-fat milk or sugar-free sweetener, so I'd like a shapely drink with full fat and maximum sweetener."

Jamie blinked. That was certainly a new one, but she could comply. "A shapely medium mocha is on the way."

This was normally the kind of noteworthy interaction Jamie would text to Leighton. They'd go back and forth dissecting the woman's angle, appreciating her take, and laughing about the uniqueness of the exchange. But none of the texts she'd sent to Leighton these days had come back. She'd send this story anyway. Wherever she was, maybe she'd appreciate the new term.

"You know you've been a mopester for a couple of months now," Marjorie said. "Is it the workload that has you down? It's gotta be a lot, overseeing both stores."

"It's not the workload," Leo said and gave his head a shake. That guy was too intuitive.

"Is it the weather? I wish it would warm up," Marvin said and slid farther beneath his cardigan. "I'm convinced cold weather brings out serial killers."

"That might be the weirdest thing you've ever said," Clarissa told him. "Now I'm wondering if you're a serial killer."

"I'm a day trader," he corrected.

"Prove the difference." She sent him a hyperbolic gaze of suspicion.

Jamie held up a hand. "I'm clearly not the only moody one around here. If you must know, I'm just going through some things. It'll pass."

Genevieve closed her laptop and folded her arms. "We haven't seen Leighton in a long time, and Marvin's checked out both stores."

"Don't tell her about my missions," Marvin said, tossing up an exasperated hand.

Jamie turned to him. "Are you spying on me, Marvin?"

"Just taking one for the team." He looked over at them for backup. "We were worried."

Clarissa hadn't said much. She knew the story and gave Jamie's hand a squeeze in solidarity, having told her—from the night it had all happened and she'd come over to comfort Jamie on the couch—that she'd done the right thing. "It's never wrong to be honest about your feelings," she'd said as Jamie had cried on her literal shoulder.

"I'm not sure Leighton would agree."

"She was caught off guard. Give her time."

She had, wanting more than anything to just put things back how they had been. She'd accept a friendship, would support Leighton's marriage, and would bury her feelings until she found a way to resolve them. She could do all of that if it would bring Leighton back into her life.

"Listen, all of you," Jamie said, addressing the regulars. "I don't want you to worry about me. I'm doing just fine, and from what I can tell, Leighton is on vacation. Her office email has an autoreply that says as much." She shrugged. "She'll be back, right?"

"She will," Genevieve said with such force it was startling. "I guarantee it. She would be a fool not to, Jamie."

"And we know she's not that," Clarissa offered. She stood. "It's the first day of our big clearance sale at the store, and my mother will be on edge all day. I better get over there."

"Oh, save me one of those turquoise scarves for my mom's birthday."

"Half-off today." Clarissa kissed Jamie's cheek and waved to the regulars. She'd check in on Jamie diligently throughout the day via text, good friend that she was.

As for Jamie, she would limp along through the rest of her day, go home, and try to find a little joy in a good book or a rerun of *Modern Family*, until it was time to get up and do the whole thing over again. Meanwhile, she watched the clock, wondering when, if ever, Leighton would return.

❖

When you needed to escape reality, a strawberry farm in the middle of small town California might just be the best place to do it. Leighton knew Tanner Peak from her visits to see Courtney here, along with their grandmother, whom she missed so much that it hurt. Her mom, too. She didn't delve too far into the other people she'd been missing these weeks she'd been away, but the fresh air had been good for her. The long walks through the strawberry fields had become a daily practice. She'd been staying in the little cottage on the property that she was told used to be Maggie's. In the evening, she'd sit on the porch and watch the sunset, her heart squeezing at the display of color. New York would always be her city, but even she could concede that they didn't have sunsets like these.

Early one evening, just as the show in the sky got underway, Maggie appeared at the bottom of the steps. She'd knocked off her real estate job for the day and now wore jeans and a simple white T-shirt, dark hair pulled back in a ponytail. She was such a big part of this place. "Courtney just called from Chicago. She wanted an update on how you were doing, and quite honestly, I don't think I have the latest."

"So here you are."

Maggie placed a flat hand beneath her chin. "It's me. Here for the check-in."

Leighton nodded. "This respite from the real world has been good for me. I don't think there's anything like an abundance of time on your hands to help you clear your thoughts."

"Country life for you. It's good for the soul." Maggie placed a hand on Leighton's chest.

After the past few weeks, Leighton believed it and wondered about investing in a cottage or cabin like this one somewhere. "You can say that again. Though my problems aren't resolved, I have a peace about everything that, one day, they will be. I will be eternally grateful for you letting me hide out and clear my head."

Maggie shrugged. "Well, I really like having you here, and we needed somebody to help eat the strawberries." They shared a laugh because Leighton had eaten more than just a few with a dish of vanilla ice cream. "And I've been there before. This very cottage was instrumental in helping me get myself together when my whole world fell apart." She touched a beam and gave it a pat. "It won't let you down."

"Do you know what I think?" Leighton asked.

Maggie took a seat on a step. "Tell me." Her eyes were luminous and kind. In fact, everything about Maggie's welcoming presence had made Leighton's stay on the farm just what she needed. There was a part of her that never wanted to leave, clinging to the safety and distance from her real life struggles. The other part of her knew that it was time to book a flight to New York.

"I think I have to go back, face everyone, figure out what I want to do."

"And what is that?"

"I don't have a clue. But there are people who deserve to hear from me. Too many loose ends dangling. Helen. Jamie. My job."

Maggie nodded. "This place is here for you whenever you need it. You're family, and we love the hell out of you, or whatever." Maggie's cheeks dusted pink.

She was a sweetheart, and it was easy to see why Courtney loved her so damn much. Watching them together recently in the kitchen of the big house when they thought no one was looking had melted her heart. The soft stares, the casual touches, even a stolen kiss against the cabinet. As it should be, she'd told herself, leaving them their privacy. She met Maggie's eyes. "I love you both just as much. Come see me in New York? Let me take you to a baseball game. I hear Carrington's has a fancy box."

"Never heard of them." They shared a laugh. "As long as there are beer and hotdogs, I'm in."

"You're a good friend, Maggie." She looked behind her. "I better pack."

She was going to miss the little town of Tanner Peak, but she was taking a little nugget of what it had taught her along the way: Life is about the simple things. Those are the ones that count. A deep lungful of air. Good food. Laughter. Space to think. But the most important thing of all? The people you love in this world. Everything else, the details, the chaos, the noise? At the end of the day, none of it mattered.

As her plane touched down in New York City just after ten p.m., Leighton was tired yet determined. She didn't quite know how to fix her life, her heart, but she was getting there. As she made her way toward baggage claim, she saw a man with two others surrounding him as his photo was taken. What pop star had she stumbled upon this time? LaGuardia certainly had its fill of them passing through daily. As she approached, she stole a quick glance that made her veins run with ice. Logan Morrow, right there in the flesh. She'd heard a piece of news about him holding up a vote that was garnering him a bit of attention, but she'd purposefully scrolled right past the details. Maybe that was why the press were cornering him in an airport late at night. She gave her head a shake and kept walking…until she turned back and walked straight over to him.

"Hi, there," she said, offering him a tight smile. "We've never met before, but I couldn't pass up the chance." His hair had gone entirely gray over the past year or so. He looked tired but brightened when he heard her words, likely grateful for the reprieve from the reporters' rapid-fire questions. One of them was clearly rolling video on his phone.

"Hi, there. I'm Logan. It's a pleasure. I appreciate your support," he said and extended his hand.

She gave it a squeeze. "I know. We have the same last name. I'm Leighton. Your daughter." His handshake went still, and he slowly withdrew the hand altogether. "I'd say I appreciated your support as well, but I think you stopped writing child support checks when I was two." She added a laugh. "Probably because they were traceable, and you were trying to keep your reputation clean for your career."

"Leighton," he repeated. God, his brain had to have been working overtime to figure out how to handle this one. He must have been spinning out of control. She drank in every blissful minute of it. "I don't know what you're—"

"Oh, *you* know *me*. Not personally. Because you weren't there for even a second of my childhood, but you certainly know *of* me, right?"

"You know, if you get in touch with my office, maybe we can set up a time to sort out some of your concerns. Unfortunately, I have an engagement that I'm trying to make."

"This late? Wow. Well"—she gestured to the walkway ahead of them—"don't let me keep you. It's already been a whole ninety seconds you've devoted to my life. Can't bother you with any more."

He nodded and turned, looking queasy.

Two of the three reporters followed him, while one hung back with her. "Are you saying you're the congressman's illegitimate child? How do you feel about that?"

"I am. And no comment. At least not for now," she said loud enough, knowing Logan was likely still in earshot. Why not make him a little extra nervous? If his delaying a vote pulled in a lot of press, this should garner even more. Especially if the media verified her story, which shouldn't be all that hard to do.

After a good night's sleep in her own bed, Leighton woke up with a newfound sense of purpose. She'd conquered one of her greatest fears the night before. She'd confronted her father and spoken her truth, and never felt more in control of her own life. Now, the pieces of her path, the one she was always meant to be on, were beginning to materialize in front of her, and an immense sense of calm settled. She had no idea what Jamie would say when she saw her. That was for Jamie to decide. For Leighton, it was about putting aside the past, the unimportant details, and focusing on one thing: the love gathered in her heart.

She dressed for the day and gave herself a good long look in the mirror. After an empowering nod, she found her bag and headed off into the loud, busy streets of New York.

God, she treasured this city.

CHAPTER TWENTY-FOUR

I'm thinking I want…" A long pause as Jamie's new customer scanned the menu, which was odd because the line was out the door, and he had to have been standing in it for at least a short while, with plenty of time to peruse. "Hmm, what do I want?" He tap, tap, tapped his upper lip.

"Leo, over there, makes a fantastic cappuccino," Jamie offered, hoping to usher him along. The woman behind him—Jazz Hands, because she did them once—shifted her weight. "We also have cold brew you'll write home about if you're in the mood for something cold."

"Tell you what. Give me a large iced latte with two pumps of brown sugar, one of vanilla, cinnamon powder on top, and one Splenda. Oh, and with almond milk."

Jamie nodded and wrote up the really interesting drink. Not that anything fazed her anymore.

She rang up one customer, then the next, followed by another, all the while noting that the line remained virtually unchanged. While she lamented not getting ahead of the demand, she also remembered Leighton stressing the importance of revenue, over lunch one day, making several valid points and showing off her very savvy business brain. The line stood for revenue, plain and simple. But now she was thinking about Leighton again, about her kind eyes and quick but quiet wit. Her heart tugged unpleasantly. She missed her so much it ached. There was even a woman two back in line who reminded her of Leighton. All signs seemed to point to— *Hold up.* She looked more closely, craned her neck. Same height. Though she could only see a small portion of the side of the woman's face, she knew that hair, those hands.

Her heart thudded as she served the next two customers. Jazz Hands ordered her usual skinny mocha, and the new customer behind just wanted a bag of doughnuts for his walk, which led her to the next very important customer, who looked so beautiful it hurt. Leighton stood there in jeans and a soft blue T-shirt. Her hair was down and fell across her forehead just shy of her eye. "Bambi's Mother."

Leighton relaxed into a lazy grin. They stared at each other for a good couple of seconds. "Never gonna lose that one, am I?"

"I don't think so. It would be wrong." Jamie popped a cup into her hand, her gaze never moving from Leighton, a sight for sore eyes. "What can I get you?"

"Blueberry latte, please."

Jamie nodded. "We can do that. Anything else?" she asked as she wrote up the order on the side of the cup.

"You."

Her writing hand went still. She looked up in question, trying to make sure she'd heard the word correctly and understood its meaning. She tilted her head.

"I'm here for you."

Still not quite caught up, she looked at Leo, who offered a knowing smile. "Why don't you go talk to her?" he prompted. "Shannon can take the line."

"On it, boss. Take a break," Shannon said, also grinning. She stepped up to the register and greeted the next customer.

"Should we?" Jamie gestured to the door with her chin.

"Let's take a walk."

"Sure. We can do that."

"The woman of Jamie's dreams had returned," the voice-over said. "But what did she have to say?"

Jamie's entire body tingled, but her thoughts were still jumbled. Words weren't stretching into sentences properly. But she walked across the room anyway, one foot in front of the other. She noted her regulars swiveling to watch the action. Genevieve's eyes were wide. Marvin tossed an encouraging fist in the air, but the room slowly faded to the edges of her awareness. Warmth blossomed in her chest, and extra energy coursed. It was starting to feel like dawn after a very long and dark night. She couldn't quite believe it. Leighton was back. She was right there in the bar.

"I'll work on that latte while you're gone," Leo called.

"Thanks, Leo," Leighton said, opening the door for Jamie and waiting for her to pass through first.

They walked a few feet in silence before Jamie found her first question. "Where have you been?"

Leighton smiled and shook her head. "On a strawberry farm in California, if you can believe that."

"I can. That sounds peaceful. Was it what you needed?"

"To figure out what matters? Yes. It was." Leighton looked over at her as they paused on the corner for the light to change. "I ended the engagement before I left town."

"I heard. Clarissa saw a blurb about it on social."

"Yeah, Helen was good about putting the word out there pretty quickly."

"I was…shocked. But also not." She shook her head. "I'm sorry."

"I'm not. It was all wrong. I was in love with someone else."

"Oh." The butterflies joined together to create a flutter festival in her midsection.

"She knew it, too. She's said as much since then."

"Oh." The light changed, and pedestrians around them crossed the street, but they stayed right where they stood. "I don't know where your head is at, Jamie. But I'm really sorry I left your apartment the way I did. I should have been more rational. I should have stayed to talk things out."

"I blindsided you. It's partly my fault you fled."

Leighton touched her hair just as a ray of sunlight caught her eyes. Stunning. Always had been. "You were being honest, and it must have been hard for you. The problem was…"

"Yeah?"

"Those words were all I ever wanted. That's the important part."

Jamie stared up at Leighton, searching her eyes. "It's always been you, Lay. Always."

Leighton's gaze fell to Jamie's lips. It made her thighs tense. Leighton looked around. "This isn't private enough. Can we get out of here for a little while?"

Jamie nodded. "Please." She raised her arm, and in perfect timing, a cab pulled to a halt in front of them. Six minutes later, they stood in her building's elevator, unable to look away from each other, the tension in the small car near explosive as it eked its way up. Had the ride to her floor always taken this long? Jamie's body thrummed with desire. Her hands longed to touch. Her mouth needed to be on Leighton's and soon. With a ding, the doors opened, and Leighton followed Jamie to her door. Jamie took the key out, but Leighton turned her around, pressed her up against the door, and kissed her long and good. Their mouths moved and clung. Jamie parted her lips and pushed her tongue into Leighton's mouth, up on tiptoes for better access. Leighton pushed closer as they kissed, her hands wandering madly, both of them gasping for air, but needing more. Jamie's hands slipped beneath the back of Leighton's shirt, pulling her closer still, reveling in the warmth of her skin. She wanted to make Leighton come, to take her to heights she'd never experienced before. This damn door was in the way.

"Keys," Leighton murmured.

"On the floor," Jamie said, realizing she must have dropped them. But her fingers were all thumbs, and it took a minute to get the key in the lock with Leighton kissing her neck from behind. *God*. Her knees were weak, and her mind was one-track, but she needed to get into this apartment. Finally, the lock clicked, and she pressed them inside. Turning, she took Leighton by both hands and walked them backward into her bedroom. Flashes from the last time they'd been in there together overwhelmed her memory. This felt different, though. There was a freedom to the way they kissed and touched each other, born from the feelings they'd admitted to, uniting them fully.

"Where were we?" Leighton asked, hauling Jamie in. She very much liked the commanding version of Leighton. *More, please*. She slid her fingers into Leighton's hair and gripped, lost in her eyes. Why was eye contact with Leighton sexier than with any other human?

"I think your hands were on the move," Jamie said. Leighton grinned and nodded. Jamie's shirt hit the floor. Leighton's hands found her breasts and squeezed, causing Jamie's center to throb intensely, so she slammed her eyes closed.

"And where were you?" Leighton asked.

Jamie unbuttoned Leighton's pants, pulled down the zipper, and slid her hand into Leighton's underwear. Leighton moaned when Jamie began to stroke her slowly. Her hips rocked and her hands went still, all the while still cupping Jamie's breasts. "How's that?" Jamie whispered in her ear, which pulled another moan. Leighton dropped her head back, leaving a waterfall of blond hair, beautiful and thick.

"Jamie," she breathed. She loved the sound of her name on Leighton's lips. But she wasn't about to take Leighton standing up in her bedroom. No. She wanted her naked and horizontal beneath her. With one last thorough stroke, she removed her hand and then every last piece of Leighton's clothes. She cupped her ass and melded their hips together. "What are you doing to me, Jamie?"

"You're about to find out." She sat Leighton on the bed, and with sunlight slanting through the blinds, she undressed slowly, captivated by the way Leighton watched each and every inch of skin as it was revealed to her, her eyes dark, signaling her desire. "Now where do you want me?"

Leighton extended her hand to Jamie and guided her until she stood between Leighton's legs. "I want to be inside of you," Leighton breathed, kissing her stomach. She wrapped an arm around Jamie's waist and touched her intimately between her legs, causing Jamie's thighs to tremble. Leighton entered her with purpose, and she heard her own voice cry out. She was so close. Too close. If Leighton so much as moved, she might tumble. Very slowly, Leighton, her eyes on Jamie's face, began to ease her fingers in and out, causing the pressure to build to astronomical levels that made Jamie squeeze Leighton's shoulders for support. Brain cells were inaccessible, but she knew one thing for certain. She wanted Leighton to take her, claim her, right then and there. The second Leighton picked up speed and moved within her in rhythmic motions, Jamie broke, and her entire world came to a stop on its axis, and she shot in a million different directions. She saw light behind her eyes, and pleasure rained down hard and intense as she rode Leighton's hand into sweet oblivion.

"Too good," she murmured, as the shock waves receded. Her limbs were liquid.

"No such thing," Leighton said back, pulling Jamie forward until she was settled on top of Leighton's lap, straddling her. She closed her eyes and pulled Jamie tight to her stomach. "This is everything," she said, kissing Jamie's collarbone, nipping at her breast, before sucking on a nipple. "Stay here forever."

"No, no. Work to do first," Jamie said, still in recovery but very much capable of enjoying her skin pressed to Leighton's. She gave Leighton's shoulder a little shove until she lay back on the bed. Jamie followed her down and settled her hips between Leighton's legs, aware of how wet she was, how ready. "Now, this is everything." She began to circle her hips as Leighton squirmed beneath, her breathing shallow. Jamie dipped her head and kissed one breast and then the other, curling her tongue around a nipple, biting ever so softly. That inspired a hiss from Leighton, so she did it again, lavishing each breast with individual attention until Leighton was whimpering, asking for release. She nodded, slid down the bed, more than eager. She palmed Leighton's thighs and parted them, marveling at her beauty for a few moments before tracing Leighton intimately with her tongue. Soft at first, and then again with more purpose. The sounds of approval, the pleas that came strangled in Leighton's throat when she began to suck, only encouraged and guided Jamie's path. With a few well-placed swipes of Jamie's tongue, Leighton tensed and called out, intertwining their fingers as she reveled in pleasure.

"Oh, God," Leighton said. Her eyes were closed with her hair spilled out around her on the pillow. She looked so incredibly beautiful that an uncomfortable lump formed in Jamie's throat as she realized how very lucky she was.

"I've got you," Jamie said, wrapping her arms around Leighton.

She looked up at Jamie and their gazes met. "I believe you. And I have you right back." Leighton kissed her softly. "Jamie, I love you."

"I love you, too. Let's be happy together now. It's been long enough."

Leighton smiled, beautiful and sincere. "I'm never letting you go again. Just know that."

She stroked Leighton's hair, feeling anchored and relaxed. "Why did it take us so long?"

"Because perfection takes time. And look at us." Leighton laughed.

"Did I mention I love you?"

Leighton slid on top. "No. So you should probably say it again. I will, too. I love you." A kiss, deep and thorough.

"I love you back." She pulled Leighton's mouth to hers and kissed her slowly, like they had all the time in the world, and in reality, they did. They had a lifetime stretched out to laugh over wine, cuddle on the couch, and fall into bed together when they simply couldn't keep their hands to themselves.

With her hair spilled over Jamie's arm, Leighton stared intently at Jamie. "This is it for me. You know that, right? You're everything."

"This is it," Jamie murmured against her mouth.

She'd never felt more vulnerable, as open to another person, or as happy as she did in this very moment. She'd lived so much of her life underselling herself on what she thought she deserved that she never once dared believe that she could be this fulfilled and full of love. But Leighton, in her arms, made her feel complete.

"Please say you'll be mine," Leighton said, tracing her cheek with one finger, the love in her eyes a caress all its own.

"I already am. Always and forever." She glanced over her shoulder with a grin. "Do you think Leo's got the latte ready?"

❖

Leighton loved Saturday mornings these days. Especially since Jamie'd committed to taking every other one of them off. That meant they slept in until midmorning when they'd lie twisted in bedsheets, flirting, kissing, and making plans for their day.

Today, they'd decided on hitting up the little farmers market that popped up each weekend on Fifty-Fifth not far from the bar. They strolled slowly, holding hands and getting to know the vegetables.

"What if we did a zucchini, onion, and pepper scramble for breakfast tomorrow? I'll be the chef. You can cheer me on with little to no clothing."

"Sold," Leighton said. "I have the best little number for breakfast cheerleader. I think you'll be impressed."

Jamie went still, onion in hand. "Unless you just want to do that today."

Leighton laughed and leaned in, hovering just shy of Jamie's lips. "Patience, my love. But I love it when you get that little dazed look on your face," she said, her voice lower. "It means you're turned on."

"What can I say, these onions do things to me."

Leighton laughed, and they made the purchase only to turn around to see Helen and her sister approaching the stand. Leighton and Helen had seen each other a few times over the past couple of months and had actually smoothed things over rather well, considering. Helen had released a lot of the anger over the broken engagement and had even wished her and Jamie well. In the end, she'd agreed that it had all been for the best. She hadn't been in love with Leighton either and could admit that would have been a problem.

"You're in the paper again," Helen said, pointing at Leighton without hesitating. "Hi, Jamie. Did you get the onions? These guys have the best."

Jamie held up the bag. "Couldn't resist."

"Why am I in the paper this time?" Leighton asked innocently, knowing full well the likely reason. "One of my many good deeds? I did pick up trash in the park and return it to the bin."

"More like Logan Morrow's approval rating is in the toilet because of that viral video of you two at the airport. It's been interesting watching him scramble."

Leighton nodded. "It certainly has." She hadn't set out to destroy the guy's reputation, but it wasn't an awful bonus. His office had reached out to her several times, hoping to smooth things over. Logan himself had left two messages as well, suddenly interested in speaking with her, hearing how she was. Awfully convenient. Those calls were left unreturned. Leighton had released any and all lingering feelings about her second parent, and it was honestly the most freeing decision ever. Whether he got elected again or not was not up to her, nor would she follow his campaign. She gave Jamie's hand a squeeze. She had an amazing life now and was focused entirely on enjoying it. "Do you two have big plans for the weekend?"

"This one does," Tamara said with a mischievous grin.

"I don't even want to tell you," Helen deadpanned. "You wouldn't believe me anyway."

Jamie leaned in. "Then you definitely have to."

Helen took a deep breath. "Here goes. Do you two remember the double date from hell?"

"It's seared into my memory for all time," Jamie said. "I feel like I should apologize again to all of you."

"Same," Leighton said with a wince.

Helen laughed and turned to her sister. "Why I didn't know that night it was these two all along is beyond me." Tamara shrugged, and Helen pressed on. "Anyway, I'm having dinner with Tegan tonight."

"Stop it," Jamie said. "I never would have guessed that you two…"

"She has a unique style I kinda liked, and we ran into each other at this little martini bar and decided to set something up."

Leighton couldn't have written this better herself. "If this goes anywhere, I think we're gonna need another one of those doubles. This is all too good not to."

Helen laughed. "I'll keep you posted. Enjoy those onions."

Jamie held two of them in her hands and sent Leighton her most suggestive look.

"God, I love you. We should get out of here and get you some action."

"Now, I love you back. It's like you can read my mind."

They shared a kiss and continued on their way. "Wanna try this new merlot I'm thinking of ordering for the bars later tonight?"

"You realize that I will never turn down a glass with you."

"A woman after my own heart."

Leighton looked over at the woman who lit up every room she walked into. She'd done the same for Leighton's life, sparking it into color the moment they'd found their way to each other. Jamie took her breath away daily and enriched her life with kindness, laughter, and warmth. "I love your heart," she said back.

"It's yours."

About the Author

Melissa Brayden (www.melissabrayden.com) is a multi-award-winning romance author, embracing the full-time writer's life in San Antonio, Texas, and enjoying every minute of it.

Melissa is married and working really hard at remembering to do the dishes. For personal enjoyment, she spends time with her Jack Russell terriers and checks out the NYC theater scene as often as possible. She considers herself a reluctant patron of spin class, but would much rather be sipping merlot and staring off into space. Bring her coffee, wine, or doughnuts and you'll have a friend for life.

Books Available From Bold Strokes Books

Blood Rage by Illeandra Young. A stolen artifact, a family in the dark, an entire city on edge. Can SPEAR agent Danika Karson juggle all three over a weekend with the "in-laws" while an unknown, malevolent entity lies in wait upon her very skin? (978-1-63679-539-3)

Ghost Town by R.E. Ward. Blair Wyndon and Leif Henderson are set to prove ghosts exist when the mystery suddenly turns deadly. Someone or something else is in Masonville, and if they don't find a way to escape, they might never leave. (978-1-63679-523-2)

Good Christian Girls by Elizabeth Bradshaw. In this heartfelt coming of age lesbian romance, Lacey and Jo help each other untangle who they are from who everyone says they're supposed to be. (978-1-63679-555-3)

Guide Us Home by CF Frizzell and Jesse J. Thoma. When acquisition of an abandoned lighthouse pits ambitious competitors Nancy and Sam against each other, it takes a WWII tale of two brave women to make them see the light. (978-1-63679-533-1)

Lost Harbor by Kimberly Cooper Griffin. For Alice and Bridget's love to survive, they must find a way to reconcile the most important passions in their lives—devotion to the church and each other. (978-1-63679-463-1)

Never a Bridesmaid by Spencer Greene. As her sister's wedding gets closer, Jessica finds that her hatred for the maid of honor is a bit more complicated than she thought. Could it be something more than hatred? (978-1-63679-559-1)

The Rewind by Nicole Stiling. For police detective Cami Lyons and crime reporter Alicia Flynn, some choices break hearts. Others leave a body count. (978-1-63679-572-0)

Turning Point by Cathy Dunnell. When Asha and her former high school bully Jody struggle to deny their growing attraction, can they move forward without going back? (978-1-63679-549-2)

When Tomorrow Comes by D. Jackson Leigh. Teague Maxwell, convinced she will die before she turns 41, hires animal rescue owner Baye Cobb to rehome her extensive menagerie. (978-1-63679-557-7)

You Had Me at Merlot by Melissa Brayden. Leighton and Jamie have all the ingredients to turn their attraction into love, but it's a recipe for disaster.(978-1-63679-543-0)

Appalachian Awakening by Nance Sparks. The more Amber's and Leslie's paths cross, the more this hike of a lifetime begins to look like a love of a lifetime. (978-1-63679-527-0)

Dreamer by Kris Bryant. When life seems to be too good to be true and love is within reach, Sawyer and Macey discover the truth about the town of Ladybug Junction, and the cold light of reality tests the hearts of these dreamers. (978-1-63679-378-8)

Eyes on Her by Eden Darry. When increasingly violent acts of sabotage threaten to derail the opening of her glamping business, Callie Pope is sure her ex, Jules, has something to do with it. But Jules is dead…isn't she? (978-1-63679-214-9)

Letters from Sarah by Joy Argento. A simple mistake brought them together, but Sarah must release past love to create a future with Lindsey she never dreamed possible. (978-1-63679-509-6)

Lost in the Wild by Kadyan. When their plane crash-lands, Allison and Mike face hunger, cold, a terrifying encounter with a bear, and feelings for each other neither expects. (978-1-63679-545-4)

Not Just Friends by Jordan Meadows. A tragedy leaves Jen struggling to figure out who she is and what is important to her. (978-1-63679-517-1)

Of Auras and Shadows by Jennifer Karter. Eryn and Rina's unexpected love may be exactly what the Community needs to heal the rot that comes not from the fetid Dark Lands that surround the Community but from within. (978-1-63679-541-6)

The Secret Duchess by Jane Walsh. A determined widow defies a duke and falls in love with a fashionable spinster in a fight for her rightful home. (978-1-63679-519-5)

Winter's Spell by Ursula Klein. When former college roommates reunite at a wedding in Provincetown, sparks fly, but can they find true love when evil sirens and trickster mermaids get in the way? (978-1-63679-503-4)

Coasting and Crashing by Ana Hartnett. Life comes easy to Emma Wilson until Lake Palmer shows up at Alder University and derails her every plan. (978-1-63679-511-9)

Every Beat of Her Heart by KC Richardson. Piper and Gillian have their own fears about falling in love, but will they be able to overcome those feelings once they learn each other's secrets? (978-1-63679-515-7)

Fire in the Sky by Radclyffe and Julie Cannon. Two women from different worlds have nothing in common and every reason to wish they'd never met—except for the attraction neither can deny. (978-1-63679-561-4)

Grave Consequences by Sandra Barret. A decade after necromancy became licensed and legalized, can Tamar and Maddy overcome the lingering prejudice against their kind and their growing attraction to each other to uncover a plot that threatens both their lives? (978-1-63679-467-9)

Haunted by Myth by Barbara Ann Wright. When ghost-hunter Chloe seeks an answer to the current spectral epidemic, all clues point to one very famous face: Helen of Troy, whose motives are more complicated than history suggests and whose charms few can resist. (978-1-63679-461-7)

Invisible by Anna Larner. When medical school dropout Phoebe Frink falls for the shy costume shop assistant Violet Unwin, everything about their love feels certain, but can the same be said about their future? (978-1-63679-469-3)

Like They Do in the Movies by Nan Campbell. Celebrity gossip writer Fran Underhill becomes Chelsea Cartwright's personal assistant with the aim of taking the popular actress down, but neither of them anticipates the clash of their attraction. (978-1-63679-525-6)

Limelight by Gun Brooke. Liberty Bell and Palmer Elliston loathe each other. They clash every week on the hottest new TV show, until Liberty starts to sing and the impossible happens. (978-1-63679-192-0)

Playing with Matches by Georgia Beers. To help save Cori's store and help Liz survive her ex's wedding, they strike a deal: a fake relationship, but just for one week. There's no way this will turn into the real deal. (978-1-63679-507-2)